The Sunflower Letters

A Mid-century Life of Discoveries

by

Rebecca Willman Gernon

HRH Dolland Press
Covington, Louisiana 70433

The Sunflower Letters

Published by: HRH Dolland Press
Covington, LA 70433

Second Printing 8/2023

The characters and events portrayed in this book are fictitious. Any similarity to real persons, living or dead is coincidental and not intended by the author.

Photographer and Cover Design by: Laura Siebert

Cover Model: Victoria Mentel

ISBN-13: 979-8-218-23460-7

Printed in the United States of America

Dedication

This book is dedicated to everyone who lived during the fabulous 1950s and 1960s (or wished they had) and enjoyed life at a slower pace in a friendly neighborhood, danced to the best music, drove some of the most uniquely designed cars ever manufactured, and enjoyed the simple pleasure of sharing secrets with their friends at the local soda shop.

Table of Contents

Ackknowledgements			5
Chapter	1	My Humble Beginnings	6
Chapter	2	The Great Escape	13
Chapter	3	Hog Heaven	23
Chapter	4	There's No Place Like Home	31
Chapter	5	Late Night Adventure	38
Chapter	6	Not Alone Anymore	43
Chapter	7	Making Friends	47
Chapter	8	Names and Old Photos	53
Chapter	9	The Secret Passage	59
Chapter	10	Alley Oops!	66
Chapter	11	Stupid Questions and Sweet Revenge	71
Chapter	12	A Seed is Planted	78
Chapter	13	Sheesh! What a Question	82
Chapter	14	Christmas Greetings	89
Chapter	15	One Picture is Worth a…	96
Chapter	16	Birthday Wishes	104
Chapter	17	The Cost of Gambling	109
Chapter	18	Gaining the Bathroom	114
Chapter	19	In the Heat of the Game	122
Chapter	20	Drama: Comedy and Tragedy	132
Chapter	21	A Spirited Graduation	140
Chapter	22	Summer Revelation	147
Chapter	23	First Date	155
Chapter	24	Spring Flowers	169
Chapter	25	Stripping Gears	179
Chapter	26	Surprised Parties	187
Chapter	27	All that Glitters	191
Chapter.	28	Summer: What a Drag	202
Chapter	29	Senior Moments	213
Chapter	30	Discoveries	218
Chapter	31	New Beginnings	225
Epilogue		Today's Comments by an Older Rebel	235
About the Author			236

Acknowledgments

My writer friends are too numerous to mention, but I want each one of them to know I appreciated their reading and critiquing my numerous drafts of this manuscripts and for encouraging me to continue writing despite my frustration with rejection.

I owe special thanks to Janet Lococo, who not only nudged me to self-publish *The SunflowerLetters*, but took time away from her romance writing career to typeset my book and to assist me in publishing it. Her last published novel is *Until Death… or Not?*

The photography and editing talents of Laura Siebert produced my book cover.

Victoria Mentel, a natural redhead posed as my Rebel.

Of course, I would like this work to be perfect, but I'm fairly certain there will be errors. All errors spotted are my own.

Chapter 1
My Humble Beginnings

"Go away, Rebel. You're a pest. Amherst and I are playing checkers," says Columbia. She's ten, my oldest sister, and never lets anyone forget she should always be first since she's the oldest.

My sister Amherst is nine. She's taller than Columbia. People often think Amherst is the oldest because of her height. Columbia gets stinky when someone says to her, "Are you sure you're the oldest? Amherst is taller than you." I think that's funny. Columbia doesn't.

As I watch them play, I stack unused black and red checkers into a small tower on the edge of the card table. I am wearing my cowboy boots, a recent birthday gift from Daddy for my fifth birthday. They make a clumping noise on the oak floor of our living room.

"Leave those alone," Amherst says. "Checkers is for two people, Rebel. Go chase yourself."

I run around the card table, looking over my shoulder while trying to chase myself. On my second lap my boot snags a table leg and the table collapses. The checkerboard, along with red and black checkers clatter onto the floor like hail.

"Now look what you've done!" Columbia screams. "I was going to win."

"Fat chance of that ever happening," Amherst says. "I always win."

"Don't be a smarty pants, Amherst. I'm the oldest. I should win," Columbia snaps. She lowers her voice to a mean whisper and says to me, "Let me tell you something you red-haired, freckle-faced brat, you're not really my sister. You're adopted. Now go away."

What? Mother never told me I'm adopted. If I don't belong here, where do I belong?

Amherst usually defends me, but today she says, "Columbia's right. You don't belong here. No one else in our family has red frizzy hair and green eyes."

"You were left on our front porch one day like a stray dog," Columbia adds.

"Mother and Daddy should have chased you away with a broom," says Amherst.

Tears fill my olive-green eyes. I turn away before my sisters call me a crybaby. I run toward the front door.

"Hey, orphan, come back here," Columbia calls. "You have to pick up these checkers."

Columbia and Amherst laugh as the screen door closes behind me. I climb onto our porch swing, my thinking place. The swing is wide enough for Mother, Daddy, and me to sit together. I love the evenings we sit and swing. I wish I was surrounded by them now, but Daddy is at work and Mother's busy in the kitchen.

I stretch out on the swing, tuck my hands under my head, and rock away my tears. I hate Columbia calling me freckle-face. I don't want a different family. I want this Mother and Daddy. Tears refill my eyes. Amherst is right. I do look different. Mother has light brown hair with soft curls. She pins them back from her face with bobby pins. Her eyes are as blue as the sky. Her hands are soft with long, smooth fingernails. Sometimes she wears pale pink nail polish. My nails are short because I gnaw on them.

I don't look like Daddy either. His hair is blonde and straight. His eyes are blue. Amherst and Columbia have straight hair like him, but it's brown like Mother's.

I've never seen anyone in the whole wide world with hair like mine. My hair is the color of the new pennies Daddy gives me to put in my piggy bank. My curls fly away from my face like kites blowing in the wind. When Mother combs the snarls from my hair, it hurts. And worse yet, I have horrid freckles across my nose and cheeks. Maybe I am adopted. If I am, where do I belong? No one wants a girl with penny-colored frizzy hair and freckles.

Before more tears run down my cheek I realize, if I'm adopted, then Columbia and Amherst aren't my sisters. Yeah! Maybe I have nice sisters somewhere who won't pick on me and call me a crybaby. I need a cookie.

Mother baked white cookies with cinnamon on them this morning. Snickerdoodles. What a weird name for such a good cookie.

I rise from the swing and push it away. The swing returns bumping my legs, nudging me toward the living room window. A small white flag with a red border and one gold star hangs there, a Remembrance Flag.

Last week Mother told Daddy, "Let's put the flag in a drawer."

Daddy said, "No, the flag makes me feel close to my brother."

I asked Mother, "How does a flag with a gold star remind Daddy of his brother?"

She said, "A gold star flag was given to families who had a family member die in the war. Your father's brother, Edward, died in World War II in 1944, two years before you were born." Mother showed me on our globe where Uncle Edward died. It's on the other side of the world a long way from Schoenfeld, Kansas, where we live. He died on a tiny speck of land in the ocean. Mother knows everything. She used to teach school. There's a photo of Uncle Edward on the piano in his soldier's uniform. Maybe he has curly, red hair under that hat.

I pull open the front door. Columbia and Amherst are seated at the kitchen table doing homework. Mother's peeling sweet potatoes for supper. Ugh! Sweet potatoes make me gag. This is the worst day of my life. First, I learn I'm adopted, and now we're having sweet potatoes."Mother, do you love me?" I ask.

"Of course. What a silly question," she answers.

"Even though I'm adopted and have a real family somewhere else?"

"What are you talking about, Rebel?" Mother frowns.

"I don't want you to give me back to strangers. I want —" I wipe the gooey stuff coming from my nose away with my fingers.

"Where do you come up with this nonsense? You're not adopted." Mother tightens her jaw and glances at my sisters. They grin and push their chairs away from the table. The chairs make a screeching sound on the linoleum floor as they hurry outside.

"Columbia said I'm like a stray dog. And Amherst says I don't belong here because I have red hair," I say between sniffles.

"You're not the only person in this family with red hair," Mother says.

"Really? Who else has red hair?"

"No one you've met." Mother keeps her eyes downcast, focused on peeling the dreadful sweet potatoes.

"Who else has red hair? Does Uncle Edward have red hair under that army hat?"

"No. His hair was blonde like your father's."

"Who has red hair?" I demand.

"I'm not sure I have a picture of her," Mother says. "Don't worry. You belong here."

Mother is silent with a faraway look in her eyes, the one she gets when thinking deep thoughts. A secret maybe. She never talks much after her eyes become foggy-looking.

"Maybe you brought home the wrong baby from the hospital."

"Not possible. When you were born, the doctor said, 'You have a healthy red-haired daughter.' He held you up by your legs and I saw you."

"Tell me about me being born."

"Okay." Mother stops peeling the sweet potatoes and sits. "You were born on a Friday. That morning, as we finished saying grace, right here at this very table, the ceiling fell onto the table. Your sisters' bowls of oatmeal were filled with chunks of plaster. Your father's coffee splashed all over his shirt. What a mess."

"Wow! Did a star fall from the sky and crash into the house like what happened to *Chicken Little*?"

"You and your imagination, Rebel. No, nothing that dramatic. Your father was using a steamer to remove wallpaper in the upstairs bedroom, the room Columbia and Amherst share now. Wet wallpaper sat on the floor upstairs for days. The water soaked though the floor, made the kitchen ceiling soggy and it fell onto this table with a big splat."

Phooey. A falling ceiling is not special. I want an exciting life. One as different as my red hair.

Mother stands. "I need to finish preparing supper. Your father will be home from work soon."

I grab her hand to keep her away from the sweet potatoes. "Why does everyone call me Rebel if my real name is Redcliffe Rose?"

Mother sits again. "Your father and I are college graduates. A good education is important, Rebel. Never forget that."

I nod.

Mother continues, "After we married, we decided we'd name our children after famous colleges. I chose Columbia's name hoping it would inspire her to be adventuresome like Christopher Columbus and to expand her horizons beyond Schoenfeld."

"What's wrong with Schoenfeld?"

"Nothing. But it's just a wide spot in the road compared to St. Louis. That's where your Grandpa Michael and Grandma Rose, my parents live, and where I grew up. I miss riding street cars, going to museums, and shopping in big department stores."

"I like Schoenfeld. We can walk everywhere. There's a school for Amherst and Columbia, a library, our church, and the grocery store sells ice cream bars."

"I know you like Schoenfeld. It's a good place to raise a family." Mother stands, brushes her hands on her apron, ready to return to the sweet potatoes.

"Who named Amherst?"

"Your father chose her name."

"And what about me? Who named me?"

"We both did. The day before I came home from the hospital with you, your father and I still hadn't decided your name. I wanted a stylish name. Something romantic and elegant, but it had to be the name of a famous college. I'd just finished reading *Wuthering Heights* about the brooding Heathcliff—"

"Can I read that book? I know how to read."

"When you are older. You haven't finished *The New Adventures of Dick and Jane* yet. What was I saying… oh yes, Heathcliff reminded me of Radcliffe, an exclusive girls' college back east. I thought that would make a great first name. Your father suggested Rose for your middle name to honor me and your Grandma Rose. So, we named you Radcliffe Rose."

Mother has that faraway look again. Before I can ask what she's dreaming about, she says, "I wonder what happened to that old sepia photo of me sitting on the lap of my mother with dad standing by her?"

"It's probably in that chest in your bedroom with all those other old photos."

Mother's cedar chest is off limits. I sat beside her once when she opened it. Mostly it's filled with old clothes, blankets, and photos. Nothing very interesting except an old doll, but she says it's fragile and I can't play with it, but maybe I can when I am older. The doll is beautiful and has fancy clothes to wear.

"I hope you are right, Rebel. I'd hate to lose that photo."

"But Mother, my name is RED-cliffe, not RAD-cliffe. I know

because you showed me my birth certificate and my name's spelled R-E-D. That spells red. My name is not —"

"I know, I know. The nurse misspelled your name on your birth certificate. I told her to correct the spelling, but she said, 'What's done is done.' Your father and I would have to fill out a bunch of forms to have your name changed. We've never taken the time to do it. Do you want your name changed?"

"No, besides no one ever calls me Redcliffe or RAD-cliffe. Everyone calls me Rebel. Why?"

"When your father brought you and me home from the hospital, you cried until your face was as red as your curly hair. Your father sang lullabies, turned on the radio, adjusted the heat, and patted your stomach to calm you. Nothing worked. After fifteen minutes of crying he said, 'Redcliffe's a rebel, isn't she?' I agreed, so we've always called you Rebel. You don't mind do you?" She leans over and hugs me.

"No."

Mother looks at my sisters' homework and shakes her head. "Rebel, tell your sisters to come inside right now and finish their homework."

Yippee! I get to tell my sisters what to do. "Columbia! Amherst!" I shout out the back door. "Mother says come in the house right now and do your homework!" I smirk at them as they enter the house. I stomp across the kitchen really loud in my cowboy boots. "You better finish your homework before Daddy comes home."

"Pipe down, Rebel." Columbia shuffles to the kitchen table. "And quit stomping around in those boots. I can't think with all that racket."

My boots are not her problem. Columbia's problem is homework, especially arithmetic. I sit at the table and stare at her while she arranges her pencils. Amherst is already hard at work.

"I only have four more math problems," Amherst says.

"You pipe down too, Amherst." Columbia writes something on her Big Chief table, then erases it, tearing a small hole in her paper. "Now look what you made me do, Rebel."

"Me? I didn't do anything. I'm just sitting here."

"Finished." Amherst folds her paper inside a schoolbook and runs from the room.

"How can you be finished already?" Columbia jerks another piece of paper from her Big Chief tablet. "I've ruined this page. I'll have to start over. I hate long division."

"I hate sweet potatoes." I say.

"Sweet potatoes are good for you. Daddy grew these in the garden," Mother says.

"I don't care."

"How much is sixty-four divided by twenty-three?" Columbia sniffs and wipes her eyes with the back of her hand.

I stomp around the kitchen hollering, "Sweet potatoes are y-u-c-k-y. They make me sick, sick, sick!"

"Quiet! I can't think. I'll never finish these problems." Tears trickle down Columbia's cheeks.

"Cry Baby. Cry Baby. Columbia's a cry baby." I run from the kitchen.

Chapter 2
The Great Escape

On Sunday afternoon Daddy suggests we go for a ride. Mother loves the Sunday rides since she does not drive this gives her an opportunity to escape the confines of Schoenfeld. This Sunday after a great dinner of roast beef and mashed potatoes, white potatoes this time which I love, Mother says, "You girls go the bathroom and then get in the car."

Columbia yells, "I'm the oldest. I get a window." Amherst usually sits by the other backseat window, but I hurried and am now sitting by a window behind Daddy. Amherst is squashed in the middle of the back seat of our 1950 Dodge.

Minutes later we pass pastures with huge black and white cows. Daddy says they are Holsteins, milk cows. Fields of golden wheat ready to be harvested stretch as far as I can see. "See that big green machine?" Daddy says. "That's a combine. It's used to reap the wheat. Those blades cut the wheat, thresh the grain heads, and store the wheat inside the machine. The chaff and straw are blown out onto the ground. When I was a boy on the farm, my Dad plowed with horses and a huge steam driven tractor with metal wheels came to help with the harvest."

"Did you ride the horses?" Columbia asks.

"No. They were large draft horses, used for work, not pleasure," Daddy replies.

"Did the horses have names?" Amherst asks.

"Yes, Maud and Bessie."

"Bessie? Like Aunt Bessie, Uncle Waylon's wife?" I ask.

"Yes," Mother says.

"Does Aunt Bessie know she has a horse name?" I ask.

"No, and let's not tell her." Mother turns from the seat and winks at me. "It will be our secret."

"In 1928 my dad bought a tractor and put Bessie out to pasture," continued Daddy. "Tractors make farming much easier, but I liked driving the team of horses."

"Look, everybody. It's a sign just for me," I say. Daddy stops our car a few feet from the familiar round, yellow road sign with a black X and two Rs. "R-R, that's for me. Rebel Rose Rothberg." I point at the railroad crossing sign.

"Why does she get a sign and I don't?" Whines Columbia. "I'm the oldest. I should have a sign first."

"You're a ninny, Columbia," snipes Amherst. "That's a railroad crossing sign."

"Well," Columbia huffs, "The signs should say 'train.' Rebel shouldn't have a sign with her initials on it; after all, I am —"

"The oldest," Amherst and I say in unison.

Our car bumps over the railroad track. The flat landscape of Kansas is dotted with big red barns and tall silos. Cottonwood trees grow along the few rivers that cross the prairie. Sunflowers, the state flower of Kansas, are blooming in the ditches. I love sunflowers. They are yellow, my favorite color.

"There's a roadside market at the next intersection and a fireworks stand." Daddy turns toward Mother and says, "Shall we stop, Bonnie?"

"Yes, that would be nice, Henry," Mother replies. "I'd like to stretch my legs. I'm enjoying the ride, but uncomfortable sitting in one position this long."

At the roadside market Daddy buys a bushel of fresh sweet corn. My sisters and I select silver and gold sparklers at the fireworks stand, and Daddy buys a few fountains and rockets for our celebration this weekend.

"I'm glad my parents are coming for the Fourth of July. Mom can help me can this corn," she says.

Daddy pats Mother's arm. "Are you feeling, okay?"

"Just a little tired, that's all. I'll feel better in a few weeks."

Daddy helps Mother into the car. "We'll be home in fifteen minutes. Then you can rest."

"When are Grandma and Grandpa coming?" I ask.

"Friday," Mother says. "Your father will pick them up at the train station after work."

As we pull into our driveway, Daddy says, "Columbia, carry the bushel of corn into the house."

"It's heavy, Daddy. Why can't Amherst do it?" Columbia says.

"She's bigger than me."

"I thought you'd want to do since you're the oldest." Daddy winks at me.

* * *

On Wednesday morning while Columbia and Amherst are at Vacation Bible School at St. John's Lutheran, Mother says, "Rebel, help me with the laundry. I want everything clean before your Grandma Rose and Grandpa Michael arrive."

Our laundry is done in the basement with a wringer washer. Usually Mother loads all our dirty clothes in a big wicker basket, carries it to the basement, and sorts the laundry into piles on the floor. Dark clothes, white clothes, and Daddy's work clothes. But lately Mother has sorted the clothes on the kitchen floor and carries one small load at a time to the basement.

The washer is round and white and stands on four sturdy legs. The wringer is attached to the back. I can't see into the washer because I am too short. Beside the washer is a table with two large metal tubs. Behind the wringer is another table that holds another wicker basket.

Mother fills the washer with water from a hose, puts in the white clothes, adds soap powder, plugs in the machine, and turns it on. The clothes swish back and forth. Next, she fills the tubs beside the washer with water for rinsing. We sit on a bench while the clothes slosh around and I read from one of my books. Today I'm reading *The Pokey Little Puppy*. After a few minutes, she pulls wet clothes from the washer and drops them into the first big tub of rinse water. She hands me a fat pole, almost as tall as me. I push the clothes around in the rinse water to get out the soap suds. Then Mother puts them into the other tub of water for a second rinse. Then comes the magic.

She pulls a piece of wet laundry from the rinse water and feeds it into the wringer. The wringer looks like two rolling pins together. Mother puts a corner of a wet towel between the two rollers and pushes a button to start the wringer. I can't do this because the wringer is dangerous, and my hand could be crushed. The wet soggy clothes are pulled through the wringer and come out the other side like flat, damp leaves. I make sure they fall into the wicker basket and don't fall on the dirty basement floor.

Next we do the same thing all over again with more dirty clothes.

When all the clothes are washed, she hands me the clothes pin bag. It has a metal handle on the top that fits over the clothesline outside. She picks up the basket of wet clothes and I scamper up the stairs to open the back door for her.

Mother sets the basket on the ground and rubs her back. She's wearing a blue checkered dress with a huge, flowered bib apron over it. Usually, she ties the apron around her waist with a big bow in the back, but today the apron strings hang at her side. She puts several clothespins in the pocket of her apron, rubs her stomach, and says, "Hand me a towel."

I grab the edge of a towel, shake it loose from the other wet laundry in the basket and hand it to her. She sighs.

"Are you okay, Mother?"

"Just tired, Rebel."

Humph. Lately Mother's always tired. Two times this week while reading a book to me after lunch she fell asleep. One day she did not wake up until Columbia and Amherst came home from school. I don't like to take naps, but Mother does.

I hand Mother two socks. She removes a clothespin from her mouth and snaps the socks onto the line. "Grandma Rose and Grandpa Michael will return to St. Louis after the Fourth of July. You will go home with them and spend a few weeks in St. Louis before you start kindergarten this fall."

"Really? How will I get there?"

"On the train. This is something special just for you." She clips a towel to the line with two snapper clothespins.

"You mean Amherst and Columbia aren't going?" My eyes sparkle with delight.

"No, I need them here to help me with the gardening and canning. Hand me another towel."

I hand her a tea towel. One Amherst embroidered flowers on. "A trip just for you and me, great!"

"I'm not going either. This is something only you get to do," Mother whispers as if conveying a top secret message.

"Why aren't you coming with me?" I ask with suspicion.

"If I did, then it wouldn't be something special just for you, would it? You'll be the first person in our family to ride the train from

Schoenfeld to St. Louis."

"First?" I squint and stare at Mother, not certain I'm hearing her correctly. I stamp my boots and stick out my chin, "Are you sure Columbia hasn't done this? She always does everything first."

"No, neither she nor Amherst has ridden on a train. This time, you'll be first."

I'm actually going to do something before Columbia does, hot diggity dog.

When Columbia and Amherst return from Vacation Bible School, I run out to meet them. "I'm going on a big train ride, and you can't go. I'm going to be first! You have to stay here and work in the garden. Ha ha ha."

Columbia doesn't whine to Mother that she should be first. This is not like her, but I don't care. I'm going to be first.

* * *

Friday evening, after Daddy helps Grandma Rose and Grandpa Michael into the house, he returns to the car and returns with a large box. Grandma Rose and Grandpa Michael hug Mother, and then she sees Amherst. "My goodness, girl, you're already as tall as I am."

"Yeah, she's going to be a giant," Columbia says.

"No, she isn't," Grandpa says. "Amherst is going to be tall like me."

Grandpa is the tallest man I've ever seen. He's taller than Daddy. Grandpa and Grandma have white hair. She has on a black hat with a large brim that is covered with red roses. The flowers on her hat match the flowers in her dress.

"You look like a bouquet," Mother says.

"Thank you, Bonnie," Grandma says. "Once a LaFleur girl, always a flower girl."

"Were you a real flower girl, in a wedding?" I ask.

"No," Grandma says. "Lafleur, which is French for Flower, was my last name before I married your Grandpa and became a Cassidy. My sisters and I all had names of flowers."

"Sisters?" Columbia says. "I thought you only had one sister, Aunt Lily?"

Mother clears her throat. Daddy inhales deeply, and Grandpa sighs.

"I do, Columbia," Grandma says. "A little slip of the tongue. I must be getting old."

Now Mother sighs, Grandpa coughs, and Daddy exhales. Everyone seems to be waiting for someone to talk, so I say, "What's in the big box? A present for me?"

"It's not polite to ask for presents," Mother says.

"It's something for you," Grandpa says. "Bet you can't guess what it is."

"Bonnie," Grandma says, "You certainly have your hands full with this one." She points at me. "Keep after her or she'll be nothing but trouble later on."

"Now, Rose," Grandpa says, "Rebel's just a child. Curious, That's all."

"What is it?" I ask.

Daddy takes out his pocketknife, slits open the box, and removes a shiny red tricycle.

"Wow!" I sit on the seat. "It's perfect." The tricycle has a basket on the handlebars and a small bell that rings when you push a lever. Riiiing. Riiiing.

"We have bicycles for you girls," Grandpa says. "Early birthday presents. We had Sears ship them to the post office. We'll pick them up tomorrow."

"Thank you. Thank you," my sisters say.

"I hope mine is purple," Columbia adds.

On Saturday the Fourth of July, Mother fries chicken, Grandma makes potato salad and fresh ears of corn are boiled and slathered with butter.

After supper Daddy places three metal lawn chairs in the back yard. Mother spreads a blanket on the ground for my sisters and me. We don't sit in the grass because chiggers might bite us. I've never seen a chigger, but if they bite you know it because your skin itches for days. At dusk, the lighting bugs start winking on and off. I catch two and show them to Grandpa. At 10 o'clock the sky is finally dark enough that we can light our sparklers. I twirl around the yard as gold and silver sparks fly from the end of my sparkler. "Look. I'm a ballerina."

"I certainly hope not," Grandma says.

After the sparklers burn away, we put the hot wires in a bucket of water. They sizzle when submerged. My sisters and I lie on the blanket and watch the dark sky explode with red, blue, green and silver rockets that Daddy and our neighbors are lighting. It's a magical display of colors.

* * *

By Tuesday my sisters have mastered bike riding. They have Band-Aids' on their knees and scratches on their elbows covered with orange Mercurochrome, but they can now pedal around the neighborhood without Daddy running along beside them to hold the bike steady. Daddy picked baskets of fresh peas before he left for work. Amherst and Columbia are sitting in the shade of our apple tree shelling them. I can't do this as I smash the peas in the pod before I can get the pod to split open. With my sisters occupied, Mother suggests that Grandpa and I pedal to the Post Office to buy stamps, so she and Grandma Rose may talk without interruption.

Grandpa puts on his straw hat with a wide brim. I pedal down the sidewalk with Grandpa close behind.

"Grandpa, Rexall is right by the post office."

"Is that so? What do they sell there, snips, and snails and puppy dog tails?"

"No, Grandpa. Ice cream!"

"Oh, I scream, you scream, we all scream for ice cream."

"Yes, I want ice cream!"

At the Post Office, Grandpa buys a dozen purple 3-cent stamps for our letters and puts them in my tricycle basket. At the Rexall Drug Store, I sit on a high stool that swivels around by the lunch counter. Grandpa orders me a chocolate covered vanilla ice cream on a stick. Trying to pedal and steer my tricycle while eating my ice cream bar is difficult. A piece of the hard chocolate shell falls to the ground. Phooey. That's the best part. At home I burst into the house with chocolate on my face and fingers and thrust the stamps toward Mother.

"My goodness," Grandma Rose says. "You're a mess. Wash your face."

As I walk toward the bathroom, Grandma says to Mother, "For a minute I thought my eyes were playing tricks on me. She looks just like my sister did when she was that age. Rebel has her disposition too, sassy and dramatic. You better hold a tight rein on Rebel or she'll turnout just like you-know-who."

Mother shakes her head. Grandpa says, "Sorry, I should have picked up napkins at Rexall's." Grandma harrumphs her displeasure.

After supper I flounce into the upstairs bedroom my sisters share. "I had ice cream today."

"Big deal." Columbia opens a book from the library. Her books are filled with words, no pictures. I like books with pictures.

"I had a chocolate-covered ice cream bar."

"Tell me something new," Amherst says. "That's all you ever eat. You have no imagination."

"What's 'magination?" I ask.

"You're too young to understand," Columbia says.

"I'm not too young. I can read. I know lots of things," I reply.

"Imagination is something you'll never have," Amherst says.

"Who wants 'magination when they can have ice cream?" I stomp from the room.

My excitement over having an ice cream bar is diminished, but not so much that I refuse Grandpa's offer the next day. I might not have any 'magination, but I'm not stupid.

Thursday, Mother says, "Rebel, take off your culottes and shirt and put on the clean clothes on your bed. When your father comes home from work, he'll take us to the train station."

In my small bedroom next to theirs, my blue Sunday dress which Mother made is on my bed. On the floor, white socks protrude from my brown oxfords. I slip off my dirty play clothes, pull the blue dress over my head, and kick the hideous brown oxfords under the bed. I'm not embarking on a record-setting adventure wearing those clodhoppers. A trip of a lifetime requires special attire. I pull on my cowboy boots and tip toe to the back door. "I'll wait in the driveway for Daddy." When he pulls into the driveway, I get in the backseat of the car.

Moments later, Mother, Daddy, my sisters, grandparents, and I are wedged into our Dodge. Daddy, Columbia, and Grandpa sit in the front. Grandma, Amherst, Mother and I squish together in the back. I can't sit still. I'm excited to start my 'first' real adventure.

"Sorry Mother," I say. "I didn't mean to kick your leg."

Mother leans over to rub her shin and notices my booted feet.

"Rebel, where are your oxfords?"

"Under my bed."

"You can't go to St. Louis in those boots." Mother says.

Daddy consults his watch. "Yes, she can."

"What will people think?" Mother's fingers knead the creases in her brow.

"Whatever they want." Daddy says. "We don't have time to go home and get her shoes."

"Hurrah!"

"I'm glad I don't have to be seen with her," Columbia says.

Grandma pats Mother's arm. "It's all right, Bonnie. I'll buy Rebel shoes in St. Louis."

Maybe Grandma will buy me black patent leather slippers or Mary Janes. Nothing like fancy shoes to make you feel special.

At the station, Grandma and Grandpa assure my parents they will take good care of me. They hug my sisters goodbye, shake Daddy's hand, and tell Mother to take care of herself. They give Mother a final hug and allow the conductor to assist them onto the train. They wait in the vestibule of the coach for me to climb onto the small metal conductor's stool and board the train.

"Remember your manners, Rebel. Don't give Grandma and Grandpa any trouble," Mother warns me. I shake my head indicating "yes" to the manners and "no" to the trouble causing.

Daddy gives me a final hug. "Good-bye Buckaroo."

My chest swells with pride. I grab my striped cardboard suitcase and climb onto the small metal stool near the massive train. "Bye Daddy. Bye Mother." Amherst and Columbia wave.

The distance between the step stool and the train is a wide chasm filled with monstrous steel wheels, sharp cinders, and hissing steam. Maybe I can't make history after all.

"All aboard!" The conductor yells. He hoists me under his arm where I dangle and squirm like a sack of snakes. My boots flail the air as he bounds onto the train. The last thing I hear is Columbia and Amherst's hysterical laughter. Inside the passenger car, the conductor sets me down and escorts me to a seat by a huge window.

I gaze at my family, who suddenly seem small and far away. I wave to Mother and Daddy as the train lurches forward. As the steam whistle pierces the air, I put my thumbs in my ears, wave my fingers, and stick out my tongue, my final salute to Amherst and Columbia. Yippee! I am making history.

The rhythmic click of the iron wheels is hypnotic. I watch mesmerized as farms and small villages appear and disappear as we travel through the approaching darkness away from my family. Miles away.

Chapter 3
Hog Heaven

While wallowing in the lap of luxury at my grandparent's apartment in St. Louis, I forget my sisters. I'm in hog heaven. Life is great. When I say, "I've always wanted a pet," Grandpa rode home from work on the streetcar the next day carrying a bright yellow canary in a cage.

"What will you name your bird?" Grandpa asks.

"Daisy, because it is bright yellow like a daisy."

"Over my dead body," Grandma murmurs. "What about Tweety?"

"No. It needs a yellow name."

"What about Sunflower?" Grandpa suggests.

"No, that's too big of name for a little bird. I'll call it Sunny."

"That's not much better," Grandma mumbles.

Within a few days, Sunny is eating small seeds from my hand; his beak tickles. Sunny's cage hangs by an east-facing window. When the sun's first rays hit his cage, Sunny trills and chirps. His singing doesn't stop until I cover Sunny's cage at night with a floral pillowcase.

Grandpa says, "There's no need to set an alarm clock with that bird in the house."

One night I forgot to put the cover over Sunny's cage. Every time a streetcar turned the corner, its headlight illuminated the living room, and Sunny burst into song. In the middle of the night, Grandma got up and covered Sunny's cage so we could sleep.

The next morning it rained. Dark clouds covered the sun. Sunny didn't sing. Grandpa missed the early streetcar that passes their apartment and was late for work.

"That bird is a fair-weather friend," Grandpa said. "I'll set my alarm from now on."

* * *

"Grandma, Sunny got out of his cage," I scream. I chase Sunny around the apartment until I'm frazzled and still can't catch him. "I'm sweating like a pig, Grandma."

"Rebel, ladies do not sweat. Horses sweat. Men perspire, but women glow."

I run into a closet and shut the door. The darkness closes over me.

I wipe my damp forehead and look at my hand. I see nothing. I burst from the closet shouting, "I'm not glowing, Grandma. I told you I was sweating."

"I declare, Rebel. You could try the patience of Job."

"Come here birdie. Stop! Come here, Sunny."

"If you'd quit running around hollering like a wild animal," Grandma says, "Sunny will land."

I sit on the couch, as still as I can. Finally Sunny lands on my shoulder. In one quick motion Grandma grabs Sunny, puts him in his cage and latches the door. She picks up her Bible and sits beside me. She smoothes her white hair that is drawn into a tight bun at the nape of her neck. A pink rose clip holds it in place.

Yesterday she read a story about a man who was swallowed by a big fish. It reminded me of *Pinocchio*, the movie we saw last week. That wooden boy was eaten by a horrible blue fish.

"I don't want another fish story, Grandma. Being inside a fish would be scary and stinky. Once Columbia was sick and she threw up her tuna fish sandwich all over the rug, and it stunk to high heavens. I don't want to be eaten up and spit out. I'd rather be a queen like the lady you read about the other day. Then I could wear a fancy crown and beautiful dresses. If I was a queen, I'd wear black, shiny Mary Jane shoes on my feet."

"Land of Goshen child. You have an imagination like nobody's business. You need to forget all these wild ideas before they lead you down the road to perdition." When she opens her Bible, a sepia-toned photo flutters to the floor.

I jump off the couch to get it. "Where's the road of purr-dishes? Is that the path Little Red Riding Hood was on when she met the Big Bad Wolf that wanted to eat her? I don't want to be eaten by a wolf either!" I hand Grandma the photo of three girls in strange clothing.

"Little Red Riding Hood had trouble because she didn't obey her mother. If you do what your mother tells you, Rebel, you won't have to worry about big fish or wolves eating you?"

"Who are the people in that picture?"

"Me and my two sisters," Grandma replies.

"Is it Halloween? You have on weird clothes."

"No. This photo was taken when I was six years old. Those clothes were in style then."

"Which one are you?"

"The one in the middle. I had an older sister and a younger sister."

"I'd like a baby sister. Big sisters are no fun. I wish a big fish would eat Columbia and Amherst and never spit them out."

"Rebel, what a thing to say." Grandma replaces the photo in the Bible. "You have two very nice big sisters."

"No, I don't." I swing my booted feet. The heels thump the couch. "They never play with me and always tell me I'm too young to understand."

"Well, let that be a lesson to you." Grandma shakes her finger at my swinging feet. "Soon you'll be a big sister. Be sure you don't act like that."

My boot swinging stops, not because Grandma's gnarled finger points at my feet, but because she said I was going to be a big sister. "How can I be a big sister? We need a baby. Grandma, where do babies come from?"

Grandma sputters, "Uh, you don't need a baby to be a big sister. You can be Sunny's big sister."

"Sunny's a bird, not a sister." My frown softens, but a seed of curiosity remains.

***

"Today we'll ride the streetcar across town to see my older sister," Grandma says. "Your Aunt Lily and her daughter, Pansy. Do not ask Lily about Uncle Zeke. She and Zeke were divorced last year."

"What's a divorce?"

"Something decent people don't do. Lily has a difficult time getting along with people. She's too bossy. Zeke got tired of it and left," Grandma said.

I'm wearing my good blue dress and Grandma has on a green dress with yellow roses on it. She usually wears a dress with roses because that is her name. She has a real rose stuck in the bun at the back of her neck.

After a long streetcar ride, we get off and walk two blocks to Aunt Lily's house. She lives in a small chocolate-brown house. "I wonder what Lily will be wearing today?" Grandma says.

Aunt Lily answers the door in a bright orange dress with black spots. "Come in, come in. So glad to see you. Rebel, come hug me."

Aunt Lily is a tiny woman covered with wrinkles and freckles. Her gray hair curls around her impish face. I've never met anyone so old. She gives me a tight hug.

"Not so hard, Aunt Lily. You'll squeeze the juice out of me!" I say.

"Now don't that beat all?" Aunt Lily turns toward Grandma. "Rebel speaks her mind, doesn't she?"

"Yes, but that kind of behavior can lead to trouble," Grandma says.

"She's a child, Rose. Don't be hard on her. Here, Rebel. I bought these especially for you." She points toward a plate of Fig Newtons on her coffee table. I reach for one, but stop midair when Grandma makes a single 'tut' noise with her tongue. I sigh. My favorite treat is so close and yet so far away. I sit on the couch and wait.

"You're dressed like a tiger lily today." Grandma frowns. "Orange really isn't your color."

"And why not? I like bright colors," Aunt Lily says.

"At your age I think you shouldn't be so flamboyant," Grandma says.

"I'm only three years older than you. Not ancient and decrepit yet," Aunt Lily says.

"You've always been headstrong, just like Daisy," Grandma says. "I was the only one in our family with a lick of common sense."

I edge toward the coffee table and pop one Fig Newton in my mouth and grab two more.

"Rebel!" Grandma's scowl reminds me of my manners.

"Thank you, Aunt Lily." Cookie crumbs fall from my mouth.

"Rebel, don't talk with your mouth full," Grandma says.

"But Grandma, I thought you wanted me to tell Aunt Lily 'thank you.'"

Grandma shakes her head. "I can't win with this child."

I gnaw off the cake part of the Fig Newton, then pop the gooey filling into my mouth and lick my fingers.

"Use a napkin, Rebel," Grandma says.

"Why? I'm not going to wrap this other cookie up for later. I'm going to eat it right now."

"Use the napkin on your sticky fingers," Grandma says.

I lick my fingers again. "Look. See. They're clean now."

Grandma shakes her head and sighs again.

"Aunt Lily, where's Cousin Pansy?" I ask.

"Teaching school. First grade this year. She'll be here later."

"Aunt Lily, you've got more freckles than me. You're spotted all over. Will I look like you when I'm old?" I rub my nose and cheeks that are peppered with copper spots that match the color of my curly hair.

"I doubt it. You take after your mother. She doesn't have freckles, but your grandma had a boatload of freckles." Aunt Lily exhales with a 'whew.' "Your grandma's face was one big freckle when she was a child."

Grandma Rose scowls at Aunt Lily, purses her lips, and drums her fingers on her thigh, something she never does. She's always the picture of poise, serenity, and refinement. If looks could kill, Aunt Lily would have died right then and there. I stare at Grandma. Her pale skin is covered with fine wrinkles without a hint of freckles. "What happened to your freckles, Grandma? You don't have any now."

"They fell into my wrinkles and disappeared," she snaps.

I touch her cheek to pry open the crease near her lips to discover her hidden freckles.

"Rebel." Grandma jerks away. "Don't touch me with your sticky fingers. See what you started," she hisses at Aunt Lily.

"Sorry. The comment about her grandma just popped out." Aunt Lily stares at me. "She doesn't look a bit like Amherst or Columbia, does she? They look like their father's side of the family. Brown straight hair and blue eyes. Rebel looks just like —"

"Hush up, Lily!" Grandma glares at her sister.

"I never thought I'd see the spittin' image of you-know-who sitting right here in my living room." Aunt Lily says. "Don't you see the resemblance, Rose?"

"Yes. And now that you've had your say, be quiet." Grandma clenches her jaw and fists.

Aunt Lily adjusts herself in her wing-back chair, assuming a regal pose, like only an older sister can do. Aunt Lily juts out her chin and sticks her nose in the air. Grandma and her sister are acting just like Columbia and Amherst, fighting each other with words.

They sit in a stony silence. Aunt Lily's lips are in a pout and Grandma's are clenched. They squint their eyes and make prune faces at each other. When my sisters act like this, Mother says they must say, "I'm sorry, and ask to be forgiven," but neither Aunt Lily nor Grandma speak. Are they going to be stinky all afternoon?

I reach for another cookie. Grandma frowns. Aunt Lily smiles and pats my curls. "I hate freckles. I hope mine fall off and never come back."

"Nonsense. Freckles make you special," Aunt Lily says.

"Says who?"

"Not everyone receives a sprinkle of stardust from the angels." Aunt Lily pauses while my frown softens.

I laugh. "Aunt Lily, you have funny wrinkles on your forehead. Grandma's wrinkles go up and down when she frowns, but yours go straight across your forehead. Why?"

"Rebel, I told you, it's not polite to ask personal questions," Grandma says.

"Rebel's not rude, just direct," Aunt Lily says. "Gets right to the point. I like that."

"Why do you have sideways wrinkles?"

"So I can screw my hat on and the wind can't blow it off."

"Oh, I see." But I don't see at all. I take another cookie. While she and Grandma talk about people I don't know, I frown and feel small wrinkles on my forehead. I push a Fig Newton onto the wrinkles. The cookie falls off. I try again. No luck. When Aunt Lily and Grandma's voices change to hushed whispers, I pay attention. Secrets are always whispered. I like secrets.

"Are you going to Uncle Grover's funeral?" Aunt Lily asks.

"Probably not. When is the funeral?"

"Next Thursday in Francisville." Aunt Lily leans toward Grandma. "They're going to bury him beside Aunt Millie in the family plot. Thank God we got that mess straightened out. Plot poachers! Can you believe it? I've never heard of such a thing."

"That cemetery mess was all caused by her." Grandma's disgusted tone of voice tells me she is angry. "She was spoiled rotten, just like you."

"I was not spoiled," Aunt Lily huffs. Tears well in her eyes.

"You can store your tears, Lily. I'm wise to your ways," Grandma says.

Aunt Lilly scrunches her nose. Her freckled face resembles a prune again.

"She never understood the word 'no.' Our dad gave you and her anything you wanted. When he finally told her 'no,' she went wild. She was no good, and as usual, I had to cope with the mess she left behind. I never wanted to —"

"Watch what you say, Rose. Little pitchers have big ears," Aunt Lily says. "It was your choice to —"

"Lily, be quiet?" Grandma clamps her jaw shut and hisses between her false teeth. "It's over and done with. Let sleeping dogs lie."

"You can bury bodies, but you can't bury the past," Aunt Lily says. "One day a certain person in this room, who I will not name, or one of her sisters is going to find out what happened, and then the fat will hit the fire. Just you wait and —"

The clock chimes four. Grandma jumps to her feet. "My goodness, it's late. Rebel. We have to leave."

"Aren't you going to wait for Pansy to come home?" Aunt Lily asks.

"Not today," Grandma says.

"I want to see my Cousin Pansy," I whine.

"Some other time, Rebel," Grandma says. "We must leave now to catch the 4:15 streetcar or we won't be home by five to cook your Grandpa's supper."

"I'll have Pansy visit you soon." Aunt Lily gives me a final hug and whispers in my ear, "I know how to get your grandma's goat."

"She has a goat," I say. "Where is it?"

"Shhhhhh," Aunt Lily cups her hand around my ears, "It's an expression, means I know how to make her mad. I can have the last word in any argument. Watch me."

"You're not filling that child's head full of foolishness, are you, Lily?" Grandma says. "Rebel has more than enough silly notions of her own."

"Of course, not Rosy." The corners of Lily's lips twitch into a smug smile.

"It's a secret. Right, Aunt Lily?" I say.

"Don't call me Rosy, you know I don't like that," Grandma snaps.

"Yes. Another family secret," Aunt Lily says. "Something we don't mention, right Rosy?"

Grandma jerks my hand. "Come along now Rebel. There's no time to waste.

"Good-bye, Rosy," Aunt Lily calls at the door. "Bye, Rebel." She winks at me.

Grandma pulls me down the steps and does not say good-bye to her sister.

* * *

My days in St. Louis become weeks. We ride the streetcar to the circus where I ate cotton candy that was frothy and pink. I tell Grandpa it tastes like a cloud. He tells me I have a vivid imagination.

Another time we visit the zoo. The hippo which looks like a huge hog snorted misty water and snot onto my face. Grandma wiped it off with a handkerchief trimmed with lace.

There's always Fig Newtons in their kitchen and I don't have to share them with anyone. Grandma bought me a tea set with pink roses on it, because we share the same name, Rose. I don't like tea, so we use water and pretend it is tea.

Yesterday, Grandpa and I went to a huge store that sells everything in the whole world. There are moving stairs that take you from one floor to another. There is nothing like this in Schoenfeld. He bought me Mary Jane shoes. They are black patent leather, shiny with a bow on the front that looks like a white rose. My every wish is their command, and yet, I miss my family.

Chapter 4
There's No Place Like Home

"I received a letter from your mother today," Grandma says.

"What does it say? Can I go home?"

Grandma opens the letter and reads it to herself and then says, "Your sisters have a piano recital next week. They're playing a duet. Your father took a business trip to Topeka last week. The tomatoes are doing well. Plenty to be canned."

"Did she say when I can go home? I want Mother and Daddy. I don't want to be here. I want to go home. Tell her I won't tattle on Columbia and Amherst again." I stomp my feet in my new patent leather shoes. They make a soft slapping sound on the linoleum in the kitchen, not nearly as loud as stomping my boots, so I jump up and down screaming, "I want to go home."

"Stop that Rebel, you'll wake the dead." Grandma pulls me onto her lap. "Don't get yourself all worked up. You'll be going home soon."

"Are you sure?" I rub my dripping nose on her shoulder.

"Yes, of course. I don't know what gets into the curly head of yours thinking your family would abandon you."

"Because that's what happened to that boy in the Bible. Moses. He was put in a basket, floated away and never saw his family again." I sniff. "Columbia and Amherst said if Mother can find a big basket, she will float me away in the Kansas River."

"Children aren't abandoned like that now. It's not right." I look at her eyes to see if she is telling me the truth. She has a faraway look. The same one Mother gets when she is thinking. "Your sisters were just teasing. The saints preserve us, Rebel. You beat all. Now blow your nose on this, not on my dress."

She hands me a white handkerchief edged with lace that has a pungent smell.

"This stinks. What's that smell?" I wipe my nose on the handkerchief, but it makes me sneeze.

"That's lavender. I have a sachet of it in my dresser. Lavender is soothing. Did you know Lavender is my middle name? Rose Lavender, such a pretty name, don't you agree?"

Grandma continues to hold me on her lap which is nice, but her hugs are not like Mother's. I sniff again. I miss Daddy. The lap of luxury is a lonely place. I even miss Amherst and Columbia griping about practicing the piano and having to shell peas and pick beans. Nestled in Grandma's loving arms, I imagine what my family might be doing right now, and I wish I was home.

* * *

Three days later as I lay on my bed nibbling on Fig Newtons, Grandma says, "Rebel, get your suitcase out from under the bed, so I can pack your clothes. You're going home today." She dumps a load of clean laundry on my bed.

"Yippee! Really? I'm going home to Schoenfeld."

"Yes, you're going home to the beautiful fields. That's what Schoenfeld means. It's German. I'm sure many of first settlers were from Germany. You fit right in. Your father's side of the family is German."

"What's a German?"

"Someone who lives in Germany or came from Germany? Now scoot under the bed and get your suitcase."

"Okay." I crawl under the bed. The floral bedspread hangs to the floor transforming the area under the bed into a dark tent. I sweep my arms back and forth in search of my suitcase, dust bunnies stick to my arms.

Grandma's black shoes nudge my feet. "Hurry up. Don't take all day under there."

"Ouch! My hair is caught. I'm stuck, Grandma. I can't get out." I clutch my suitcase handle.

Grandma kneels on the floor. She slips her arm under the bed to free my hair by pulling it.

"Don't! That hurts. Stop it!"

"Hold still." She tugs my hair again. "It's caught on the bed springs."

"Ouch! Stop! Don't do that! Help. Ooooow!"

"Shhh. Be quiet. The neighbors will think I'm killing you."

"I'll never get to go home," I moan. "I'll be stuck here forever."

"Hush now. Don't cry." Grandma pats my bottom before she stands.

"Where are you going? Don't leave me here."

"I'm going to get the scissors."

"Noooooo! Don't cut my hair."

Minutes later, my bangs look as if they have been gnawed on by rats, but I am free. I toss my suitcase on the bed, unbuckle my Mary Janes, and shove them in the suitcase. "Soon as I put on my boots we can go." I run toward the front door carrying my boots.

We're not leaving until your grandpa comes home from work."

I sink to the floor, and press the soles of my flowered cowboy boots against the front door. Sunny's chirping fills the room. Warm moist air from the open window wafts over me. Beads of sweat form on my upper lip. I'm too far away from the floor fan to feel a breeze, but I'm not moving. At noon, Grandma lures me away from the door with a peanut butter sandwich, but minutes later I'm at my post by the door. I have no intention of missing this train ride. When Grandpa arrives, I shout, "Come on everybody, let's go."

"Don't you want to say good-bye to Sunny?" Grandma calls as I go out the door.

I spin on my heels, stick my head inside the apartment and shout, "Good-bye Sunny."

A horn toots twice, announcing the arrival of our taxi. Grandpa locks their apartment and follows Grandma and me to the waiting Yellow Cab. The driver stows our suitcases in the trunk. I sit in the back seat between them. My smile is almost as wide as the backseat.

This time, I don't give the conductor a chance to boost me onto the train. I bound from the small step stool onto the steam-belching train. If necessary, I would jump a chasm of fire and snakes to go home.

As the sun sets, I watch village lights wink on across the summer landscape. I press my nose against the window, creating a greasy spot. When the train makes a sweeping turn, I see the massive beacon on the front of the engine cut a swath of light across the countryside. The rhythmic clickety-clack of the steel wheels over the rail joints lulls me to sleep.

When Grandma wakes me, the sun is rising. She takes me to the tiny toilet room at the end of our train car. By the time we return, a porter is pushing a cart down the aisle with drinks and warm cinnamon rolls. He pulls up a small table that was flat against the wall under our window and locks it into place. He sets a small glass of juice, a large glass of milk and two cinnamon rolls on a plate before me.

"Here's breakfast for the curly, red-haired girl," he says. "Enjoy."

Usually, I'd say don't call me a curly, red head, but I'm hungry, so I just say, "Thank you." Grandma and Grandpa have steaming cups of coffee with their rolls.

I press my nose against the window as the train speeds through a flat, treeless landscape with miles of tall corn and fields of grass, some with cattle munching large bales of hay. The small towns we pass are marked by church steeples and huge grain elevators that reach toward the sky. "Grandma, I see a white horse. That's good luck, isn't it?"

"Yes, you can make a wish."

I wish I were home.

Midmorning the train slows, and the steel wheels scream in protest as the huge engine hisses to a stop. I look out the window, wipe away my greasy nose print with the sleeve of my dress and see a wonderful sight: Daddy, Columbia, and Amherst. Home at last. I'll never tell Columbia and Amherst this, but I am actually excited to see them.

I rush to the exit before the conductor places his step stool on the platform. I descend the train's three steps and take a gigantic leap of faith. I don't care if I land with a splat on the ground and my sisters laugh until their skin bursts, I want off this train! I'm home.

Daddy catches me midair, saving me from skinning my knees. "Hey, it's my little Buckaroo."

After everyone hugs everyone several times, I ask, "Where's Mother?"

"She's home resting. She has a surprise for you," Daddy says.

"What is it?"

"Won't be a surprise if I tell you. Now get in the car."

Daddy opens the door of our green Dodge, and I jump in the front seat. Grandpa Michael sits beside me. He always sits in the front seat. Daddy puts our suitcases in the trunk while my sisters and Grandma Rose settle into the back seat. Daddy starts the car and turns on the radio. "It's almost time for the news."

"Good morning. You're listening to KDOG-AM. We have a nose for news. Last night Mayor Wacker asked the city council to enact a…"

"Is that Waylon?" Grandpa asks.

"It must be," Grandma says. "No one else has a voice like our son."

"Yep, that's Uncle Waylon," Columbia says.

"I thought you'd be surprised," Daddy replies.

"When we gave Waylon money to invest in a radio station, I never imagined he'd want to be on the air again. I thought he gave that up years ago," Grandma says.

"He really seems to enjoy being on the radio," Daddy says. "He's a big dog here in town. Everyone knows him."

"I hope he sticks with it," Grandpa says. "I'm retiring soon. I can't afford to give Waylon money every month, even if he is our son. It's high time he did —"

"How are Bessie and Wanda?" Grandma says.

"Aunt Bessie and Cousin Wanda are fine," Amherst says. "They wanted to come with us, but we all can't fit in one car."

"They live about ten blocks from us, but soon we'll be on the same block," Columbia says. "Daddy's having a new house built for us in their neighborhood."

"Bonnie Rose never wrote about a new house in her letters to me," Grandma says.

"We just got the loan yesterday," Daddy says.

"When will it be finished?" Grandma asks.

"In five or six months," Daddy says. "Bonnie's excited, She's already selected paint and carpet colors."

"If you need any money, let me know," Grandpa says. "I can trust you to pay me back, unlike Waylon."

"Now Michael, don't start that," Grandma says.

I look over my shoulder and see Grandma's scowl, but Grandpa doesn't turn. He keeps on talking. "Waylon's never been responsible. He's certainly not frugal like we are Rose. Waylon's like your sister Lily. He spends every dime he has and then borrows more. Now, Bonnie Rose, there's a daughter you can be proud of."

"Michael, that's enough," Grandma says.

Even without turning to see her face, I know Grandma has clamped her teeth shut and set her jaw like that of the painting of George Washington at the library. The tone of her voice means further talk on this subject is forbidden.

Grandpa keeps quiet.

"Thanks for the offer, Michael, but we don't need any money." Daddy stops at a red light. "My job with the Kansas Department of Roads pays well."

"Don't hesitate to ask," Grandpa says. "Henry, you're like a son to me, better in many ways than the one we have."

"Michael!" Grandma hisses.

"Well, Henry is more responsible," Grandpa says. "Waylon spends money like some hotshot movie star, and then expects me to pay off his debts."

"Michael, that's enough," Grandma snaps. "Little pitchers have big ears."

We ride in an uneasy silence for several blocks. Daddy points out the window to a building under construction. "That's going to be a Dairy Queen. They sell soft serve ice cream and chocolate dipped ice cream cones."

"That's different," I say.

"That's not the only thing that's different," Columbia says. "Now Amherst and I have to share our bedroom with you."

"Wow! Since I'm sleeping in your room that means I'm all grown up. You can't call me a baby anymore."

"For your information, you're not the baby anymore," Amherst said. "You've been replaced."

"Yeah, now you're just our snotty little sister," Columbia adds.

"Replaced by what?" I ask.

"A new ba . . ." Amherst says.

"You keep your trap shut, Amherst," Columbia says.

"Tell me," I whine.

"You girls quit teasing your sister." Grandma's stern voice hushes Columbia and Amherst.

You haven't been replaced, Rebel," Daddy says. "You're one of a kind. All my girls are special."

After Daddy parks in our driveway, I nudge Grandpa out of the car and rush into the house in search of Mother. She's sitting on our blue sofa near the radio wearing a white apron over her blue print dress. Her wavy brown hair is combed in her usual short bob, but instead of listening to a favorite radio program, the radio is silent. Mother's attention is directed toward a squirming, squeaking item in a pink fuzzy blanket that she cradles in her arms.

"Mother! Mother!"

Mother puts a finger to her lips to quiet me. She moves one arm from around the bundle, draws me to her side, and kisses my cheek. "I'm so happy my little Rebel is home. I've missed you." She looks at my ragged bangs. "What happened to your hair?"

"Grandma cut it. I was stuck under the bed, and she had to cut me out. Where's my surprise?"

"Right here."

"What is it?" I ask.

Mother pulls the blanket back from the squeaking bundle.

"A baby!" I exclaim. "A real live baby. I thought it was a mouse. It sounds like one."

"Well, it's not a mouse. She's your baby sister."

"A baby sister. Wow! This is much better than a canary. What's her name?"

"Bryn Mawr."

"Bryn Mawr? Weird name. Her nose twitches just like Mickey Mouse's does in cartoons." I smile at Bryn Mawr, and she makes more squeaking sounds. "Hi, little mouse."

"Do you want to hold her?"

I sit beside Mother on the couch, and she places Bryn Mawr in my lap. I hold out my finger and her doll-like fingers curl around it. "Look, Mother. Mouse is holding my hand." I sigh with happiness. "Hello Mouse. I'm your big sister."

Chapter 5
Late Night Adventure

A week later I start kindergarten at Pawnee Grade School. Kindergarten is a half-day only. I'm in the morning class. Amherst and Columbia, who are in the fourth and fifth grade, walk me to school in the morning and home at noon for the first few days, and then they say, "You're on your own. We want to walk with our friends, not a pesky little sister." None of the kids in my kindergarten class walk home in my direction, so I walk alone.

My life is as flat and boring as the Kansas landscape until Halloween night. After collecting a sack of candy, I fall asleep holding a half-eaten Snickers bar. I'm having a wonderful dream about playing with my cousin Wanda when a hand on my shoulder shakes me awake. "Rebel, wake up. Put on your house slippers and robe and get in the car." Mother rouses Columbia and Amherst.

"Mother, I can't go outside like this, I'm only wearing my pajamas!"

"You'll be fine. No one will see you. Hurry up." She nudges me toward the front door.

Holy cow! What's happening? A car ride in the middle of the night must mean the world is coming to an end. And my "stay-at-home, never-do-anything-exciting" family is actually going to witness this big event. Hot dog!

I rush outside into the dark night. I trip over the garden hose, stumble forward, turn in a circle trying to balance on one foot, and fall flat on the driveway. Dazed and bruised, I grab the massive chrome bumper on our car and pull myself upright. I shuffle to the back door of the car and sink onto the soft seat. "Aaaah."

"That was some fancy dance, Buckaroo." Daddy snickers.

"Sheesh," I check my knees and elbows for scrapes and bruises.

"That pirouette you did before you landed flat on your face was spectacular."

"Did I look like a ballerina? I want to take dance lessons, but Mother says I can't."

"Uh, well, uh… you listen to your mother. If she says no dancing, then there will be no dancing."

"But Daddy, if I took dance classes, I could wear a pink dress.

Ballerinas never wear blue. Mother always makes me wear blue clothes, because she likes blue, but I don't. Daddy, please tell Mother I should take dance lessons. Please, pretty please with cream and sugar on top."

"Won't do any good, Rebel. Your Mother and Grandma are dead set against dancing."

"Cousin Wanda takes dance lessons, and Grandma doesn't care, so why can't I?"

"Here come your mother and sisters. I need to move that hose before they trip on it."

I slump in the back seat. Everything I want to do, Mother's answer is always 'no.'

Daddy backs the car out of the driveway. Mouse is asleep on Mother's lap. Columbia and Amherst are too drowsy to quarrel, so I am able to keep my place by a window. Soon the street lights of Schoenfeld disappear and the night sky surrounds us like a black velvet curtain.

"Where are we going?" I ask.

"See that orange glow straight ahead," Daddy says. "That's a huge fire."

Daddy turns on the radio. "I'm Waylon Cassidy with a special KDOG-AM news bulletin. If any of you night owls are awake, look to the south and you can catch a glimpse of the fire of the century in Hendrix. Flames were reported shooting through the roof of Marshall's Egg Processing Plant at midnight by Willis Jones. Fire departments from seven towns have responded to the blaze. The cause is yet to be determined. Citizens within three blocks of Marshall's should evacuate…" Daddy turns off the radio.

"Marshall's is by a Department of Roads' equipment lot," Daddy says. "If the fire spreads, the gas tanks there could explode and destroy all the snow removal equipment for western Kansas."

"Oh, no," Mother says. "That would be terrible."

Hendrix is a jumbled parking lot of fire trucks, police cars, ambulances, station wagons, pickups, tractors, and anything with wheels that could be driven into town when we arrive. I stare wide-eyed out the back window as savage orange tongues of fire lick the black sky. Our car is engulfed in a hellish glow. I roll down my window. Fire sirens wail in the distance. The heat from the inferno warms my face. The acrid smoke makes my eyes water. The distinct smell of rotten eggs, burning wood and hot chemicals assail my nostrils.

Columbia jerks upright, pushing Amherst off of her. "Phew. Shut the window you idiot-stick. You'll kill us." Columbia covers her nose.

"It smells terrible," says Amherst. "Like the bathroom does after Uncle Waylon uses it."

"Amherst," Mother says. "That's not ladylike."

"Maybe, but it's true," Amherst says. "If Uncle Waylon ate a bowl of chili and drank a few beers on a windy day he could asphyxiate half of Schoenfeld."

Mother holds her lips together, but Daddy laughs. After clearing her throat, Mother says, "Rebel, roll up the window."

I slowly crank up the window. Amherst and Columbia are asleep again. Car doors open and close. People outside appear as dark silhouettes moving toward the blaze as if pulled by a mysterious magnetic force.

"Daddy's out there with his camera!" I open the door and run after him. "Wait! I'm coming with you."

"No, Rebel, go back to the car. You could get lost out here or hurt," Daddy says.

"But I want to see the fire up close."

"It's too dangerous. Something might explode." He turns around. "Your Mother's outside by the car. I'm sure she's worried. Go back."

"But, Daddy, I want —"

"Rebel, where are you?" Mother calls. "Rebel, answer me. Rebel!"

Mother pacing by the car shouting my name reminds me of Henny Pennywho ran around yelling 'the sky is falling.'

"I'm coming." I walk backwards toward her so I can watch the flames.

Mother hugs me tightly. "Don't run off like that again. Something could have happened to you. It's a cold cruel world for a little girl who doesn't have her mother or father with her."

"I wasn't alone I was with Daddy, and you were here."

"Get in the car."

That tone of voice means the discussion is finished. Over. Done. I can whine till the cows come home and she'll never budge. I get in and slam the door hard enough to wake Columbia and Amherst.

"Are we home?" They mumble.

Home? How can they be thinking of home at a time like this?

What in blazes is wrong with everyone? We're at the fire of the century and all Columbia and Amherst want to do is sleep.

We sit for what seems hours in the car with the windows rolled up because of the smoke and chilly night. Daddy finally opens the car door. "What took you so long?" Mother says. "I was worried."

"I wanted to make sure the fire was contained. If the Department of Roads facility caught fire, I'd be neck deep in paperwork for a month."

"Was anyone injured?" Mother asks.

"No. The last shift at Marshall's left at 10 o'clock. The building was empty."

"I suppose all the eggs there are hard boiled now," Mother says.

Daddy laughs and looks at his watch. "Good grief, it's two in the morning. I didn't know it was so late." He turns and looks in the back seat. Columbia and Amherst are slouched together sleeping. "You asleep, Rebel?" He asks. Late at night when parents think you are sleeping, they share secrets. I say nothing. "They're all out like the lights," Daddy says to Mother.

"They'll be tired tomorrow. It's Saturday, they can sleep late," Mother says. "Isn't that Waylon over there?"

"Yeah. He's gathering information for tomorrow's newscast." Daddy starts the car.

"Well, at least he's still working. Not expecting another handout."

"Now Bunny, don't be that way." Daddy drives slowly between parked vehicles.

Bunny is Daddy's pet name for Mother. He only calls her Bunny when she's upset. I asked Daddy once why he calls her Bunny, and he said, 'Go ask your mother.' When I asked Mother, she said, 'That's layovers to catch meddlers, and you're the first meddler I've caught.' I figure that's another way adult's tell kids, 'it's none of your business.'

"Waylon's operated the radio station here for a year. I think he'll stick with it," Daddy says. "At least I hope he will."

"Did you ever tell Mom and Dad that we bailed him out of jail?"

"No. It would upset them, and I like your parents."

"Waylon's their favorite," Mother says. "Always has been, always will be. They spoiled him rotten. I was never good enough to even be second best."

"I know, Bunny, but it's best to let bygones be bygones."

“I do, most of the time.”

Mouse whimpers and Mother rocks her. “Shhh, Mousey. Waylon’s selfish. Thinks he’s the center of the universe. He never says he’s sorry. I’ve forgiven him seven times seventy, just as Jesus said, but if Jesus met Waylon, he’d say seven times seven thousand.” Mother sighs. “How much money do you think my folks gave Waylon to buy KDOG-AM?”

“I have no idea. Your Dad offered me money to help build our new house.”

“I didn’t know that. Did you take it?”

“No. We don’t need it. Your parents will be retiring soon. They need to save their money.”

Mother caresses Daddy’s shoulder. “That’s one of the reasons I love you, Henry. You’re kind and honest. Always thinking of others. Not the least bit selfish.”

Daddy gives Mother a brief smile. I gaze out the window at the stars, knowing I’m blessed to be in a loving family, even if I do have two older sisters who bug me.

Chapter 6
Not Alone Anymore

For months I have slept in the upstairs bedroom with Columbia and Amherst. I hoped they might share secrets with me or let me play games with them, but they pushed their bunk beds to one side of the room, drew a chalk line on the floor and told me their side of the room is off limits. When I am home from school in the afternoon, I often lie on their beds, not because I am tired, but because I can. Ha!

The week of Easter is special. First, we have no school. Second, Mother made us all new dresses to wear on Easter Sunday. Mine is blue gingham, which is really just blue checked material, but it does have tiny pink roses in some places. Our church, St. John's Lutheran, will be filled with beautiful-smelling Easter lilies, and trumpets will play before we sing Hallelujah. And third and best of all, Daddy's taking the week off from work and we are moving into our new house. On Monday Columbia, Amherst and I will not return to Pawnee Grade School. We are now in the Cherokee school district. I hope Wanda and plenty of girls will be in my class.

For weeks,Mother's been busy sewing curtains and packing boxes. On Saturday several men who work with Daddy and Uncle Waylon arrive with a U-Haul truck. After it is filled, we get in our car, and Daddy drives us to our new home and Uncle Waylon follows in the U-Haul.

There are many new houses on Arapaho Street where we'll live. A few of the yards have newly planted trees. There aren't many trees in western Kansas. It's flatter than the pancakes we eat on Sunday morning.

"Our street is named for one of the Indian tribes that lived in Kansas before the Pioneers moved west," Mother says.

Daddy points to a two-story house with a huge porch. "That's where your Uncle Waylon, Aunt Bessie and Cousin Wanda live, Buckaroo."

"Here's our house." Our car bounces over the curb and into the yard. "This curb will be replaced by a driveway next week."

Scrap lumber and unused cement blocks are stacked near the porch. A cottonwood tree with large limbs stretches over our yard.

"Can I have a swing?" I ask.

"We'll see," Mother says.

When Mother says, 'We'll see,' that usually means 'no.' But Daddy saves the day. "Sure thing, Buckaroo. I think a swing is just what that tree needs."

Inside the house we walk from one empty room to another. It's like opening presents on Christmas morning. The kitchen is light blue. Flowered café curtains Mother made are hung on the windows. The living room has a fireplace. I imagine my Christmas stocking there. The dining room has a bay window with a bench, a perfect place to sit and read. Mother and Daddy's bedroom is painted aqua, which is a different color of blue, no surprise there. A small alcove in their room will be Mother's sewing area. Two smaller bedrooms down a long hall are for Columbia and Amherst. Pale green for Amherst, lavender for Columbia.

"Where's my room?" I ask.

Daddy opens a door to a large bedroom. "You and Mouse will share this room."

Sky blue. I should have known. Windows stretch across one wall. I gaze at a big backyard that slopes away from the house. Across a weed-filled alley is a large building.

"What's that building?"

"An apartment house," Daddy says.

"Do some kids live there?"

"No, it's for retired people," Daddy says.

"Like your grandma and grandpa," Mother says. "They'll be moving there soon."

"Wow! Really? That means Grandpa can buy me ice cream every day."

"Maybe not every day, but often."

"Yoo-hoo. Anybody here," a voice calls.

I run to the front door. "Come in, come in. Mother! Aunt Bessie and Wanda are here."

Mother enters the empty living room holding Mouse on her hip. "You're our first visitors. Good to see you, Bessie."

"I'll take Mouse and Rebel off your hands today," Aunt Bessie says, "so you can unpack."

I grab Wanda's hand, excited to have a girl to play with. "Let's go."

"Wait a second, Rebel," Aunt Bessie says. "Bonnie, tonight the neighbors are having a potluck at six o'clock. Please come. It will give you the opportunity to meet your new neighbors, and your girls might make a friend or two before they start classes at Cherokee on Monday."

"My goodness," Mother says. "I've no idea which box has my kitchen utensils. I can't get anything baked by tonight."

"Don't worry about bringing anything. I've made plenty of potato salad and a huge pan of brownies. I'll pick up more hotdogs."

"That's so thoughtful," says Mother. "Bessie, you are like a sister to me. Where's the potluck?"

"On the vacant lot next door to you." Aunt Bessie takes Mouse from Mother's arms. "Come on Wanda, you too Rebel. Let's get out of the way so the men can get to work."

* * *

By six o'clock more than thirty people are setting up tables and BBQ grills in the vacant lot. The men are shaking hands and drinking beer while tending the grill s. A booming voice proclaims, "I'm the voice of KDOG," which tells me that Uncle Waylon is here. Columbia and Amherst drift toward a group of kids their age around a table with a metal wash tub filled with ice and bottles of root beer and Coke. Baby strollers and women sit in the shade of a young elm tree. I stand beside Mother while she talks to a bunch of women I don't know. Boring.

"Twins keep me busy," a woman says. "Skip and Sandy are always into mischief."

"How old are they?" Mother asks.

"Six, they'll be in first grade next year."

"Is Sandy here?" I ask.

The woman's reply is muffled by another woman screaming, "Come down out of that tree before you fall and break an arm."

A boy is swinging from a branch of our huge cottonwood tree like a monkey. "That's my son, Jimmy," his mother says.

"Geronimo!" Jimmy jumps from the tree.

His mother gasps. "He's going to be the death of me."

"Boys will be boys," Mother says. "I don't know much about boys, all I have are girls."

"Is this one of your daughters?" A lady points at me.

Mother turns toward me. "Yes, this is Rebel. She's our third daughter."

"She looks about the age of my Jaylynn. How old are you Rebel?" The lady asks.

"Six. I'm in morning kindergarten, but I can already read."

The lady nudges a blonde girl toward me. "This is Jaylynn. She's in morning kindergarten too. We live on the other end of this block. You girls should get to know each other."

And that's how I met my best friend.

Chapter 7
Making Friends

Before I finish kindergarten, Grandma Rose and Grandpa Michael move into the apartment building across the alley from us. They live on the ground floor and when they sit on their back porch, they can see my sisters and me playing in our backyard. Most of the time that's okay, but sometimes Grandma calls Mother and tells her she should watch me closer, or I will get into trouble playing in the alley with other kids. Phooey.

Today Mrs. Thomas, Jaylynn's mom, telephoned and invited me to come play with Jaylynn. Mother actually said, "yes." Not her usual, "We'll see." Whoopee!

"I'll walk you to Jaylynn's house to make sure you get there safely. I'm sure you can walk home by yourself," Mother says.

She puts Mouse in her stroller and off we go. I take my baby doll Nancy with me, hoping Jaylynn likes to play with dolls as much as I do. The sidewalk is new and smooth. My sisters and their friends roller skate on it. I'm not good with skating yet. I spend more time falling down than moving forward.

We walk down our front sidewalk, which curves to the right before it meets the public sidewalk. "We'll walk to this corner first." Mother points in the opposite direction of Jaylynn's house.

"Why? That's not where Jaylynn lives."

"I know, but Mouse needs fresh air, and the exercise will be good for me."

I shuffle along, not happy about having my playtime delayed. First, we pass a vacant lot. Next is an empty house with a 'for rent' sign in the front yard. The next house is a huge, two-story, white house with a giant lilac hedge separating it from the house for rent. The lawn is a bright green with no dandelions. Our lawn is new, and Daddy sprays it often with something that stinks to kill the dandelions. I like the dandelions. They are bright yellow, my favorite color. I inhale the fragrance of the lilacs.

"Who lives there?" I ask. "Do they have kids my age?"

"The Benson's. They have a son, Bobby. He's Columbia's age, and an older daughter."

"They must be rich to have such a big house."

"Maybe so," Mother says. "He's a doctor. But money isn't everything, Rebel."

The next house is on the corner. It has a sloping roof that covers a wide front porch. The front yard is perfect. The evergreen bushes are neatly trimmed. A crab apple tree blooms near the house. Large peony bushes with deep pink flowers line the front sidewalk. The grass is trimmed so that not one blade touches the sidewalk. An old lady wearing a sunbonnet is sweeping the porch steps.

"Hello," Mother calls. "Beautiful day isn't it."

I lean down to smell the peonies.

The old lady looks up and nods. "Don't pick those flowers!"

"Rebel wouldn't do that," Mother says.

"Some of the kids around here have no respect. They roller skate on my driveway and skid off into the grass. I like my yard neat."

Mother turns the stroller around making sure not to let it touch the lawn. "I'll tell my older girls to be careful when they're skating."

"You the new family that moved in with all the girls?"

"Yes. We have four daughters."

"Hummmph. Hope they are not as wild as the boys in this neighborhood. Hard to keep my yard looking nice with them cutting across my lawn to save a few steps."

"Being on the corner does have its drawbacks," Mother says. "I'll tell my girls to be careful."

"Good. I'm Miss Penstemon. Retired from teaching third grade last year. Kids today have no discipline."

"Some don't. That's for sure. I know. I taught school for several years before I married."

"Then I'm sure you know how to keep children in line." Miss Penstemon sweeps the few blades of grass and twigs she had gathered into a dustpan. "Good day."

Mother walks quickly down the street. After we pass Dr. Benson's house, and the house for rent I say, "Miss Penstemon must be an old maid. She looks just like the woman on our old maid cards."

"Calling her an old maid is not kind. She's a maiden lady."

"She sure was crabby."

"That's not polite to say. She may have her reasons. Just see that you keep off her lawn."

Mother doesn't tell me not to call her crabby, and I know why. You can't argue with the truth.

We pass our house and continue toward Jaylynn's house. The vacant lot on this side of our house has stakes driven into the ground. Daddy says they mark where the basement of a new house will be dug. Next is a red brick house with a single garage. Two kids, a boy and a girl, wave at their huge picture window as Mother and I pass.

"That's the Prescott house," Mother says. "We met them at the potluck."

"I know. Skip and Sandy. They're twins." I return their wave. "They were in afternoon Kindergarten."

Next to the Prescotts is a long ranch-style house painted white with a small front porch and a double attached garage. The front door is open. A large box fan is in a front window. The blades turn slowly. Inside the house a woman shouts, "Go outside and play!"

The screen door flings open. Jimmy Randall charges out.

He rushes across the yard and stands with arms out and his legs wide apart on the sidewalk in front of us. "Halt! Who goes there?"

"Neighbors, out for a walk. I'm Mrs. Rothberg. This is Mouse." She pushes the stroller ahead a few feet. "And this is, Rebel."

"Weird name." Jimmy says. "I've seen you before."

"Yes," I mumble. "You're in my Sunday School class."

"Rebel's her nickname," Mother says. "Her real name is Reddl —"

"Red! That's a perfect name. Red, the red-haired girl," he says.

"Don't call me, Red." I say. "That's rude."

"Red, Red, Red," he says.

"Jimmy! Stop teasing that girl." His mom opens the screen door and walks toward us. A little boy follows her. "Don't mind, Jimmy. He's full of baloney. I'm Mrs. Randall. We met at the potluck a few weeks ago. This is Tommy, our younger son."

"Nice to meet you again," Mother replies. "You remember Mouse and Rebel, don't you?"

"Come on, let's go." I try to push past Jimmy.

"Not so fast there, Red. You have to say the magic word," Jimmy says.

"Please."

"Okay, you can pass. Where you going, Red? Can I come along?"

"It's none of your business, and no, you can't come along." Jimmy grabs my doll. "Give me my doll!"

"Jimmy!" Mrs. Randall yells. "Give Rebel her doll. Now go in the house." She sighs. "Boys. Enough to drive you crazy."

Mother and Mrs. Randall say goodbye, and we continue walking toward Jaylynn's house. Beside Jimmy's house is another ranch style house, this one made of brick. A sign in the front window says, 'Reelect Councilman Roberts.'

"That must be where our councilman lives," Mother says.

I don't know what a councilman is, nor do I care. I want to play with Jaylynn. She's outside waving at me. I run past Councilman Robert's house toward her.

"You brought your doll. That's great," she says. "I have a walking doll. You want to play Cootie?"

Jaylynn's house is tan with green shutters. A long driveway leads to a single garage in the backyard. The front yard has several newly planted trees and evergreen bushes shaped like gumdrops along the house's foundation.

As we run up the steps to the front door, Mother calls, "Be home in two hours, Rebel."

Mrs. Thomas opens the front door and waves to Mother.

Jaylynn has her very own bedroom. Her room is painted pink and there is a canopy over her bed. Along one wall are bookcases filled with storybook dolls and games. Her large walking doll, wearing a yellow dress stands in the corner. She grabs Cootie from a shelf. We sit on the floor and sort the pieces into piles.

"Your room is beautiful. Looks like it belongs to a princess."

"I'm an only child. I'm glad you could come play. I never have anyone to play with."

"Well, I have three sisters, and I don't have anyone to play games with either. Columbia and Amherst, they're my older sisters; they always tell me I'm too young to understand. And my little sister Mouse would eat these pieces or throw them around the room."

"Would you girls like a snack?" Mrs. Thomas calls from the kitchen.

"Sure." Then I remember my manners. "That would be very nice, Mrs. Thomas. Thank you."

Jaylynn and I sit at a yellow Chromecraft table in the kitchen and eat molasses crinkle cookies and drink root beer. Life can't get better than this. I have a friend and root beer to drink.

When the clock chimes four, I say "I have to go home. I've had a great time. Thanks for inviting me."

"Come anytime," Mrs. Thomas says.

"I'll walk you part way home," Jaylynn says.

Outside, I look across the street and see Uncle Waylon getting out of his big fancy car, a Cadillac. "Hello, Uncle Waylon. Is Wanda home?"

"Yeah. She and Bessie are inside. Don't be a stranger, come over and say hello."

Jaylynn and I run across the street.

"Did you find yourself a playmate, Red?" Uncle Waylon says.

"Yes, this is Jaylynn, and don't call me Red."

"Red you are, and red you'll be. Jaylynn, nice to meet you. Come in and say hello to my wife and daughter."

"I better stay outside," Jaylynn says. "Mother will worry if she can't see me."

The screen door snaps open. "Aunt Bessie!" I run up the steps to receive her hug.

"Well, aren't you a sight for sore eyes. What brings you to this end of the block?"

"I came to play with Jaylynn. I'm on my way home. Is Wanda here? I want her to meet my best friend, Jaylynn." Best friend. Those words roll off my tongue like butter melting on a steaming ear of corn.

"Wanda!" Aunt Bessie calls. "Someone here to see you."

Wanda looks like a smaller version of Jaylynn. Jaylynn is tall, a head taller and me, and has long blond hair that she holds back from her face with barrettes. Wanda is short like me. Her hair is long and blonde too, but has gentle waves. Today she's wearing it in a pony tail.

"Jaylynn, this is my cousin Wanda. Guess what? We'll all be in first grade next year. You two could be twins," I say, "except one of you is short and the other tall."

"Skip and Sandy are twins," Wanda says, "and they don't look alike."

"Of course not," Aunt Bessie says. "One's a boy, and one's a girl."

I look down the block and see Mother in our front yard. "I better go. See you later. Bye, Uncle Waylon. Bye, Aunt Bessie. Come down and play sometime, Wanda."

Aunt Bessie walks to the curb and sees Jaylynn and me safely across the street. "I had fun today, Jaylynn. I love your storybook dolls."

"If you want to borrow one, you can."

"Really? My sisters never let me touch their stuff."

As Jaylynn and I pass Councilman Roberts' house, Jimmy jumps out from behind a bush. "Dolls! Is that all your girls ever talk about?"

"Run, Jaylynn!" I shout.

She turns and runs toward home, and I hurry in the opposite direction.

"Come back, Red. I want to talk with you," Jimmy calls.

"I've got nothing to say to you, Jimmy, except, don't call me Red."

Chapter 8
Names and Old Photos

Grandpa told me time moves faster when you get older. I'm not sure how that works, because there are still 365 days in a year, and I only get one birthday a year, but it seems like yesterday I was the new kid on the block, and now I feel like I've known Skip, Sandy, Jaylynn, and Jimmy for a hundred years. Actually, it's just been three years. We all passed third grade, which is an accomplishment because Mighty Munson the Warden of Cherokee Grade School was our teacher. We've earned our summer vacation and I plan to spend most of it with Jaylynn and Wanda.

One scorching July afternoon, Jaylynn and I are leisurely skating toward my house. I rarely fall now unless I forget to lift my skates when passing over the crack in the sidewalk by Dr. Benson's house. The steel-wheels of our sidewalk skates click in unison as we roll over small cracks in the sidewalk.

"Jaylynn, guess what?" Before she can say what? I say, "My Aunt Steve from Wisconsin is visiting us next week."

Jaylynn furrows her brow, "Aunt Steve? Don't you mean your Uncle Steve?"

"No, my aunt," I reply with obvious disgust.

"Why does your aunt have a boy's name?"

"I don't know. She just does!"

"I can't believe you don't know why your aunt is called Steve. You always have an answer for everything."

At my house we skate onto the lawn, our surefire method of stopping without scrapping our knees or scuffing the toes of our shoes. We collapse under the shade of our cottonwood tree. Daddy never attached a swing to the tree, but that's okay, I have a friend.

"Jaylynn, look, a cicada." We watch it crawl up the tree trunk.

"Why do you think your aunt is named Steve?" Jaylynn says.

My diversionary tactics haven't worked. "How should I know? I wasn't alive when she was born."

"Ask your dad. She's his sister, isn't she?"

"Yeah. I'll ask him sometime," I say.

"Why not now? He's home."

"He's probably busy." I've no desire to open an unknown can of worms in front of my best friend. I don't suffer humiliation well, and my life gives me plenty of opportunities to experience embarrassment. None of the kids in the neighborhood will let me forget what happened at Jaylynn's Halloween party last year. When her dad sprang out from behind the couch dressed as a ghoul, Wanda and Sandy screamed and ran to hide. Jimmy and Skip were crying like girls, but I choked and snorted root beer out my nose transforming a plate of cookies into a soggy, snotty plate of mush. Nope, I'm not asking Daddy anything about Aunt Steve's name.

"Come on, let's ask him." Jaylynn takes her skate key from a string around her neck. She fits the end of the key into a bolt on the front of her skates and loosens the clamp so she can slip her skates off her shoes.

"Oh, all right. Give me the key."

Daddy's watching a White Sox game on our twenty-one-inch black and white TV. The picture is snowy, since the TV station is far away in Topeka. A turquoise aluminum tumbler of iced tea sits on the end table sweating a pool of water onto a stack of his engineering magazines.

"Daddy, why does Aunt Steve have a boy's name?"

"She's always been called Steve," Daddy says.

"Steve's her nickname isn't it, like me being called Rebel?"

"The Sox have three men on. Watch this next play. It could be a grand slam."

"Yeah, but Daddy why is she —"

"That wasn't a foul ball! Looked fair to me," Daddy shouts at the TV.

I ask several more questions about Aunt Steve. None receive a straight answer. Finally, he says, "Go on now. I'm watching the game."

End of discussion.

"Come on Jaylynn, let's get a snack."

"Mr. Rothberg, is Steve really her real name?" Jaylynn asks.

"No," Daddy says. "Her name is Stephanie, but no one ever calls her that."

* * *

The next day when I visit Grandma, she's in one of her storytelling moods. She tells me for the umpteenth time her last name was Lafleur, (flower in French) before she married my grandpa, Michael Cassidy, and that she and her sister were called the Flowers of Francisville. I'm bored, but I know not to interrupt. After she tells me, again, "Your Aunt Lily named her daughter Pansy to carry on the Flower tradition," I ask, "Why didn't you name Mother for a flower?"

"She already had a name," Grandma says. "Bonnie. Your grandpa liked the name Bonnie. Said she was a bonny girl. Bonny means pretty in Scottish. Your grandpa has Scottish heritage, you knew that didn't you?"

"No. Wait a sec. You said Mother already had a name. Babies aren't born with names."

"Did you know my father called me Ross not Rose for years?" Grandma says.

"No, why?" This stuns me. I forget about Mother having a name before she was born.

"My father wanted a son," Grandma says, "many men do. Your Aunt Lily, my older sister, was born first. Papa doted on Lily like she was the Queen of Sheba. Humph!"

The passage of years has not tempered Grandma's feelings toward her sister. Seems as if the "forgive and forget" message she's always preaching doesn't apply to her and Lily who always bicker when they're together.

"What does Aunt Lily have to do with you being called Ross?" I ask.

"Hold your horses. Don't interrupt. Do you want to hear this story or not?"

I nod yes.

"Now where was I?"

"You were telling me about Aunt Lily being the Queen of Sheba."

"Well, as I was saying, my father wanted a son. He forced me to wear trousers."

"That's not so bad. I wear pedal pushers in the summer."

"But ladies did not wear trousers in the 1890s. A few suffragettes bucked tradition and wore them, and when bicycle riding became fashionable women wore bloomers, but trousers with suspenders like I wore then were only for men."

"That's terrible." I know what it is like to be out of fashion. Most of my clothes are Columbia's hand-me-downs.

That night before falling asleep I think about names. Daddy has a sister called Steve. Grandma was called Ross. It's a miracle they didn't become crazy axe murderers, like Lizzy Borden. The jump rope chant we sing springs to mind. Lizzy Borden took an axe, gave her mother forty whacks, when she saw what she had done, she gave her father forty-one. I fall asleep and dream about having a normal name like Mary Anne.

* * *

Mother and Daddy's room is off limits, unless invited in. Mother's beautiful red maple cedar chest sits in a corner of their room. Mother keeps her treasures in the chest. The only time I can peek inside is on the rare occasions when she opens it. Today, Mouse and I stand by Mother as she lifts the lid. The pungent smell of cedar floods the room. Mother removes a large quilt and in that instant Mouse snatches an item from the corner of the chest.

A fuzzy blur whips by my eyes. "What did she take?"

"An old puppet," Mother replies.

"Why does she get something, and I don't?"

"You wouldn't want that old thing. The children at the Monroe Orphanage played with it. After they were tired of it, my great-aunt Martha who worked there gave it to me."

"You mean it's a hand-me-down toy?"

"Yes, I guess you could call it that," Mother says. "Rebel, you're not the first person to receive used toys and clothes."

Mother must read minds because I was just thinking how tired I am of hand-me-down clothes from Columbia.

Mouse leaves the room singing a lullaby to her puppet. Mother and I are alone by the mysterious cedar chest. Mother brushes lint from a black photo album. Her hand lingers too long on the worn cover to just be brushing off dust. I don't want to look at photos of dead people. I want something special from the chest. A necklace, a ring, or perhaps a chance to play with her old doll.

Mother sits on the floor and holds the photo album on her lap. Even though I'm beside her, she seems far away as she scans the pages.

"This is your Uncle Waylon when he was a baby," she says.

"He sure was fat. Grandma and Grandpa had dark hair then. What color was it?"

"Brown. About the color of Columbia's."

There's a photo of Uncle Waylon in the arms of Grandma by a church altar. I don't comment on his long dress. This is his baptism, an occasion when a long white gown on a boy is acceptable. There are pictures of Waylon on a pony; in a wagon; on a sled in the snow; and one of Waylon holding the hand of a thin little girl with no smile.

"Is that you?" I ask.

"Yes. I was three then. Waylon was twelve."

"You don't look very happy?"

"I suppose I wasn't. It was strange to have a big brother."

"Why? You grew up with him."

"I wasn't close to him. Maybe it was the age difference."

Mother must have read my mind again. Columbia and Amherst are four and five years older than me. We have nothing in common. They are snotty know-it-alls and consider me their little sister, who is not worthy to be in their presence.

Mother turns more pages. All filled with photos of Waylon. "Where are your baby pictures?"

"Uh… more pictures were taken of Waylon than me. He was special, their first child."

"I know. I've seen gobs of photos of Columbia when she was a baby, some of Amherst, and far less of me and Mouse. Daddy took the most photos of Columbia because she's his favorite."

"Your father and I don't have favorites. He took more photos of Columbia because he had a new camera, and she was our first child."

Mother flips to another page. "Uncle Waylon sure looks mad. I've never seen him frown like that. He's always laughing or joking now."

"Might be the liquor talking." Mother replaces a corner tab on a loose photo.

"What do you mean?"

"Oh, nothing. Forget I said it. Aunt Bessie is a saint to put up with Waylon's antics. Your Uncle Waylon was almost the death of me on more than one occasion. Did I ever tell you about the time he left me in the park when I was three years old?"

"Yes, about fifty times." As soon as I say those words, I want to take them back. Mother snaps the album shut and stands. A brownish photo falls to the floor. I pick it up. Staring at me is a young woman with a nest of curls piled atop her head. I know the photo is old because of the style of her clothes. She holds a baby on her lap and a small man, no larger than a gnome stands beside her.

"Who are these people?"

Mother takes the photo. Her eyes sparkle with surprise. "Where did you find this?"

"On the floor. It must have fallen out of the album."

She exhales deeply, something she never does except when Columbia asks for help with her math homework. "Oh Rebel. I'm so glad you found it. I haven't seen this photo in years. I thought it was gone." Mother takes a manila envelope from the chest and slips the photo inside.

"Who are those people and what's in that envelope?"

"Layovers to catch meddlers and you're the first meddler I caught." She gives me a big hug, which is nice, but I want answers.

"What's layovers to catch meddlers mean?"

"Would you like to change the dress on my doll?" Mother asks.

Mother often shows us her old bisque doll, but we are never allowed to change her clothes. I don't know why I'm blessed with this honor today, but I don't ask, afraid she might change her mind.

"You bet! Can I put on her ruffled dress?"

"Whatever you want."

I dress the doll under Mother's watchful eyes. "What color was the curly hair of the lady in the old photo? Her hair looked like mine does on Sunday morning when you fix it."

"Do you want to put another dress on the doll?" Mother pulls a red taffeta dress from the doll box, a dress I've never seen. "This is my doll's party dress."

With the unexpected pleasure of being allowed to change two dresses on her doll I forgot my question about the lady with the curly hair.

Chapter 9
The Secret Passage

This afternoon I tighten my roller skates onto my nasty oxfords. They were my school shoes this year, but I'm forced to still wear them as Mother did not buy me sandals this summer. I've had a great afternoon playing with Jaylynn and Wanda, but now it's time for me to skate home. I pray I can pass Jimmy's house without being seen.

As I approach Jimmy's driveway, he charges from his house screaming like Tarzan. I stumble then rise to examine my skinned knees. The scabs from last week are ripped off. I spit on my fingers and wipe off fresh blood. "You're gonna kill me some day, Jimmy."

"You okay, Red?"

"Leave me alone. I can't stand the sight of your ugly face."

"Curly head, curly head, hair so red. Curly head, curly head, go to bed." Jimmy gives another Tarzan yell and follows me.

"I'm sick of your stupid poems. Go away and stay away." I skate toward home before he can see my tears.

Despite being nine-years-old, I can't stop my tears. "Mother," I cry as I pull open the door to our house. "Jimmy makes fun of my red hair like Uncle Waylon does. Uncle Waylon says red hair means trouble and that I'm no damn good."

"Rebel, ladies don't say damn."

"But that's what Uncle Waylon said."

"I'm sure he did." Mother clenches her jaw, a vein on the side of her forehead pulses. "I'll ask Waylon to stop, but I doubt he will. Waylon is pigheaded."

To solve the problem of passing by Jimmy's house, Jaylynn and I enlist the help of Sandy Prescott who lives next door to Jimmy. Before venturing out, we telephone Sandy and ask where Jimmy is. If he's in his backyard, we skate on the sidewalk. If he is lurking in the front yard, Jaylynn and I meet in no-man's-land. Ha! Sometimes I can beat Jimmy at his game of spying.

No-man's-land is the fifteen-foot-wide unpaved alley behind our houses. Sunflowers, the state flower of Kansas, blue, pink and purple larkspur, ragweed, daisies, and other wildflowers grow along the edges. I often pick the flowers to give to Mother or Grandma. Mother loves all the flowers, but Grandma tells me daisies and sunflowers are nothing but weeds. She likes the spikes of larkspur I give her. I'm partial to the sunflowers that tower over my head since they are yellow.

Moms often gather in the alley after finishing their morning chores to chat. When the Mom Patrol convenes, no kid is safe from their all-seeing eyes and chastising voices. After work and on weekends, our dads meet in the alley to smoke, talk sports, or drink a couple of beers. They keep an eye out for us kids, but for a different reason. Telling a dirty joke or two is part of their ritual. The last thing they want is one of us repeating their jokes at the dinner table.

When Uncle Waylon joins the men, the laughter is always loud. Obviously the 'no swearing' rule Grandma enforces on Mother doesn't apply to her son. Mother told me Uncle Waylon was a traveling salesman for years before Grandma and Grandpa helped him buy KDOG-AM, which is why he has an encyclopedia of jokes.

Buying KDOG meant Uncle Waylon had to move from the big city of Chicago, where he was a radio announcer, to Schoenfeld, a town of about fifteen thousand. Most people would consider this a demotion, but not Uncle Waylon. In Chicago, he was a nobody, an unknown voice on one of the many radio stations in the area, but in Schoenfeld, his booming voice is recognized all over town.

Every morning, Uncle Waylon's voice wakes the residents of Schoenfeld with, "This is KDOG-AM, 1435 on your dial. We have a nose for news." Sometimes after the news, he mentions something one of the kids in the neighborhood has done. I would love to hear my name on the radio, but he never talks about me. Columbia and Amherst are often mentioned, and they hate it. Guess there is no pleasing some folks.

The middle of the alley is full of ruts caused by Floyd's Fly-By-Night garbage truck as it barrels down the alley after a thunderstorm. Usually Floyd picks up garbage on Wednesday, so on Tuesday my friends and I scrounge the alley for treasures. The alley allows us to snoop on each other and is sometimes used as a playground since the vacant lots in our neighborhood have dwindled to zero.

Today is Tuesday. Jaylynn and I are strolling the alley for treasure. Several people on our block have remodeled their bathrooms. Old toilets and bathtubs are hidden in the hedges of their back yard. "I'd hate to have an old toilet in my back yard," I say.

"Me too," says Jaylynn. "Looks crappy."

"Ha ha, very funny. You better not let your mom hear you say 'crap.'"

Without warning, Jimmy breaks through the bushes behind his house. "What are you guys doing?"

"Nothing that concerns you," Jaylynn says.

"Taking a walk and minding our own business. You should try it some time," I say.

"Okay. I'll walk with you," Jimmy says. "I've nothing better to do."

"I meant mind your own business," I snap.

"Look, Buck Arpkey has flowers growing in his old toilet," Jaylynn says. "Guess they are pee-tunias."

"Pee-tunias, I like that," Jimmy says. "Pee Pee pee. Purple peeeee-tunias."

"Jaylynn," I say. "Don't encourage Jimmy. Look, Mr. Arpkey has a bathtub Mary, too." The interior of an old bath tub painted light blue is upended and sunk about two feet into the ground. In the niche is a statue of the Virgin Mary.

"He must be a Mackerel Snapper," Jaylynn say.

"Must be," I agree.

"What's a Mackerel Snapper?" Jimmy asks.

"That's for me to know and you to find out," I say.

"Come on, tell me what it means?" Jimmy whines.

"Go home," Jaylynn says. "Go play with Skip."

"He's not home."

"Get lost," I say.

"Nope, I'd rather be with you."

"Aren't we lucky, Jaylynn?"

"Look at the deer head on Mr. Witkowski's shed?" Jimmy says. "It's a 6-point buck. I've never seen it there before."

"He put it out there last week," I say.

"How do you know that?" Jimmy asks.

"The Mom Patrol. I overheard them say his new wife refused to watch TV with a dead deer staring at her," Jaylynn says, "so he had to move his hunting trophies outside."

"Maybe he'll throw it in the garbage," Jimmy says. "I'm gonna check back every Tuesday night."

"You do that," I say.

Mr. Powell is in his back yard beside an old boat with a gaping hole. "What happened to your boat?" Jaylynn asks.

"I was fishing on Milford's Pond and a sea monster chomped through it," Mr. Powell waves his hook hand at us. "Bit my hand off too."

"What kind of sea monster was it?" Jimmy asks.

"Last week you told me your hand was chopped off during a sword fight with a pirate," I say. I twirl my finger at the side of my head to indicate Mr. Powell must be crazy.

"Might have been," Mr. Powell replies. "Or could have been a lion at the zoo. I don't recall."

"Which was it, the lion or the sea monster?" Jimmy asks. "Did you keep your hand?"

"Bye Mr. Powell." Jaylynn and I kick clods of rock-hard clay as we continue our walk. The skeletal remains of an old swing set, its spindly legs surrounded by uncut grass are in one backyard. We walk slower as we approach Old Man Market's backyard. A huge shed there covers half of his back yard.

"I wonder what's in that shed," I say.

"I don't know," Jaylynn says, "but the Dad Patrol complained to Councilman Roberts last week about an explosion in the middle of the night. My Dad was really upset because the next morning there was stinky yellow powder all over our new Pontiac."

"He has an airplane in it," Jimmy says.

"I don't believe you," I say.

"Me either," adds Jaylynn.

"Wait up! Wait up!" Skip Prescott hollers as he runs up the alley to join us. "He does have an airplane in there. I've seen it. And guess what? There's a skeleton inside the plane."

"You're full of baloney," I say.

"Yeah, so full it's coming out of your mouth," Jaylynn says.

"You're not supposed to go into Old Man Market's yard." Sandy, Skip's twin pushes through the tall weeds to join us. "I'm going to tell Mom."

"You blab, and I'll tell Mom you broke her vase," Skip says.

"It was an accident," Sandy says. "Besides, you pushed me."

"Did not," Skip says.

"Did too," Sandy shouts.

"Jimmy," Skip says, "I dare you to climb over Old Man Market's fence and take a bone from the skeleton."

"I've got better things to do," Jimmy says.

"Chicken!" Sandy says.

"Yeah," Jaylynn says. "Cluck, cluck."

"I double dare you to do it," Sandy says.

"I double-dog dare you," Skip says.

Jimmy walks toward Old Man Market's fence. He pushes down the barbed wire, carefully climbs over it, and disappears into the chest-high weeds in Old Man Market's back yard.

"Don't go! Come back, Jimmy," I shout.

"Afraid he'll get hurt?" Sandy says. "Look who's got a boyfriend. Rebel and Jimmy swinging in a tree, k-i-s-s-i-n-g."

"He's NOT my boyfriend, but Old Man Market's dog —"

"Help! Save me!" Jimmy runs toward the fence with old man Market's dog, Vermin, in hot pursuit. As Jimmy straddles the barbed wire fence, Vermin bites out the seat of his shorts.

"I saw the skeleton move," Jimmy exclaims.

"Skeletons can't move, they're dead," Jaylynn says.

"You have a hole in your pants," I say.

Jimmy puts his hand over the back of his shorts, but not before Sandy says, "I see London, I see France, I see Jimmy's underpants."

"Shut up, Sandy!" Jimmy races toward his house.

"I don't believe Jimmy saw a skeleton or that it moved," I say.

Jaylynn and I say goodbye to Skip and Sandy and continue walking toward the end of our block to check out Miss Penstemon's back yard. Last week my skate left the sidewalk and rolled over her grass. She came out of her house screaming like an injured cat. At Miss Penstemon's we peer between the slats of her five-foot high fence and see a riot of weeds.

"Look!" Jaylynn says. "She steals road signs."

On the back of Miss Penstemon's garage hangs a STOP sign, a ONE-WAY sign, and a yellow school crossing sign.

"Maybe we should report her to Councilman Roberts," I say.

"And what would he do about it?" Jaylynn says. "Make another law?"

As we return to our yard, the Dad Patrol is having a heated discussion in the alley. We crouch behind the raspberries bushes in our yard to listen.

"I get off work at two in the morning," Buck Arpkey says, "I'm dead tired when I get home. Just as I doze off, that $%#&@ rooster Councilman Roberts has starts crowing."

"Dandy the rooster drives me crazy too," says Old Man Market.

"The city council should impeach Roberts," says Mr. Prescott. "Roberts is worthless. Plus raising chickens in town is illegal."

"Why don't you expose him on KDOG?" Jaylynn's dad says.

"I'm not sure that would help my cause," Uncle Waylon replies. "I might run for public office some day and —"

"I didn't know you were thinking about going into politics," Daddy says.

"Seems like a natural progression," Uncle Waylon says. "I'm pretty famous here in Schoenfeld and civic-minded. So, why not?"

"I wouldn't do that," Mr. Prescott say. "Politics is a dirty business. Promising one thing and doing another. It involves lying."

"True, but that's no different from what goes on in most families. Everyone has dirty laundry to air, don't they, Henry?" Uncle Waylon looks at Daddy.

The men turn toward Daddy expecting him to reveal a secret. Daddy scowls, waits a few seconds and says, "I've read if you don't have time to do your genealogy, you should go into politics and the press will do it for you."

The men laugh. Jaylynn's dad says, "You better check your closet for skeletons Waylon before you throw your hat in the ring."

"It's not my closet that has the problem." Uncle Waylon stares at Daddy again.

"What's your Uncle Waylon talking about?" Jaylynn whispers.

I shrug my shoulders.

"I don't give a hoot about politics," Buck Arpkey says, "but if that dang rooster wakes me one more time at 4:00 in the morning, I'm going to wring that @#&@ chicken's neck."

"I'll help you," Old man Market adds.

"Me too," says Uncle Waylon.

"And then I'm taking a bowl of chicken and dumplings to Roberts," says Buck.

The guys snicker. Buck grins. His eyes are dilated with anger or humor. I'm not sure which.

After supper, Daddy tells Mother about the men's conversation. "Nobody in their right mind should aggravate Buck. He's a couple of doughnuts short of a dozen."

"He and Waylon are a pair to draw to, that's for sure," Mother says.

"Waylon's thinking about going into politics," Daddy says. "He insinuated we have skeletons in our closet. That jailbird has some nerve bringing you into the conversation."

"Was he drunk?" Mother asks.

"No, just full of himself, as usual," Daddy says.

"Forget it. Waylon won't say anything that might make him look bad."

"I've never understood why your parents made a small incident thirty-some years ago a top-secret event," Daddy says. "It's nothing to be ashamed of."

"Don't say that to my mom. She says she can't forget the past because Rebel looks just like her. I don't know if that's true, because I don't remember her."

This conversation puzzles me. Who do I look like? I can't ask Mother what she and Daddy were talking about because I've been eavesdropping, and that's a big no-no.

Chapter 10
Alley Oops!

It rains on the last week of fourth grade. Friday is our school picnic at Riverside Park and if the weather doesn't clear, we'll be eating our sack lunches in the gym. Riverside Park contains Schoenfeld's only swimming pool, a small dugout cave, numerous picnic areas, tennis courts, and several playgrounds that have tall swings on chains and killer metal slides. The tallest slide has 20 steps to the top and after several kids have slid down it on sheets of wax paper the slide is so slick you fly five feet off the end before landing in a gully dug by the heels of hundreds of shoes landing in it. Most of the kids remain standing when they land. Falling on your butt is really embarrassing, I know. There are several Merry-go-rounds too, but I don't like them. I get off feeling dizzy.

The day before the picnic the rain stopped. We rode big yellow school buses to the park. Four hours later we returned to Cherokee Grade School exhausted and filthy because the gully under the swings and at the bottom of the slide were filled with muddy water.

Rain is a crummy way to start summer vacation. We are forced to play in our front yards, no sneaking around in the alley. Prudent people or those already baptized in mud, stay out of our alley after a torrential rain. The ability of that muck to suck the boots off grown men is well documented. More than one member of the Mom Patrol has received a full-body mud bath, better than the one the local beauty salon offers, when she lost her balance trying to pull her foot from the mud's grasp and fell into the gooey slop.

Jimmy delights in making mudpies from the glop which he dries on a discarded piece of sheet metal. The first week of summer vacation after we had all finished fourth grade, one of Jimmy's dried disks hit Jaylynn in the face. Jimmy's mom tanned his hide with a willow switch. Jimmy said the whippin' didn't hurt, and I guess it didn't because he was flinging disks again the next day. Jaylynn wore her black eye with pride for two weeks. She was our neighborhood hero because she'd taken a direct hit from one of Jimmy's mud grenades and lived to tell the tale.

Jimmy swears being a garbage man is the best job in the world, because you can save all the good stuff for yourself. I figure no treasure is worth working around stinky stuff all day, but since today is Tuesday, and Jaylynn and I are bored, we are searching for trash treasures.

In Doc Benson's trash we find a moth-eaten, stuffed raccoon wearing a Superman cape. I hoist the raccoon over my shoulder and lug it into the house. "Look what I found!"

"Yikes! Drop that filthy thing and go wash your hands," Mother says.

I watch her toss it in our garbage can. I wash my hands and then sneak outside to retrieve the raccoon. I lug it across the alley to my grandparents' apartment.

"That's quite a monstrosity you have there, Rebel," Grandpa says. "What are you going to do with it?"

Before I can answer, Grandma says, "She's going to put it right back in the trash where it belongs. Ye gods, Rebel, that flea-bitten critter probably carries the plague. Go home and bathe immediately. And be sure to wash your hair." She mutters something under her breath about washing my hair several times to get rid of that hideous red color.

I leave the raccoon by my grandparents' trash can and trudge home across the alley. The next morning, I wake early hoping to reclaim the raccoon before Fly-By Night garbage service zooms by. I'm too late. It's gone!

I run to Jaylynn's house. "Someone stole my raccoon from my grandparents' trash," I wipe sweat from my brow.

"I saw Jimmy lug it into their garage last night."

"Sheesh. I'll never get it back if Jimmy has it."

"Probably not, but let's try."

Jaylynn and I avoid Jimmy as much as possible, speaking to him only when we have backup from Sandy or Wanda. Neither of them is home, but our desire for the raccoon compels us to confront Jimmy alone.

"Hi, Red. Jaylynn. How you do'in'?" Jimmy says. "Nice to see you."

"Don't call me Red, and we're not making a social call, Jimmy. You swiped my raccoon from my grandparents' trash, and I want it back."

"Finders keepers, loser weepers," Jimmy snipes.

"If you don't give it back," Jaylynn says, "we're, uh we're gonna —"

"You're gonna what? Tell my mom? Won't do you any good to rat me out," Jimmy says. "My dad took the raccoon."

Why would he want it?" I ask.

"Uh, I don't know?" Jimmy stammers.

"You're lying," I say. "What did you do with my raccoon after you swiped it?"

"I don't remember."

"Come on, 'fess up. You'd never misplace something like that." Jaylynn is six inches taller than Jimmy. In fact, she is the tallest person in our class. She looks down on Jimmy like a robin eyeing a wiggling worm. "Spit it out. What did you do with our raccoon?"

"If it was your raccoon, and I'm not admittin' it was, why did you throw it in the trash?" Jimmy says.

"That's none of your business. Just fork it over!" I scream.

"I don't know where it is. That's the truth." Jimmy shifts on his feet and coughs. "I haven't seen you two skating lately. Did you lose your key?" He jams his hands in his pockets as if he is hiding a great treasure.

"That old trick won't work, Jimmy." Jaylynn pulls a string from under her blouse. Our skate key gleams in the sun.

"We're not here to discuss skating. What did you do with my raccoon?" I demand.

"I lost it."

"I thought you said your dad took it?" I snap.

"He did. I think."

The more questions we ask the more nonsense Jimmy spouts, which is not hard for him to do. Frustrated, we leave. We knock on the Prescott's door. Skip and Sandy are now home. They are excellent spies except for one small detail: they can't keep a secret, which could prove useful today.

"What did Jimmy do with our raccoon?" Jaylynn asks Sandy. "He told us his dad took it."

"He did," Sandy says. "That raccoon caused a real stir last night."

"Spill your guts. We're all ears," I say.

"Jimmy showed it to us before he took it into his house," Sandy says.

"He told me he was going to hide it in his room," Skip says, "but he didn't. Sandy and I watched him from our bedroom window. Jimmy stuck it in their bathtub behind the shower curtain."

"That was dumb," I say. "It's probably soaking wet now."

"Nope," Sandy says. "An hour after he hid it in the shower, you should have heard the whoopin' and hollerin' when Mrs. Randall jerked back the curtain to take a shower."

"She ran butt naked from the bathroom screaming about a huge rat in the house," Skip says. "I saw her boobies."

"You're disgusting!" Jaylynn says.

"They weren't very big," Skip adds.

I am too dumbfounded to even say sheesh.

"So, where's the raccoon?" Jaylynn says.

"Jimmy's daddy charged into the bathroom, swinging a baseball bat, screamin' he was going to beat that dang varmint to death," Sandy says.

"How do you know this?" I ask.

"We saw it all from our bedroom window," Skip says.

"I told my mom what we saw, and she told Mrs. Randall to close their bathroom blinds before taking a shower," Sandy says.

"No! You rat fink!" Skip says. "Now I'll never see Mrs. Randall's boobs again."

"Is that all you ever think about?" I ask. "A woman's breasts?"

"Where's the raccoon now?" Jaylynn asks.

The twins shrug.

We leave. It's hopeless. Jaylynn and I scour the alley, hoping to find the raccoon discarded in another trash can, but it's long gone.

* * *

Mother always listens to the KDOG morning call-in program. Today folks are complaining about the lousy garbage service. I go outside. Fly-By-Night garbage service was right on schedule this week. My racoon is probably buried under tons of trash in the dump by now.

At supper that night, Mother tells Daddy that someone on the call-in program thought the Mayor should appoint Waylon to the Waste Management Board. Daddy says, "The Waste Management Board is just the place for Waylon. Those folks are all full of bull. Your brother will fit right in."

"Now, Henry," Mother pleads. "Children are present."

"Well, it's the truth. That board wastes money like some folk's waste water washing their hair." He looks at me.

"If I wash my hair twice a day, it won't be so red," I say in my defense.

"Boy are you stupid," Amherst says.

"This beats all. You're dumber than I suspected, Rebel." Columbia wipes a milk mustache off with the back of her hand.

"At least I know enough to use a napkin," I snipe.

"I like red hair," Mouse says. "I wish mine was red and curly like yours. You look like little orphan Annie."

"No one wants to look like a cartoon character, especially one with red hair," I shake pepper on my tomatoes, so I'll have a reason to fake a sneeze and cover my eyes that are welling with tears.

"Who told you washing your hair would change its color?" Mother scans the faces of my older sisters. Deciding they looked innocent, she asks again, "Who told you this?"

"No one," I whisper. "But Grandma said only cheap women have red hair, and I thought if I washed it a lot, maybe the color would go away."

"Your Grandma's been taking stupid lessons from Waylon," Daddy says. "She's as full of bullsh —"

"Henry, that's enough." Mother's jaw tightens the same way Grandma set hers when the conversation is over.

"What's the big deal about red hair?" Daddy says. "Her sister has red hair."

"Aunt Lily doesn't have red hair," I say. "Hers is grey."

"Her hair was reddish when she was younger," Mother says.

"Is that why I have red hair?"

"Rebel, washing your hair won't change its color," Mother pats my hand. "Your hair is lovely just as it is."

Chapter 11
Stupid Questions and Sweet Revenge

Daddy does not suffer fools or foolish questions. Unlike Mother and my schoolteachers who say, "There's no such thing as a stupid question," Daddy's mantra is, "Ask a stupid question, you'll get a stupid answer."

In late August while setting the breakfast table, Mother says, "This is our last jar of plum jam."

"I've seen plum thickets along the back roads when I've driven to road construction sites," Daddy remarks. "Columbia, Amherst, you want a take a ride with me to pick plums?"

"Not really," Columbia says. "I need to go to the Rexall to buy nail polish?"

Holy cow. All Columbia thinks about is being beautiful. She spends most of her allowance on perfume, lipstick, and scented soaps. She wouldn't give me a nickel if I needed it to save my soul, but she willingly spends thirty-five cents every month to buy a copy of *Seventeen Magazine*, which she reads like it's the gospel.

"How about you, Amherst?" Daddy asks.

"Oh, Daddy," Columbia says sweetly, "I need some money for gas. The Bel Air is on empty."

Columbia got her Driver's License this year, and Daddy bought a used 1952 Chevy Bel Air for her to drive to school and to take Mother on errands. The car is really cool, even if it is five years old. It's a 2-door cherry red convertible. Has white cloth interior, and whitewall tires. There's a lot of shiny chrome trim on it. Jimmy Randall's dad sells cars, so he got Daddy a good deal, but I think $400 is a lot of money.

"I gave you $2 last week." Daddy pulls his wallet from his back pocket. "You're only supposed to be driving to church and school, not all over town for pleasure. Here's $1. Go the Phillips 66 station on 4th street. The gas is only 29 cents a gallon there."

"Columbia, if you're going into town," Amherst says, "You can take me to the library."

Amherst's read every book in our house and makes two trips a week to get more books from the library. I like to read, but books with 400 hundred pages and no pictures are a bit much for me, but not for

Amherst.

"Columbia, drive carefully," Mother calls from the kitchen.

"I'll go with you, Daddy. Can I ask Jaylynn?"

"Sure. What about you Bonnie? Do you and Mouse want to come?" Daddy asks.

"I'd love to, but I promised to take Mom grocery shopping. You know how she gets if the plans change at the last minute. I'll take Mouse with me. I don't think Mouse would be much help to you."

"Okay, Rebel. It's you, me and Jaylynn. Let's go before it gets any hotter," Daddy says.

Daddy picks up Jaylynn at her house, and we drive to the outskirts of Schoenfeld. Daddy turns off the highway onto a gravel road. After several minutes he stops the car.

"There they are. Lot of plums, just waiting to be picked."

Jaylynn and I grab our buckets. We push through tall grass, ragweeds, and sunflowers in the ditch to reach the plum thicket. As we drop the small brightly colored red fruit into our buckets, black and white dairy cows in the pasture stare at us. Before my pail is half full, the cows move closer until they are less than two feet away. Their massive heads shake from side to side as they pull grass into their huge mouths. They are chomping monsters, separated from us by one thin wire.

A cow slips its head under the wire and pulls wild oats into its mouth. I hear its teeth pulverizing the grass.

"Let's get out of here, Jaylynn."

"I'm way ahead of you." Jaylynn beats a hasty retreat from the brambles to the safety of the road.

"Are your buckets full?" Daddy asks.

"No. We're tired of picking. We'll wait in the car," I call from the ditch.

"Afraid of the cows, aren't you? Don't worry about them. They won't bite. Keep picking."

"Are you sure those cows won't barge through that puny wire and crush Jaylynn and me?" I don't understand how one thin wire can stop those behemoth animals from stomping Jaylynn and me into pancakes, as flat and nasty cow pies strewn over the pasture.

"That's an electric fence." Daddy tosses a handful of plums into his bucket.

I know electricity is dangerous, but I can't stop myself from asking, "What will happen if I touch the wire?"

"You'll jump so high you can kiss the moon," Daddy says.

Imagining the thrill of soaring through the sky, I grab the wire. A zillion volts of electricity shoot up my arm rendering me speechless. I tumble backwards into the weeds. "Yikes!"

"Are you all right?" Jaylynn asks.

After Daddy determines I have only suffered minor scratches and a bruised ego, he smirks, shakes his head and returns to picking plums.

"What did that feel like?" Jaylynn asks.

"Like once is enough. Did it straighten my hair?"

"Nope," Jaylynn says. "It's as curly as ever. Maybe more so."

Besides picking three buckets of plums that day, I learn a valuable lesson about natural consequences that may occur as a result of a stupid question.

* * *

On the first day of fifth grade, our teacher Miss Wilcox said, "There's no such thing as a stupid question."

Jimmy's worried frown is replaced with a devilish grin. He considers questions, any kind no matter how stupid, the perfect way to distract a teacher. Six weeks into the school year, he's still pestering Miss Wilcox with stupid questions. He's yet to learn the necessity of engaging his brain before shifting his tongue into gear.

One rainy day, shortly after lightning struck the flagpole making it glow like a giant sparkler and a cloudburst turned our gravel and dirt playground into ball-swallowing swamp, Jimmy said, "Miss Wilcox, the recess bell just rang. Can we go outside now?"

"No Jimmy, it's raining."

"Why not?"

"Because we'd all get wet."

"Who cares about a little rain?"

"Your mother will if you ruin your new shoes," Miss Wilcox says.

Jaylynn looks at me and shakes her head. I twirl my finger beside my head. Crazy, that describes Jimmy. However, Jaylynn and I both agree with Jimmy when he asked, "Why do we have story problems in math class every day?"

As the weeks turned into months, Miss Wilcox never wavers from her belief there are no stupid questions, but I see her clench her teeth and mutter, "What do you want now, Jimmy?" more than once as he waves his Big Chief tablet to get her attention.

Since first grade, Jaylynn, Wanda and I have walked to school together. We are the TRIO3. Most mornings as we near Doc Benson's hedge, we hear a mighty "Arrrgh" and Jimmy and Skip zoom out of hiding toward us on their bikes. They are ravenous wolves. We are defenseless bunnies running for our lives. They pursue us without mercy until we collapse onto the safety of the school yard. What a way to start the day.

Monday through Thursday, Jimmy's classroom behavior generally rewards him with thirty minutes of detention, which means the TRIO3 can enjoy our walk home. We practice skipping backwards or try kicking a stone home without losing it in a storm sewer. On Friday, Jimmy rarely has detention, maybe because neither the principal nor the teachers want to sacrifice thirty minutes of their weekend to stay late with Jimmy.

Wanda has dance lessons this Friday, and Uncle Waylon will pick her up after school. To avoid Jimmy, Jaylynn and I volunteer to help Miss Wilcox clean the blackboards, empty the wastebaskets, and put chairs on our desks so the janitor can sweep. This will give Jimmy a head start home. I would scrape gum off the bottom of our desks with my teeth to avoid having Jimmy pester us as we walk home.

"I need to leave right after school today," Miss Wilcox says as she locks her desk. "You girls run along. You can help me next Friday,"

Jaylynn and I take heel-to-toe baby steps along the hall toward the big double doors. I nudge a heavy oak door open with my shoulder, look both ways and whisper, "Come on Jaylynn. The coast is clear." We tromp down the stone steps hand in hand, round the corner of the school building and are greeted by Jimmy's crooked grin.

"Hi. Do you want a…?" Jimmy says.

We don't stick around to hear his stupid question. We take off like horses heading for the barn. Skip and Jimmy pedal after us on their bikes. Jaylynn sprints like a gazelle and gains safety in Mr. Ritterbush's Grocery two blocks away. I run as fast as my short legs can go.

As I approach Ritterbush's, Skip blocks the sidewalk with his bike, and Jimmy bikes to my side. Trapped. He jumps off his bike, grabs my jacket sleeve with a talon-like grasp and swings me around to face him. I pant with fear and exhaustion. Then Jimmy plants a huge, wet, sloppy kiss on my face. Two of them. Yuck!

He takes a step back, nods his head in a manner that says, "I knew I could do it," then he and Skip zoom off on their bikes laughing. I spit on the sidewalk and wipe my mouth on my jacket sleeve to remove every trace of Jimmy's kiss. I turn to see who has witnessed my humiliation. Jaylynn is wide-eyed in the window of Ritterbush's Grocery. Mr. Ritterbush is laughing!

Jaylynn rushes to me with a tissue. "Here. Wipe your mouth. Are you okay?"

"Of course, I'm not okay. I'm sick to death tired of Jimmy Randall. That kiss probably poisoned me."

"What are you going to do?" Jaylynn asks.

"I don't know. Promise me you won't tell anyone? Not even Wanda."

"Cross my heart and hope to die, stick a thousand needles in my eye," Jaylynn promises.

Kissed in broad daylight in front of God and everybody. What can I do to even the score?

The next week is rainy. Jaylynn's mom, who now has a driver's license, takes us to and from school in their big black Pontiac. The TRIO3 rides in the backseat like princesses, making faces out the window as we pass Jimmy and Skip. They ride like demons, pedaling their bikes through puddles, parting them like Moses did the Red Sea.

Saturday the sky clears, and Jaylynn roller-skates unnoticed to my house, probably because Jimmy is occupied watching Wild Bill Hickok on TV. Thank heavens for stupid cowboy shows. We spread an old blanket in the backyard and lie on it slurping root beer Popsicles. Twenty feet away, Daddy is cultivating newly sprouted green beans with his noisy garden tractor. It chugs through the wet soil belching puffs of black smoke.

Daddy bought the small gasoline-powered tiller this spring. He told me it's a Sidlehooper. I don't know if Sidlehooper is a brand name or something Daddy made up, but the electric fence experience has taught me not to ask a question Daddy will think is stupid.

"Life would be perfect," I say to Jaylynn, "if Jimmy would move away."

"Maybe Godzilla will snatch him."

"Fat chance of that happening."

"Too bad neither of us has a big brother who could beat the livin' daylights out of him," Jaylynn says. "That's what he needs. A good thrashin."

"Arrrgh. Arrrgh." That familiar yell puts us on high alert. We rise up on our knees.

"Oh, no! Jimmy's coming down the alley to spy on us."

"He must be nuts," Jaylynn says. "After all the rain we've had this week, the alley is a swamp. The mosquitoes are the size of hawks."

"Dang skeeters. Get away from me." Jimmy shakes his head and struggles to dodge puddles. When he swats at a swarm of mosquitoes, his bike wobbles. He quickly puts a death grip on the handle bars.

Jaylynn and I stand and stare as Jimmy wobbles forward in slow motion.

"That's my racoon tail tied to his handlebar!" I scream.

"I knew Jimmy was lying when he said he didn't know what happened to the racoon," Jaylynn says. "Liar, liar, pants on fire."

Daddy and his tiller chug toward the alley. Jimmy stands on his bike pedals for traction.

"What's that thing, Mr. Rothberg?" Jimmy says. "What are you doing with it?"

Daddy guides the handheld tiller into another row of beans. He glances up to see who has asked such stupid questions. Any fool can see Daddy is cultivating the garden, but Jimmy isn't just any fool, he's a blue-ribbon fool.

Daddy squints and the corners of his mouth twitch, as if trying to hold back a smile. For the last six months, Jimmy's shenanigans have been a primary topic at our dinner. My retelling what Jimmy did today in school has given Daddy heartburn more than once.

"What are you talking about?" Daddy says. The garden tiller backfires and belches a column of black smoke. The metal beast jerks Daddy forward.

"What's that thing?" Jimmy calls.

"What thing?" Daddy says.

Jaylynn and I smirk and nod to each other. Daddy makes a big show of looking from side to side, under his shoes, and even scans the skies. "What thing? I don't see anything."

Exasperated, Jimmy jerks a hand from his handlebars and points at the tiller. "That metal machine. What is it?"

"Oh this? It's a banana peeler." Daddy turns the tiller toward Jimmy. "Watch out. It's going to fire a peeled banana any second now." He adjusts the throttle, the garden tractor backfires loud enough to challenge a sonic boom.

Jimmy clamps his hands over his ears. "Arrrgh."

His bike tilts. Gravity pulls him and his bike into the muck. After several attempts Jimmy stands, but he can't pull his bike from the slop. He walks home, a muddy version of the tar baby.

"Ask a stupid question, you get a stupid answer," Jaylynn and I chant.

I'd consider the score even; except for the fact Jimmy has my racoon tail.

Chapter 12
A Seed is Planted

In the spring I help Daddy plant the garden. After he tills the soil with his Sidlehooper, I carefully put small greenish dried peas in rows. Two months later the pea plants will produce tubs of pea pods that need shelling. I'm old enough to shell them now. It's tedious work. Small, round brown seeds we plant will produce radishes in several weeks. Larger oval seeds will grow into green beans. Cubes from a cut up sweet potato will produce more of those nasty vegetables. Tiny black seeds will become lettuce for Mother's wilted lettuce salad. And best of all, the gold hard kernels of corn will produce tall stalks of sweet corn. Seeds don't look like much on the outside, but they are wonderful surprise packages. How one little dried-up seed produces a giant plant is a miracle.

From May to October, fresh fruits and vegetables are a regular part of all our meals. This year Daddy bought an upright freezer. It's bigger than our refrigerator. Now Mother's chore of preserving our garden produce is easier, as freezing food takes much less time than canning. We have an apple tree that provides plenty of fruit for pies and applesauce. Fresh black and red raspberries are a real treat. I love the wilted lettuce salad Mother makes using hot bacon grease and vinegar to wilt it. And nothing is better than a BLT made with fresh tomatoes.

"Ugh! Sweet potatoes again. I hate sweet potatoes." I push my empty plate, except for the potatoes away from me and shove my chair back from the table.

"Daddy grew these sweet potatoes in the garden. Eat them. They'll make your hair straight." Mother pulls my chair to the table and replaces my plate with the offending sweet potatoes.

"No, they won't. You told Columbia and Amherst the potatoes would make their hair curly and they didn't. Sweet potatoes can't make one person's hair straight and another person's hair curly. All sweet potatoes do is make me puke."

"Rebel, don't say puke. It's not ladylike," Mother says.

I choke down my potatoes in two giant bites. "What's for dessert?" I hope it's Mother's warm chocolate pudding cake.

"Desert the table," Mother replies.

"What's that?"

"Desert the table." She stands and carries two plates to the kitchen. "Amherst. Columbia. It's your turn to wash and dry."

Mother returns with a pitcher of iced tea. "Do you want more tea, Henry?" He shakes his head 'no' and goes to the living room to read the paper.

"Dessert the table? Where's the dessert? I don't see anything. When do I get it?" I ask.

Columbia and Amherst grab my plate and glass. "Where's my dessert?" I clutch my spoon, despite Amherst's attempt to pry it from my fingers.

"Desert the table so we can shake the crumbs off the tablecloth," Columbia says.

"But I want my dessert," I say.

"What a bonehead," Columbia says.

"Don't you know what a homonym is?" Amherst sneers. "You should read more."

"Now, girls," Mother calls from the living room. "Don't pick on Rebel."

After several minutes I give up on dessert, grab the TV Guide, a small magazine that Mother buys weekly at Ritterbush's Grovcery, and plop in our green recliner. I flip through the TV Guide to today's date. May 6, 1957. *I Love Lucy* will be on next. My staking a claim on the recliner before Columbia or Amherst finish the dishes guarantees me the best seat in the house for TV watching tonight. If I get up, I must say 'saved' or they will claim the recliner.

You Bet your Life with Groucho is on now. Mother and Daddy think this weird guy with a moustache and glasses is funny. I don't. He looks like a clown.

"This show is boring," I say.

"Did you know your Uncle Waylon met Groucho once?" Mother says.

"Hmm. Really?" Who cares? If Uncle Waylon had met Walt Disney and could get us all tickets to Disneyland that would impress me.

I leave for the bathroom and when I return Columbia and Amherst are fighting over the recliner. "You forgot to say 'saved,'" they hiss.

"Get out my chair! Tonight, is the last *I Love Lucy* show."

"Too bad so sad," Amherst says as she pushes Columbia from the recliner.

I plop on the floor in front of the TV hoping to block their view.

"Come here, Rebel." Mother pats the couch cushion. "You'll ruin your eyes sitting that close to the TV."

"Columbia took my chair. I had it first." I shuffle to the couch but don't snuggle close to Mother as the evening is warm. Late spring and all summer Kansas is hot and dry. Large box fans or a dusty southern breeze are the only way to feel cooler. Amherst often puts a bowl of ice cubes in front of the fan hoping that the air blowing over the ice cubes will make the room cooler. It doesn't. The only places to escape the summer heat are the swimming pool, the bank, or movie theaters with air conditioning. When I saw *Davy Crockett, King of the Wild Frontier* sitting in the air-conditioned theater was like being at the North Pole.

When *I Love Lucy* starts, Mother says, "Did you know Lucy has red hair?"

"How do you know that? TV's only have black and white pictures."

"Lucy was a movie star before she was on TV. Your father and I saw her in several movies.

"Of course they were black and white too, but she was a guest on the Arthur Godfrey Show once and they were kidding each other about their red hair," Mother replies.

"They both have red hair?"

"Yes, but Lucy's not a natural red head."

"You mean she dyes her hair? Why would anyone dye their hair red?" I ask.

"Because it's different. People notice you. A number of movie actresses have red hair. Rita Hayworth. Billie Burke. She was Glinda the good witch in the *Wizard of Oz.*"

"Maybe I'll become a famous actress like they are."

"I wasn't suggesting that." Mother's body becomes rigid. She frowns, rubs her hands together and studies her fingernails. "The stage is not the place for ladies."

"Why not?"

"Because I said so."

Mother didn't say 'you're too young to understand,' but her words convey the same message.

"But why?"

"Be quiet," Columbia says. "I can't hear the TV."

"If you want to talk, go somewhere else," Amherst adds.

Mother puts her finger to my lips. I watch Lucy with more interest than usual. She's a red head and a famous actress! There's hope for me.

Chapter 13
Sheesh! What a Question

This year for Thanksgiving, Aunt Lily and Cousin Pansy, a dyed-in-the-wool spinster, Mother's words, not mine, are joining us. Cousin Pansy's not a crabby old maid like Miss Penstemon, who lives on the corner, and rats you out to your parents if you so much as touch a blade of her grass. Cousin Pansy is a schoolteacher. The kind every kid prays they will have instead of being saddled with Miss Bunlasher who made my life a misery last year.

On Wednesday evening, Aunt Lily steps off the train saying. "How wonderful to see you." She makes a big show of giving Mother, Mouse, and me a hug. Daddy hangs back, having no desire to receive a peck on the cheek from her withered lips.

Pansy lets the conductor take her gloved hand and assist her from the train. "I'm here! Say hello to your cuzzie." Pansy clutches a pale green overnight case.

"What's in there?" Mouse asks. "Do you have a present for me?"

"Mouse! It's not polite to ask for presents," Mother says.

I sigh. For once I am not on the receiving end of a reprimand.

"I have presents, but not in here." She pats her overnight case. "All my necessary skin care products are in here. I never let it out of my sight."

"Hello, Cuzzie Pansy," I say.

"Where are Columbia and Amherst?" Pansy asks.

"Home," Mouse says.

"Our car's too small for eight people," I add.

"Where's my sister *Rosy*?" Aunt Lily says and winks at me.

I can't believe Aunt Lily is already calling Grandma Rosy, a nickname she despises. If this continues, Grandma will have a snit, and no one will have anything to be thankful for on Thanksgiving.

"Mom's arthritis is bothering her," Mother says. "She and Dad are home."

"I'm anxious to see Aunt Rose and Uncle Michael," Pansy titters. She pulls her scarf tighter around her neck. "Chilly, isn't it? Of course, we are further north, aren't we, Mother?"

"Yes, Pansy," Aunt Lily says. "And remember, dear, we're on the wide-open prairie. Stick close to me. We're beyond genteel civilization. God knows what lurks out there in the dark."

"It's pretty tame here," Mother says.

"Yeah," I say. "The only wild animal in our neighborhood is Vermin, Old Man Market's dog. If he jumps the fence, head for the hills. He'll rip your throat out."

Pansy gasps and clutches her overnight case to her chest.

"Don't worry, Pansy," Aunt Lily says. "I won't let you out of my sight or out after dark."

"The car is warmer than standing on the station platform," Daddy says. As we settle into the car, Daddy hoists five suitcases into the trunk. "Sheesh. All this for a three-day visit."

Inside the car, Aunt Lily says, "I decided to visit you for Thanksgiving this year, because your grandma is my dear sweet sister."

I cough. Mother glares at me.

If the truth were told, Aunt Lily is probably visiting us this year because she and Grandma are on speaking terms, a rare occurrence. When Grandma and Aunt Lily have words with each other, which is often, they don't just nurse their grudge, they wean it, and raise it into a giant. If they die mad at each other, I'm sure when they meet in the afterlife; they'll pick up the fight right where they left off.

At home Daddy lugs the suitcases into the house. "Pansy has one suitcase full of beauty products. Can you believe that Daddy?" I ask. "I wonder what she has in that case."

"Foolish paraphernalia," he answers.

Mother wears very little makeup, just a hint of lipstick and powder on her nose.

"Your Mother is a natural beauty," Daddy says. "What God created Revlon should leave alone."

The next morning Mother rises early to put the turkey in the oven. I set eight places at our dining room table and two places on a card table that will be the children's table. Usually Wanda, Aunt Bessie, and Uncle Waylon join us, and Wanda sits with Mouse and me at the children's table, but this year they are celebrating with Aunt Bessie's family in Des Moines, so it will just be Mouse and me. I'd prefer to sit with adults. I'm almost a teenager, how old must I be to qualify as an adult?

By ten in the morning, our house is filled with the aroma of roasting turkey and spicy pumpkin and mincemeat pies. Our Thanksgiving feast will include plenty of home-grown vegetables. Mother uses our frozen corn and store-bought lima beans to make succotash, my favorite dish. Daddy calls it Squanto food and refuses to eat it.

When noon approaches, Columbia brings Grandma and Grandpa to our house. At one o'clock we gather around the table to pray. As we pray, 'forgive us our trespasses as we forgive those who trespass against us,' I look at Grandma and Aunt Lily. Their hands are folded piously on the table, despite having had a major disagreement earlier this morning about when they moved from Chicago to St. Louis. Like who cares, it was a zillion years ago.

After dinner, the turkey is no longer stuffed, but we are. "I'll serve the pies later," Mother says. We all waddle from the dining room to softer chairs in the living room. As Aunt Lily and Grandma praise Mother's wonderful dinner, again, I imagine jabbing my fork through Mother's flaky pie crust into the rich mincemeat pie.

My sweet dreams are shattered when Daddy says, "Let's take a ride in the country."

Columbia and Amherst whine, "Do we have to?"

I am not far behind with my plea. "I'll stay home."

Daddy never tires of driving past miles of corn stubble, pastures, feed lots, and farms, but I do. Our family car, a new 1958 blue Buick is comfortable for six, we can squeeze in seven, but there is no way ten of us can go. Four lucky people will be spared this epic drive.

"My arthritis is bothering me," Grandma says. "I'd love to go, but my knees would be stiffer than a priest's collar if I went. Lily and I will stay here so we can visit undisturbed." Lily nods her agreement.

This is the first time Grandma and her sister have agreed on anything today.

"Mouse, go to the bathroom and get in the car," Mother says as she scans the dining room. Two hours ago, ten hungry people made short work of her six hours of preparation. Now, every plate, bowl, cup, and glass in the house is dirty. Cleanup will require three hours of dishwashing and pot scrubbing all by hand.

"Staying here is a good idea, *Rosy,*" Aunt Lily says.

"I'd prefer to be called Rose," Grandma says.

"Everyone called you Rosy when you were younger," Aunt Lily

says. "You liked it."

"That was then. This is now," Grandma says.

"You don't need to get snippy," Aunt Lily says. "No matter what I call you, we'll always be the three little Flower girls of Francisville. Lily, Rosy, and Daisy. And I'll always be the oldest."

"And you'll never learn to keep your mouth shut," Grandma snaps.

Wow. The fat is in the fire. I definitely want to stay home and watch the sparks fly.

"Rose," Grandpa says, "Rosy is just a word. Don't let it spoil a wonderful day."

"Who's Daisy?" I ask.

"You're never satisfied until you get people aggravated," Grandma snarls to Lily. "You enjoy stirring up trouble."

"You're too touchy," Aunt Lily pauses, then adds, "Rooos-y."

"I asked you not to call me Rosie." Grandma juts out her chin. She grips the arm rests on her chair so tightly her knuckles turn white.

"Now, Rose," Grandpa says. "Calm down. It was a slip of the tongue, right Lily?"

Lily strikes the older sister pose. The same smug pose Columbia strikes when she's letting me know she is older and wiser than I am and I'm too young to understand.

"Who's Daisy?" I ask again.

"No one," Grandma says.

"But Aunt Lilly said you were the three flower girls."

"Aunt Lily is wrong. Aren't you, Lily?" Grandma glares at her sister.

If looks could kill, Aunt Lily would drop dead.

"Whatever you say, *Ros...y*," Aunt Lily says. She crinkles her nose and grins at Grandma.

Wow! I can't believe Aunt Lily keeps teasing Grandma. Can't she see Grandma is furious?

Mother re-enters a silent room. If she notices the tension, she chooses to ignore it. "Columbia and Amherst, you may stay home, but on one condition."

"Anything. I'll do anything if I don't have to go," Amherst says.

"You two have to wash all the dishes and clean up the kitchen. And I don't want any fighting. Is that understood?"

In less than two seconds, my sisters who usually grumble for thirty minutes about washing the dishes, weigh the confining heaven-knows-how-long car ride against three hours of dishwashing. It was no contest.

"We'll stay here," they say.

"I'll help." I grab two plates and take them to the kitchen.

"Not so fast young lady," Mother says. "The three of you always quarrel when I'm not here. You're coming with us. Get your coat."

Columbia smirks. I stick out my tongue. A feeble response, but the best I can muster. I wish I could glare at Columbia like Grandma is glaring at Aunt Lily.

Outside we jockey for positions in the car. Of course, Daddy drives; no one else has a driver's license. Mother refuses to learn despite Daddy's pleas. Grandpa, who has never driven a car, offers to be Daddy's co-pilot.

"May I sit up front, please?" Pansy says. "I'll feel safer between you two big men." She sits in the middle of the front seat and places her open-toed pumps near the heater. "Ooh, the heat feels great on my tootsies."

"I want a window." If I'm forced to go on this marathon drive, I want to see where I'm going.

"I beat you to it." Mouse plops on the back seat behind Daddy, slams the car door and pushes down the lock."Na-na-na-na-nah. I get the window."

I run to the other side of the car and jerk open the door. "Ha. I have my own window." Tap. Tap. Tap. The rap of Mother's knuckles on the window ends my victory. "Scoot over Rebel."

"No. I want to sit by the window."

"Some other time." Mother pushes me toward Mouse.

"Stay over there. Don't touch me." Mouse draws an imaginary dividing line on the backseat. "This is my window."

"You can have your old window. I don't want it anyway."

Daddy drives east out of town. I see a sign for the Mesa Drive-In Theater. Great! All is not lost. I've never seen a drive-in theater. Mother and Daddy told Columbia and Amherst they can't go there. Saying it's a Passion Pit and not a place for young ladies. I have to see this forbidden fruit. I edge closer to Mouse.

"Get back on your side." Mouse redraws her imaginary dividing line.

"I want to see the drive-in theater."

"You're crowding me," Mouse says.

"Don't be such a baby."

"I got the window first. You have to wait your turn."

"My turn?" I snap. "What a laugh. You'll hog the window for the whole ride."

"Well, I got it first."

"Girls, stop that bickering." Mother pulls me toward her. I twist my shoulder to break free of her grasp and fall on Mouse. I see a fleeting glimpse of the Mesa Drive-in Theater before we crest a hill and the forbidden fruit disappears.

"Ooof. Get off me." Mouse pushes me away.

"I missed seeing the drive-in and it's all your fault, I never get to… "

"That's enough." Daddy's stern voice cuts short my protest.

Mother pulls me toward her. Climbs over me and pushes me to the side. "Now, sit by the window and behave yourself, Rebel."

I press my head against the cool window and pray the ride will be short. Miles of farmland scroll by. I listen to Daddy's monologue as he explains the recent corn harvest to Pansy.

A lone coyote runs across the road. "What was that?" Pansy asks.

"A coyote," Daddy says.

"My goodness." Pansy pulls her scarf around her throat. "Do you think it will attack?"

"I wouldn't worry about a coyote," Daddy says. "But watch out for the wily jackalope. It's a killer."

"Wha… what's a jackalope?" Pansy asks.

"A six-foot monster. Looks like a rabbit but has horns and venom like a rattlesnake. You can't outrun one of them," Daddy says.

"Oh dear. Do you think it can get into the car?" Pansy asks.

I snicker.

"Henry," Mother says. "That's enough. He's teasing, Pansy."

"Is that door locked?" Pansy asks Grandpa.

"Don't worry," Grandpa says. "I'll take care of you."

We ride on in silence for several minutes. "See that field over there that looks like it's covered with green grass?" Daddy says.

Pansy points to a field in the distance. "You mean that one?"

"Yes. That's winter wheat," Daddy says.

“Winter wheat? How can the farmers harvest wheat when the ground is covered with snow?”

I snap to attention. Pansy’s question is a super stupid question. Wheat is the number one crop in Western Kansas. Every kid past the age of five here knows winter wheat is harvested in July but planted in the fall to give it the proper growing season. I anticipate a weird answer from Daddy which would make this boring car ride interesting. But his hands clench the steering wheel. I feel Mother tense beside me. I imagine Daddy telling Pansy that farmers hire Eskimos and dogsleds to do the harvesting or that winter wheat is grown to make the frozen bread you buy in the grocery store.

After ten seconds, Daddy inhales deeply and sighs. “Sheeesh.” He patiently says, “Pansy, it’s called winter wheat because the wheat is dormant during the winter and…”

I’m flabbergasted. Maybe he’s patient because the question is about farming, a topic he loves, but more than likely, he’s not giving one of his Smart Alec answers because Pansy is Mother’s only cousin, and she is a guest in our home. The boring ride continues.

When we arrived home, Amherst and Columbia are scrubbing the pots and pans. Mother serves her pies. I have a sliver of pumpkin and one of mincemeat. I use two different plates and forks. What do I care? Amherst and Columbia are washing the dishes.

Chapter 14
Christmas Greetings

Every year Daddy insists on taking a Christmas portrait of my sisters and me. While Mother encourages us to smile, Daddy snaps numerous photos until he has one worthy of being included with our Christmas cards. Before the photo shoot, we selected a seven-foot spruce tree from Ritterbush's Christmas tree lot. The tree looked perfect when we selected it, but after Daddy put it in the stand it was lopsided.

"I'll trim off the trunk a bit, then it will be straight," Daddy says. The tree now leans to the right.

"I see what the problem is." Daddy saws another piece off the trunk. The tree now tips to the left.

The tree shrinks steadily under Daddy's saw. With each piece cut off, he says, "Now it will stand up straight." But it doesn't.

When the tree is four-feet tall Mother says, "Henry, enough is enough. Let's decorate the tree before it's a bonsai."

We festoon several strings of huge seven-watt bulbs on the tree. Mother opens boxes of our ornaments, both homemade and store bought. Mother hangs Popsicle stick sleds, cotton-ball snowmen, and pipe cleaner candy canes, all stuff we made in grade school on the tree.

"Ugh, don't hang those on the tree," Columbia moans. "They're ugly."

"It's traditional. Reminds me of Christmas' past," Mother says.

Reminds me that my family never wastes money. I hang a plate-sized plaster disk with an imprint of my hand that I made in first grade. The bough sags under its weight.

Columbia and Amherst hang fragile glass ornaments, while Mouse hangs tin bells and fresh candy canes wrapped in cellophane. I open a new box of tinsel, grab several strands of the shredded tinfoil and toss it on the tree.

"Don't do that!" Columbia says. "Hang each strand individually."

"Why? That will take all day," I say.

"It looks messy when you toss it on the tree."

"Then you do it." I toss another handful onto the tree.

"Stop that! I want our tree to look perfect, just once."

While Columbia hangs individual strands of tinsel on the tree, Daddy secures the tin star he cut from sheet metal to the top of our shortest Christmas tree ever with black electrical tape. I asked Daddy for bubble lights last week, like Wanda has, but Daddy said he has no money for such foolishness, and they are a fire hazard. Seeing my disappointment, he came home the next night with eight individual blinking light bulbs. Not as good as a string of bubble light, but at least these flashing bulbs will make our tree look more up to date. I replace several standard bulbs on the tree with the blinking bulbs. Amherst plugs in the lights.

"Why aren't the lights blinking?" I ask.

"They have to warm up first," Daddy says.

"The tree looks crooked." Mother says.

"It looks fine to me," Daddy replies. "Leave it alone."

"The lights still aren't blinking ," I say. "How long does it take them to warm up?"

"Don't put the tree in front of the window," Columbia whines. "I'll never be able to show my face in school if my friends see this leaning tower of Pisa."

Columbia's fear of social disgrace is short lived. The deformed tree leans further to the right and crashes onto the floor. The lights wink out with ominous popping sounds.

"Is that how they blink?" I ask.

"No, they're broken, you idiot," Amherst says.

Mouse and I scurry around the fallen tree to salvage unbroken decorations.

"You girls get away from the broken glass ornaments before you cut your hands." Mother picks up the jagged pieces of a glass angel that held a crystal daisy. "This ornament was mine when I was a child. My mother gave it to me." She blinks to hold back her tears.

"Your mother?" Daddy says. Mother nods. "Don't be upset Bunny. I'll glue it together. Put the pieces on the table." He turns from her and yells, "Somebody get a rag. And be quick about it. I need to sop up the water from the tree stand."

I rush to the kitchen and return with a dish towel.

"Don't worry Bunny. I'll clean up this mess." Daddy swishes the towel across the floor.

Twenty minutes later the tree is no longer by the window, which relieves Columbia. It's now crammed in a corner by the recliner. Strands of tinsel festoon the sofa and floor like confetti at a New Year's party.

"Amherst, get more water for the tree stand." Daddy plugs in the lights. They flicker, shoot sparks, and blink out. "Sheesh! Water must have gotten in the sockets. Don't plug in the lights until I test them."

"Do you think the blinking lights will still work?" I ask.

Before Amherst returns with the water, the tinsel on the tree quivers, the tin star does a saintly bow, and the tree falls toward us. The few unbroken ornaments rain onto our oak floor and shatter.

"Forget the water, Amherst," I yell.

"Damn it!" Daddy rights the tree again.

"Henry!" Mother says. "Watch your language."

"Well, you can't put all the ornaments on the front of the tree," Daddy says. "Some have to be put on the back to balance it." He moves unbroken ornaments to the back of the tree. The front of the tree is now as bare as when we bought it.

"It looks horrible," moans Columbia.

"Timber!" I say as the tree topples again. Now only our second grade paperchains and tin bells survive.

Daddy says a few words I've never heard him say and don't know what they mean, and Mother sends us to our rooms. When we venture into the living room an hour later, the tree is wedged between the couch and the recliner. A strategically placed dining room chair makes it impossible for the tree to fall forward.

As if to dare the Fates, Daddy decides to take our Christmas portrait in front of our tipsy Christmas tree. We all have newly sewn finery to wear. Columbia and Amherst wear white, peter-pan collared blouses and full-circle felt skirts: green for Columbia, red for Amherst. Layers of crinolines under their skirts, the latest style, crackle when they move. Mouse and I have matching dresses. The tops are blue velvet, (what other color is there?) and the skirts are blue plaid taffeta.

Normally we stand, but this year we sit because Amherst and Columbia are taller than our tree. While Daddy sets up his tripod and positions flood lights, Mother combs and brushes our hair until it shines.

Daddy removes the chair in front of the tree and says, "Mouse, you and Rebel sit here." We sit Yoga style, pulling our plaid skirts over our knees. Daddy stands back and frames us with his hands, like a real photographer.

"Mouse, move a little closer to Rebel." Mouse nudges my knee. "Okay, fine. Don't move. Columbia, sit beside Rebel, and Amherst, you sit by Mouse." They spread their full circle skirts over their folded legs.

Large blue-colored flashbulbs are standard, but Daddy will have none of that. In order to reduce shadows, he uses four semi-professional lighting units. Each unit has a zillion watt bulb surrounded by a huge saucer-shaped metal disk. The four lights make our living room as bright as noon on the Sahara Desert and as hot.

Daddy peers into the camera's viewfinder. "Columbia and Amherst scoot back. The tree is tilting, hold it up."

"Get your shoes off me. You'll get my skirt dirty." Columbia pushes my foot away.

"My knees are cramped from sitting cross-legged," I say.

"Your leg will be broken if you don't take your shoes off my skirt." Columbia inspects her clothes. "Look, my crinoline is dirty. I haven't even worn this outfit and already you've ruined it." Columbia pinches my stubby legs before I can tuck them under my skirt.

"Ouch, that hurts. Why are you always picking on me?" I sniff.

"Can't you girls sit still for five minutes?" Asks Daddy.

"We've already been here an hour," Amherst says. "Pimples will erupt on my forehead if I sit under these hot lights any longer."

"If you didn't eat so much chocolate, your forehead wouldn't look like the surface of the moon," snipes Columbia. "My skin is perfect."

"Well, that's the only part of you that's perfect. The rest of you is rotten to the core," says Amherst.

"Quit picking on me," says Columbia.

"Now you know how I feel, Columbia," I say.

"Pipe down, Rebel," sneers Columbia. "Amherst you're just stinky because I have a date to the Christmas Prom, and you don't."

"I don't care about that stinkin' dance," Amherst says. "Roy asked me, but I told him 'no.'"

"You did," Columbia says. "Why?"

"Everyone who goes to that dance is a snob."

"Be quiet so I can focus the camera," Daddy says.

"Are you saying I'm a snob?" Says Columbia.

"You said, it not me," Amherst replies. "If the shoe fits, wear it."

"Mouse, take your hands away from your eyes," Daddy says.

"It's too bright." Mouse removes her hands, and squints until her nose is crinkled.

Columbia shoves her foot against my leg. "Move your big fat leg, Rebel."

"Make me." I turn and stick out my tongue.

Click!

"Well, that picture is ruined. Rebel, stop acting silly." Daddy wipes his brow.

"Columbia started it. She pinched me, and said…"

"Just stop it," Daddy says.

"But Daddy, I…"

"I said, stop it!"

"I hate you, Columbia." Tears well in my eyes and run down my cheeks.

Click!

"All right, everybody try to smile this time," Daddy begs.

Columbia rises to her knees and stretches her neck to see out our front window.

Click!

"Columbia, what are you doing?" Asks Daddy. "You're the oldest. Set an example."

"I thought I heard Bobby's car drive by." Columbia scrunches back into position.

"Why do you care what Bobby does? He has a new girlfriend," sneers Amherst.

"No, he doesn't. He told me Denise is just a friend," Columbia says.

"Ha. She was riding in his car yesterday seated so close to him I thought he'd grown a second head."

"No," sobs Columbia. "My life is ruined. We're supposed to go to the Christmas Prom together." Tears bounce down her cheeks.

Click!

"Would it be possible for someone to smile? Good grief, these are holiday photos," Daddy pleads.

"The lights are too hot. I feel pimples sprouting," moans Amherst.

"They won't show in the picture," Daddy says. "Now, everyone, hush up and smile!"

Click. Click.

"Our class pictures are next week. I'll look like the poster girl for Clearasil," Amherst moans.

"Amherst, that's enough. Quit blubbering and smile," Daddy says.

Click!

"Wonderful! Now three of you are crying. Mouse, why don't you cry and make it four?"

"Why should I cry?" Mouse says. "I'm happy. Santa's coming and I'm a good girl."

Daddy's sarcasm is lost on Mouse.

"All I want is one decent photo." Daddy peers through the viewfinder. "You've all moved. I'll have to refocus."

"Why is everybody crying? What's wrong, Columbia?" Asks Mouse.

"You're too young to understand. You're just a baby," Columbia says between sniffles.

"No, I'm not. I'm seven-years-old. I'm not a baby." Tears spill down her cheeks.

Click! Click!

"Mouse, ignore Columbia. She tells everyone they're too young to understand," I say.

"Sheesh! I only have two more exposures on this roll of film. Everyone please look at the camera. Keep your hands to yourself. Quit crying and for the love of God, if not for me, smile."

Click!

"That was just great," Daddy says. "Looks like a police lineup."

Only one shot left. In ten seconds, I can move my legs without getting pinched by Columbia. Something touches the back of my head.

"Columbia, stop that," Daddy says. She folds her hands in her lap. I know she's made "V" horns behind my head.

"Ready?" Daddy says. "Smile. If this one isn't good, I'll have to put in a new roll of film."

"No more lights," Mouse says. "My eyes are broken. I see colored spots everywhere."

"Don't look into the lights. Keep your eyes closed until I tell you to open them," Daddy says. He readjusts the Sahara lighting making the glare and heat more intense. Pulling a handkerchief from his back pocket, he wipes tears off our cheeks and sponges Amherst's greasy forehead. "Is everyone ready?"

The tree quivers. Click!

Our Christmas portrait this year is four dewy-eyed girls. Tinsel sparkles in our hair, and a miniature Christmas tree with a homemade tin star lays in our laps. The photo is a portrait of disaster, but our smiles are wide and genuine.

Chapter 15
One Picture is Worth a…?

Mother always hosts our family Christmas dinner, but this year the dinner will be at Uncle Waylon's. Eating there is fine, but I'll miss the aroma of turkey stuffed with oyster dressing wafting through our house. Several days before Christmas, Mother and Aunt Bessie are discussing the dinner while Wanda and I play Chinese Checkers.

"How many people will there be?" Mother asks.

"You six, of course," Aunt Bessie says. "Grandma Rose and Grandpa Michael make eight. Waylon, Wanda and I make eleven. And if the weather is decent, my brother Donald, his wife Mary Jo will join us. Thirteen. I hope that's not an unlucky number."

"Would you like me to bring the dessert, Bessie?" Mother asks.

"A plate of your Christmas cookies would be nice. I hate to ask you to bring pies too, but —"

"I'll bring two pumpkin and one pecan. Will that be enough?"

"Yes. And your succotash too," Bessie says. "It wouldn't be a family dinner without it."

The day before Christmas, Mother is 'up to her eyeballs' in pie crust. Her words, not mine. Daddy has vacation to use before the end of the year, so he's been home this week. He's not accustomed to 'taking life easy' as Grandpa says he does now that he's retired. Daddy has already fixed the leaky bathroom faucet, replaced the hall light fixture, and repainted the front entry.

"What can I do to help?" Daddy asks Mother.

"Nothing. I have everything under control in the kitchen."

"I could shell the pecans for the pies."

Mother wipes her forehead with the back of her flour-covered hand. "I bought shelled pecans." Daddy looks dejected. "Um, I could use another can of Reddi Whip. Call Dad and ask him to come with you. He hasn't been able to walk to his lodge for a week because of the cold weather. I'm sure he has cabin fever having been cooped up with Mom all week. Her arthritis bothers her when it's cold, and you know that makes her cranky."

"I'll be happy to take your dad along," Daddy says.

"Can I go?" Mouse asks.

"Sure. Get your coat."

"Can we stop at Penney's so I can see Santa? I forgot to tell him I want a tea set for Christmas?"

"Might be too late," Daddy says. "I'm sure Santa's sleigh is already packed. You want to come along, Rebel?"

"No. I told Wanda I'd play Parcheesi with her this afternoon." I button on my heavy coat, pull on my blue gloves with holes in two fingers, and tie a wool scarf over my curly hair. Wanda lives less than a block away, but winter in Kansas is cold and windy, even if there is no snow.

Wanda and I are beginning our second game of Parcheesi on their living room floor when a car horn blares. Seconds later, someone knocks at their front door. Aunt Bessie opens the door and a flurry of snowflakes and a dark-haired man whose muscles ripple under his tight tee shirt enter. He has a pack of cigarettes rolled into the sleeve of his shirt. A leather jacket is slung over one shoulder. Behind him is a woman who looks like Jayne Mansfield. A blonde bombshell.

"That's my Uncle Donald and Aunt Mary Jo," Wanda says. "Uncle Donald is my mom's brother."

"Wow! He looks like a hood," I whisper to Wanda. "Does he carry a switchblade?"

"No, he's harmless," Wanda replies.

Mary Jo enters with a million-dollar smile and turns her cheek for Aunt Bessie's welcoming kiss. Mary Jo's makeup is perfect. Her eyelashes look like hairy spider legs. Her lips gleam with cherry gloss. Her blonde hair soars upward into a gigantic beehive hairdo. She wears a pink, scoop neck sweater and skin-tight black stirrup pants, which are all the rage this year. I think stirrup pants would make me look taller, but Columbia says I am short and squat, and I better learn to live with the hard cold facts of life. Sheesh. Even with stirrup pants, I'd never look anything like Mary Jo. She's everything I'm not.

"Kiss-kiss only on the cheek," Mary Jo says to Aunt Bessie. "I don't want my makeup mussed."

"Merry Christmas to my favorite sister-in-law." Uncle Waylon rises from his recliner to hug Mary Jo, but she pushes him back into his chair.

"Don't. You'll ruin my hair," she says.

How could a hug ruin Mary Jo's blonde helmet? Hair spray has petrified her hair. Ping pong balls could bounce off that blonde dome without moving it.

"Your Aunt Mary Jo looks like a movie star," I say. "She's cool."

"She's as dumb as a post," Wanda whispers. "She was in high school seven years and never graduated. She was Homecoming Queen four times."

Wanda and I get off the floor to greet her aunt and uncle.

"How old is she?" I ask.

"Twenty-two. And she bleaches her hair," Wanda whispers.

"Yeah, but thank God, she didn't dye it red," Uncle Waylon says. "One red head in this family is more than enough."

I'd give Uncle Waylon a snippy response, but since it's Christmas, I refrain. I'm not worried about getting on Santa's naughty list at this late date. I'm sure my presents are already hidden in Daddy's closet, but Uncle Waylon's been drinking. If I challenge him now, no telling what might come out of his mouth.

After all the hellos and hugs are finished, I say, "I need to get ready for the Christmas Eve service at church. I have a solo in *Adestes Fidelis*. Are you coming Aunt Bessie?"

"Of course. Wanda is Mary in the Sunday school pageant. Waylon and I are so proud of her."

"Don't count on me going," Uncle Waylon says. "Someone has to keep the home fires burning."

"But, Daddy," Wanda says, "I'm going to be Mary."

"I'm going to be merry right here." Uncle Waylon pours a generous shot of whiskey into his eggnog.

I dart out the door, not wanting to be caught in an Aunt Bessie-Uncle Waylon drinking conversation. "Good-bye everybody. See you tonight or tomorrow."

I walk home trying to catch snowflakes on my tongue. I love going to church, even on days when Pastor Rozelle's sermon goes on forever. Church is quiet, gives me a place to ponder things I don't understand. Like why Grandma reads Mother the riot act if we miss church, but her son Waylon can drink, curse, and never attend church, and Grandma never says a word.

* * *

As we leave the church service at midnight, snow is falling heavily. "The angels are having a pillow fight," Mouse says. I agree.

At home, I stand on the back porch and watch snowflakes float to earth like wisps of cotton from the dark sky. A tiny flake is nothing, a mere speck, but when millions are dumped from the sky, they can cover our dry, brown landscape in a few hours. If the snow continues, by morning our landscape will be a sparkling white blanket. Snow softens all the square edges. Bushes, bicycles, and lawn furniture will be transformed into soft, white, unidentifiable lumps.

I have long since learned the truth about Santa Claus, but Santa still brings each of us a special gift because Mouse believes in Santa's magic. Christmas morning Santa gives me a Monopoly game and a matching hat and glove set. These are not sturdy gloves like you buy at Montgomery Wards, but have soft purple knit palms (Hallelujah! Not blue.) and white rabbit fur on the back. The matching hat is trimmed with rabbit fur. Columbia and Amherst say I'll look like an Eskimo wearing them, but their snide barbs don't bother me.

Amherst and Columbia receive pullover sweaters and small silver compacts and tubes of pale pink lipstick. And, despite Mouse requesting a tea set at the last minute, Santa heard her request because she has just opened an Alice in Wonderland Tea Set.

The phone rings. I rush to answer it, expecting to hear Grandpa's voice. "Merry Christmas."

"Merry Christmas, Rebel," Aunt Bessie responds. "May I speak to Bonnie?"

"Sure. Merry Christmas, Aunt Bessie. See you soon." I call Mother to the phone and take my gifts to my bedroom and put on my new hat and gloves. I gaze at my reflection in the mirror. I'm not as hot looking as Mary Jo, but the hat is big improvement over the wool plaid scarf I usually tie over my head. When I hear Mother say, "Well, I'll be hornswoggled and kicked by a mule. Waylon never ceases to amaze me," I return to the living room.

"What's he done now?" Daddy asks.

"He asked Vera and Buck Arpkey to join us for Christmas dinner. Bessie said Waylon was talking to Buck this morning and Buck said they were supposed to go to Kansas City to see Vera's parents, but the blizzard last night closed the roads. Buck said they would probably eat a baloney sandwich for Christmas dinner." Mother shakes her head.

"Waylon is kinder to others than he ever is to me."

"Now, Bunny, don't get upset. Maybe Waylon's overcome with the Christmas spirit," Daddy says.

"If Waylon has any spirit, it comes from a bottle of whiskey. I hope he doesn't guzzle so much spirit today that he ruins Christmas for everyone," Mother says.

At noon, Daddy picks up Grandma and Grandpa because our family car has four doors. Amherst won the battle of the car keys with Columbia, so she's driving Mother, Mouse and me, along with the food we are bringing to Uncle Waylon's in the Chevy Bel Air. Columbia goes with Daddy to help Grandma and Grandpa down the snow-packed sidewalk to the car.

By one o'clock we are all together. From the amount of laughter in the kitchen, I know Uncle Waylon is passing around a bottle of alcohol and telling jokes. Wanda shows me her Christmas gifts: a portable record player, several records, a gold locket, a perfume set, an instamatic camera, bath oil beads, and a variety of beautiful sweaters and skirts. I'm not jealous. Wanda isn't a snob. She'll let me borrow anything. She admires my new hat and gloves, telling me I look fantastic.

Shortly after one o'clock, we gather around a makeshift table that stretches from the dining room through the living room all the way to the front door. Uncle Waylon carries the huge, bronzed turkey to the table and stands behind it. "All, right who wants white and who wants dark?" He grasps a long carving knife and stabs a fork into the turkey.

"Waylon, we have to thank the good Lord first," Aunt Bessie says.

"Ah, yes, the Lord." Uncle Waylon sits but keeps a firm grasp on the knife.

As soon as 'amen' is said, he's on his feet slicing the turkey.

"Here you go, Red." He hands me a plate with steaming vegetables and turkey. "Keep it or pass it on."

"I wish you wouldn't call me Red." White meat. I'm happy to give it away.

"Better dead than red." Uncle Waylon hands me another plate and flicks one of my red curls with the carving fork. I swat the fork away.

"Waylon," Aunt Bessie says, "what a thing to say to your niece."

"I'm teasing. Rebel needs to toughen up." He passes a plate to Wanda. "Here you go, sweetheart."

She has a drumstick with plenty of crispy skin, my favorite piece.

"Here's another, Red. Do you want it?" Uncle Waylon hands me a plate with plenty of mashed potatoes, succotash, and part of a turkey leg, covered with crispy skin. Tears well in my eyes as I set the plate at my place.

"Rebel, better dead than red has nothing to do with hair color." Daddy smiles at me and scowls at Waylon. "It means you'd rather be dead than be a red communist."

"I didn't mean anything by it." Uncle Waylon hands me another plate. I pass it on.

Mother hands the plate to Grandpa. She glares at Waylon. If looks could kill, Waylon would have impaled himself on the carving knife.

I eat in silence. Grandma looks at me and shakes her head. "Waylon, just once can't you leave well enough alone?"

A silent tension fills the room. This is all my fault because I hate being teased. I'm going to keep my mouth shut the next time Uncle Waylon calls me Red or die trying. I'll focus on what Mother always tells me, "Sticks and stone may break my bones, but names will never hurt you." I don't believe that saying, but Mother does, and she's seldom wrong.

After dinner, Vera and Buck thank everyone for the great meal, pull on their galoshes and button their winter coats. Vera says, "We don't want to intrude any further on your family celebration."

"It was much better than a cold baloney sandwich," Buck says as he leaves.

Later, when the sleepy lull brought on by overstuffed stomachs has worn off, Daddy brings out his camera. Columbia rushes to the bathroom to check her hair. Wanda and I place five chairs in front of the fireplace. Mother, Columbia, Aunt Bessie, Grandpa, and Grandma will sit. Donald, Mary Jo, Uncle Waylon, and Amherst will stand behind them. Wanda, Mouse, and I will kneel in front of Grandma and Grandpa. Daddy will set a time exposure on his camera and then hurry to stand on the back row by Amherst before the shutter snaps.

We sit posed for minutes. My lips are dry from holding them in a forced smile. I want to lick them, but if I do, I'm sure that's the instant the shutter will click and my tongue will be hanging out like Vermin, Old Man Market's dog.

"Hold on a second. I need to adjust the bounce flash to eliminate that 'red eye' effect in Waylon's eyes," Daddy says.

"There's nothing wrong with your flash, Henry," Donald says. "Your eyes would be bloodshot like Waylon's if you drank a twelve-pack before dinner."

"Waylon!" Bessie turns and gives her husband a penetrating stare. "You promised not to drink a drop today. I wish once we could have a family dinner without you getting loaded and becoming obnoxious."

"Now Bessie, Honey, don't get yourself all worked up. It wasn't twelve beers, two at the most. And besides I'm as sober as a judge." Uncle Waylon sways from side to side.

"Good grief, Waylon. Turn the other way," says Mary Jo. "A whiff of your breath could asphyxiate the Budweiser Clydesdales."

"Bud, did someone say Bud?" Uncle Waylon says. "I think I'll have another."

"You stay right where you are," Aunt Bessie snaps.

Mother is right. My Aunt Bessie is a saint.

"Okay. Everybody ready?" Daddy hurries across the room and a splash of light illuminates us.

"I'm blind. I can't see anything." Uncle Waylon squints and gropes the air.

Smack! Mary Jo's palm connects loudly on Uncle Waylon's face. "Get your paws off me, Waylon."

Smack! Aunt Bessie's hand leaves a print on the other side of Uncle Waylon's face. "I've had enough of your beer-enhanced behavior, Waylon."

"Just what I like, women fighting over me." Waylon grins.

"Keep your hands off my wife!" Donald lands a punch on Uncle Waylon's jaw.

Uncle Waylon drops like a stone in a pond. Out cold on the floor.

"Lock up the guns and liquor," Grandpa says. "The fighting has started. Come on, Rose. It's time for us to leave."

I agree. It's long past leaving time.

* * *

A week later, Wanda telephones me. "I have something to show you. It's a secret. You can't tell anyone. I'm coming over now."

When Wanda arrives at our house, I suggest we go to the basement for privacy. Mouse is playing with her dolls in the bedroom we share, and Columbia and Amherst are going ga-ga over some old movie in the living room.

"I want to show you photos I took with my new instamatic camera," Wanda says as I close the basement door. "But you have to promise to never tell another living soul about them. Especially my mom."

"I promise. Cross my heart and hope to die, stick a needle in my eye."

Wanda hands me a yellow Kodak envelope. I stare in disbelief. My mouth gapes open as I thumb through the color photos. "Oh my gosh! When did this happen?"

"After supper. Long after your family left. Mary Jo was preparing the pumpkin pie in the kitchen. When she shook the can of Reddi-Whip it exploded."

Wanda has photos of Mary Jo with splotches of whipped cream in her hair, on her face and on her pink sweater.

"While Mom was bringing the pie into the dining room, my dad stumbled into the kitchen." Wanda and I study several photos of her dad licking whipped cream off Mary Jo's face and wiping it from her breasts with a dish towel.

"That's disgusting," I say.

In the next photo, Mary Jo is whacking Uncle Waylon with a celery stick stuffed with peanut butter.

"Poor Aunt Bessie. I feel sorry for your mom."

"Yeah, me too. But I love my dad," says Wanda.

"What are you going to do with these photos?"

"You know those poodle skirts that are so popular? If I show these photos to my dad, he'll buy me one."

I'm no fortune teller, but I see a poodle skirt and maybe even a real dog in Wanda's future.

Chapter 16
Birthday Wishes

Birthdays are a family event. The honoree, as Mother calls the birthday person, selects the menu for supper and their favorite cake. Daddy is always ready with his camera to record the event for posterity.

"Your father will be gone on your birthday," Mother says. "He'll be in Topeka, so you may invite the TRIO3 to supper Thursday night. I'll make pizzas."

"Really? Can we have birthday cake and ice cream too?"

"Oh course. It wouldn't be a party without them. I want you to ask Shirley Birdfoot too."

"Who? I don't know anyone named Shirley."

"Shirley and her family just bought that house two doors away that's been vacant for a long time. It will be nice to have someone living there who will take care of the place."

"It's my birthday party. I don't want to invite a stranger. I don't know this Shirley from a hole in the ground."

"I met her mother yesterday. She seems very nice. Shirley's your age. You can walk home with her from school tomorrow and get to know her."

"Jaylynn and Wanda are my friends. I don't need strangers for friends."

"A stranger is a friend you haven't met yet," Mother says.

"All right, but if she's a jerk, I'm not doing anything else with her."

"Rebel, that's not a very Christian attitude. It won't hurt you to be friendly. Imagine how you'd feel moving somewhere where you don't know a soul."

"Does Shirley have a younger sister that could be Mouse's friend?" I pray she does because then Mouse would quit bugging me to do things with her.

"I think so. The younger girl is named Beth. Shirley has an older brother who's in Amherst's class. I think his name is Charles. He plays basketball. The family seems very nice."

* * *

Shirley doesn't say much when she walks home with the TRIO3

the next day, but at least she isn't stuckup. She moved to Schoenfeld from Wichita.

"I prefer living in a small town." Shirley says.

"You won't for long," I say. "Everyone knows your business."

"At least you get noticed, "Shirley says. "In Wichita no one cares if you live or die."

"Depending on the circumstances that could be a good thing," Jaylynn says.

"Yeah, especially if my dad catches wind of what you've done. He'll make it the lead story on KDOG the next morning," adds Wanda.

"That's right. Having your name broadcast on the radio can ruin your day. Now that you're " I clear my throat. "Uh, Shirley, my birthday's this week. Jaylynn and Wanda are coming over Thursday for pizza. You want to join us?" There I did it. Asked her to come to my party. Now Mother will get off my back.

"Sure. Sounds like fun."

Thursday night everyone arrives promptly at six. Mother spreads tomato sauce on homemade bread dough in six small pizza pans. We select toppings for our individual pizzas. Mother and Mouse eat at the kitchen table so my friends and I can have the dining room to ourselves. After we have eaten our fill, Mother carries my chocolate cake to the table. Thirteen candles wait to be lit.

"Next year you can get your learner's permit," says Jaylynn.

"Yeah, but you can't get your Drivers License until you are sixteen," Wanda says.

"I hope Amherst or Columbia don't wreck the Bel Air before I get to drive it," I reply.

"Where are Columbia and Amherst tonight?" Jaylynn asks.

"At church for choir practice," I reply.

"Light the candles so we can eat the cake," says Mouse.

Mouse and Mother join my friends in singing *Happy Birthday*. Before I blow out my candles, they all holler, "Make a wish!"

For weeks I've reminded Mother daily that all I want for my birthday is a matching skirt and sweater so I can feel like part of the in-crowd. I wish, hope, and pray that the large box from my parents waiting to be opened holds my matching skirt and sweater. I close my eyes and blow out all the candles.

"What did you wish for?" Mouse asks.

"She can't tell, or it won't come true," Wanda says.

"Bet it has something to do with Skip." Jaylynn winks at me.

"No, it doesn't. He's ancient news," I reply.

"You stuck on Skip Prescott? I think he is really dreamy," Shirley says.

Jaylynn runs her thumb and index finger across her lips closing them with an invisible zipper. "My lips are sealed."

"Skip's okay, but he spends too much time with, Jimmy and Jimmy's a bad influence," I say.

"Open your presents," Mouse says. I'm glad for her interruption. I don't need my girlfriends asking about my latest heart throb with Mother less than five feet away.

"Here's mine." Wanda thrusts a flat square package into my hand. "Open it first."

I carefully remove the red bow and rip off the tissue paper. "Wow records!" I scan the titles. *Venus* by Frankie Avalon. Paul Anka's, *Lonely Boy,* and *Dream Lover* by Bobby Darin. "Thanks, Wanda."

"My dad has stacks of extra records at the radio station. I asked him to save some for you," Wanda says.

"I wish I had an uncle that worked at KDOG," Jaylynn says. "The only records at my house are Benny Goodman and Lawrence Welk. Uh one and uh two."

I put my finger in my mouth and make a popping noise like Lawrence Welk does on his TV show. We all say yuck!

Shirley's small package contains two tubes of lipstick. Passion Pink and Red Hot. "Thanks Shirley. I love them." I apply Passion Pink to my lips. "How does it look?"

"Good enough to kiss," Wanda says. "Pucker up."

I toss mock kisses to my friends.

Jaylynn hands me her present. "No more bunny slippers for you." Wanda laughs.

Shirley asks, "What's so funny."

As I open the gift, Jaylynn rehashes my wearing bunny slippers to her slumber party last year. The new slippers are leopard print with fur trim.

I kick off my Keds. "Real fur. Hot dog! Look at me now." I prance around the room. "I feel like a movie star."

"This is from Columbia and Amherst." Mother hands me a slim, narrow box.

I open the box. Inside is a silver bracelet and a small Conestoga wagon charm with the letters SHS on it.

"Oooh. It's gorgeous," I say.

"What is it? Let me see." Mouse reaches for the bracelet.

I refrained from saying, 'you're too young to understand' as Columbia would have said to me in this circumstance. "It's a charm bracelet. And the first charm is the Schoenfeld High School emblem, a Conestoga wagon."

"Let me see it, too," Shirley says.

My friends each hold the bracelet over their wrist to see how it would look on their arm. Two gifts remain. One from Mouse, the other from my parents. I shake Mouse's gift. It rattles.

"You'll never guess what I gave you," Mouse says. "It's barrettes. They are different colors."

"No need to guess now." I tug at the wrapping paper. The package is covered with tape. Finally I release the barrettes. "Thanks, Mouse."

I pick up the box from Mother and Daddy. It's the right size and weight to be a matching skirt and sweater. I hope it's not blue. I rip off the wrappings, lift the lid and hastily unfolded the tissue paper. What's this? Where's my matching skirt and sweater? I stare at a large beach towel and yellow flip-flops.

"I know you wanted a matching skirt and sweater, but you'll get more use out of a beach towel and flip-flops," Mother says. "Since you love swimming so much, I thought you should go to the pool in style. The store had lovely blue towels, but I bought yellow since I know it's your favorite color. There's a two-piece yellow swimsuit inside the towel, did you see it?"

"No," I mumble and withdrew a modest two-piece suit. Well, this might not be so bad after all. At least Mother didn't buy a hideous one-piece suit with a skirt!

"Wow! You'll get an all-over tan in that suit," Shirley says.

"You better not let Grandma see you in that," Wanda says. "You know what she'll say."

"Yeah, 'You don't have on enough clothes to flag a train.'"

"What does that mean?" Shirley asks.

"Beats me," Wanda says.

"Me too," I add.

While Mouse and Mother clean up the kitchen, my friends and I go to my room and listen to my new records, discuss boys and the film *Now that You're Becoming a Woman*, a film that was shown only to the girls last week after school.

"My mom told me all about becoming a woman months ago," Jaylynn says.

"I think my mom is too embarrassed to talk about it," Shirley says. "She gave me a book and said 'read this.' There were no pictures."

"Mother talked to me and Columbia gave me some details, but none of these books or films tell you the hard core facts," I say. "I want to know what really happens."

"I know all about the birds and the bees," Wanda whispers. "My Aunt Mary Jo filled me in on all the details."

I remember Mary Jo from our Thanksgiving dinner last year. Mary Jo was dressed like a hot babe. Uncle Waylon spent more time salivating over her than he did his turkey dinner.

"Mary Jo told you the facts of life? Did she give you specifics or just general stuff like what we saw in that film?"

"Details. I have details," Wanda says. "You want to know anything, ask me."

We spend the next ten minutes whispering so Mother or Mouse can't hear Wanda's full report on reproduction.

"No kidding? Doesn't that hurt?"

"I can't imagine my parents ever doing that."

"They must have. You're living proof."

"Yuck!"

"I bet your mom had a fit when she learned Mary Jo gave you the real skinny on the birds and the bees," Jaylynn says.

"I didn't tell her," Wanda replies. "I played dumb when Mom gave me the big talk."

Before the evening is over, the four of us are like peas in a pod. We are no longer the TRIO3. With the addition of Shirley we are the FAB4.

Chapter 17
The Cost of Gambling

Now thirteen, Grandma believes I'm old enough to learn the game of cribbage. The game uses a deck of cards and a small board with 121 holes. Small colored pegs are placed in the holes to mark your score. Grandpa loves this game, Grandma not so much which is why she's teaching me to play it. Even though she doesn't like playing cribbage, she enjoys watching us play.

"Rebel, after you deal," Grandma says, "there are forty-cards left in the deck. How do you always manage to cut the one card that will vastly improve your hand?"

"I just think about the card I need, and Grandpa or I cut it."

"Michael," Grandma says, "Rebel must have inherited my gift of Extra Sensory Perception."

"I don't know about this ESP stuff," Grandpa says, "but she's a fine card player."

"I'm not sure letting her play cards is a good idea," Grandma says.

"It's too late to change that now," Grandpa says. "Besides, you're the one who taught her how to play cribbage."

"Yes, but only because I don't want to play cribbage with you morning, noon and night, I never dreamed Rebel would have a knack for cards. I should have known better."

As I shuffle the cards, Mother enters my grandparents' back porch. "Knew better about what?" Mother asks.

"Hindsight is 20-20," Grandma says. "I never should have taught Rebel to play cards."

"Is she beating you, Dad?" Mother asks.

"Not yet, but she's giving me a run for my money," Grandpa says.

"I've seen enough." Grandma stands by pushing her palms on the table. "Rebel deals cards like a magician pulls rabbits from a hat. Who knows what she'll do with that talent."

"It's only cribbage, Rose," Grandpa says.

"Yes, but all bad habits lead to trouble later," Grandma says.

"If Cribbage is a bad habit, why did you teach me to play it,

Grandma?" I ask.

Grandma huffs in disgust.

"Let's go to the living room, Mom." Mother and Grandma disappear into the house.

After Grandpa and I finish playing several games, I say, "On *Gunsmoke*, the cowboys play poker. Do you know how to play it?"

"Yes. It's a game of some skill, the ability to bluff, and a lot of luck. Playing for fun is okay, but if you gamble on the cards, you can lose a lot of money."

"On TV the good guys always win."

"That's TV. In real games there is only one winner, and the odds are against you."

Grandpa deals five cards face up and explains the different poker hands to me: flush, full house, straight, three of a kind, and pairs.

"So how do you play? Will you teach me?"

"Yes, but promise me no gambling, at least not with money."

"Sure." This is an easy promise. I have no money. My allowance is a mere 25 cents a week.

"Okay. There are several poker games, but the most common is five-card draw."

After playing several games with his help, I say, "Let me play this one by myself. What can we use for chips?" Grandpa suggests leaves, so I run outside and strip a lower branch on a basswood tree. Before long I am spouting phrases like 'Put your money where your mouth is,' and 'Read 'em and weep,' 'I'll take a hit,' and 'Ante up,' like a pro.

"Do you and Grandma ever play poker?"

"No, she doesn't like gambling."

"Why?"

"She has her reasons."

I shuffle and deal the cards. Grandpa forms his cards into a small fan. I hold an ace, king, jack and two tens. I discarded a ten, hoping to draw a queen for a straight. "How many do you want, Grandpa?"

"Hit me with two."

"Dealer takes one." I have just dealt myself the Queen of Spades.

"I fold," Grandpa says. "I have a queen high nothing."

"Phooey! I was going to bet the farm. Look at this." I spread my cards on the table.

"What are you two doing out there?" Mother calls from the living room. "I can hear you shouting in here."

"Playing cards. Grandpa taught me how to play poker."

"He what!" Grandma stomps her cane on the floor. "Bonnie, go out there and put a stop to this immediately."

Mother's shoes click across the oak floor toward us. Grandma's cane makes rhythmic raps as she approaches. By the time Mother reaches the porch, Grandpa has the cards in a neat stack. My fists are full of leaves. Mother shakes her head. "You two are a pair to draw to."

"Bad choice of words, Bonnie." Grandpa smiles.

"Rebel, get rid of those leaves. Dad, put the cards away."

I toss the leaves outside.

"Michael, what were you thinking, teaching this child poker?" Grandma says.

"It was fun, Grandma."

"Gambling is never fun, Rebel. It ruins the lives of good people. Makes a mess of everything." Grandma's face has her famous scowl, the one she forms right before she throws the fear of God into you.

Grandpa, Mother, and I look at each other wondering who will offer an apology to appease Grandma. It isn't going to be me. Whoever speaks first will bear the brunt of her reprimand.

"I'm sorry, Rose," Grandpa says. "I wasn't thinking."

"Sorry? Is that the best you can do? You know what I think about gambling. Such behavior has caused more than one problem in this family. Our life would have been much easier if we'd only had Waylon to raise. We had to scrimp and save to provide for Bonnie because of gambling. Her gambling."

"Rose, that's enough." Grandpa stands, towering over Grandma. "Go in the house and calm down. I'll walk Bonnie and Rebel to the alley."

Grandpa puts his arm around Mother and holds my hand as we walk across their shady yard. "Pay no attention to her, Bonnie. You know your mom says things she doesn't mean when she's upset."

"I know, but it still hurts. Waylon's always been her favorite, and I understand why, but I wish —." Mother wipes a tear from her cheek.

"None of what happened was your fault, Bonnie. You were just a child. Remember that," Grandpa says.

"I know, but Mom never lets me forget what a burden I was."

"I'd say, 'pay no attention to her, she'll forget it,' but you know your mom," Grandpa says. "She's like a rat terrier chasing a squirrel. Neither will quit running until one of them is dead." When we reach the alley, Grandpa gives Mother a hug and we part.

I have no idea why a game of poker set Grandma off on one of her Holy Terrors. I feel badly that a simple game of cards has upset Mother. "I'm sorry I asked Grandpa to teach me poker," I say.

"That's all right, Rebel."

"How can gambling with a few leaves ruin everything?"

"It can't. But when people gamble with money they don't have or can't afford to lose, it makes paying the bills difficult."

"Did Grandpa gamble when you were a baby?"

"No. Cribbage is his only vice," Mother says.

"Did Grandma gamble away their money?"

"Don't be ridiculous. Just stick to cribbage in the future."

I promised to only play cribbage with Grandpa, but don't promise to give up poker, which is a good, because on Saturday night after shampooing my hair, I catch Columbia swiping bobby pins off my dresser. "Hey, give me those," I holler. "Those are mine."

"I don't have enough to set my hair," Columbia says.

"Tough Tiddlywinks." I squeeze her wrist until she drops the pins. "I bet you want my pins so you can impress Bobby Benson with curly hair tomorrow at church."

"You shouldn't be betting at all. I heard about the ruckus you caused playing poker. Grandpa probably lets you win," Columbia sneers.

"He did not! I'm a good poker player," I boast.

"Wanna bet? I can beat you with one arm tied behind my back,"Columbia snipes.

"Who taught you to play?" I ask.

"None of your business. Just get the cards."

"Deal me in." Amherst enters my room with a deck of cards.

We sit on the floor. Amherst shuffles and deals the cards. Mouse sits beside me.

"Let's make this interesting," Columbia says. "We'll use bobby pins for chips."

"Suits me fine," I reply.

By their grins, I know they think I'm a sucker waiting to be fleeced. In short order I prove I can hold my own. Due to Grandpa's shrewd teaching or my ESP, within fifteen minutes I possess all the bobby pins.

Weeks later I become bored with poker, and Columbia finally has curly hair Sunday morning. I don't know if her curls impressed Bobby Benson, because she got snippy when I asked.

Chapter 18
Gaining the Bathroom

The FAB4 all finish the seventh grade with flying colors. Our plans to go swimming daily are put on hold as June is rainy, very unusual for Kansas which is usually hot and dry all summer except for severe thunderstorms. The Midwest is in tornado alley, a huge section of the United States often hit by devastating storms. Because of this, most houses have a basement where you seek shelter from the storms.

In the summer everyone's house is like an oven. Box fans in the windows of each room just blow the hot air around. Nights can be really miserable if there is not a southern breeze. Doc Benson installed several room air-conditioners in the windows of his house recently. Columbia, who is still dating their son Bobby, says their living room is delightful, cool and refreshing. Well big deal.

Yeah, yeah, yeah, Uncle Waylon has a finished room in his basement. The walls are paneled in knotty pine. There is an area rug on the floor, an old sofa, a card table and chairs, a radio, and a record player make it the perfect place for the FAB4 to hang out when it is rainy or scorching hot.

Soon the summer becomes hotter than normal. Every day the temperature rises to 100 degrees. In July when wheat harvest begins, crews of huge combines arrive from Oklahoma that cut the wheat and spew the straw into the air. With the fields now bare, the prevailing southern winds blow prairie dust, as fine as powdered sugar over everything. Mother dusts the furniture daily to no avail. We can't close the windows or we'd suffer with stifling heat.

Most Saturdays, Daddy or Jaylynn's dad takes us to the swimming pool. Sometimes Sandy Prescott joins us, but usually it is just the FAB4. Summer jobs occupy Columbia and Amherst. Columbia is a part-time clerk at J.C. Penny's, and Amherst shelves books at the library. When not working, Columbia spreads a bath towel in the back yard and lies on it to tan, slathering on baby oil with Iodine. She pulls the straps of her swimsuit down, so she won't have tan lines. She thinks Mother will make her a strapless dress for the Senior Prom next spring. Ha! That will never happen. Grandma would have a stroke.

There will be no family vacation for us this summer because Daddy is busy overseeing Interstate 70 construction. President Eisenhower, who is Kansas' favorite son and a war hero, thinks the United States needs a better road system. Last year we took a day trip to Abilene, Kansas, to see Eisenhower's museum. Daddy drove on the new Kansas Turnpike, a fantastic four-lane highway. You have to pay a toll to drive on it, but it's worth it. We zoomed down the turnpike at 80 miles per hour passing cars. Mother kept telling Daddy to slow down, but I thought zipping past miles of boring fields and not getting stuck behind a tractor creeping along a two-lane road was great.

In August, Jaylynn, Wanda, and Shirley all go on family vacations. I receive a picture post card of Pikes Peak from Jaylynn. "It is cool here. There's snow on the mountain," she wrote. And Wanda, that lucky dog, is in Disneyland with Aunt Bessie and Uncle Waylon. I hope she brings me mouse ears. Shirley is in Wichita visiting her grandparents.

Jaylynn comes home first. She gives me a small doll in an Indian costume. "It's beautiful. Thanks. Jaylynn."

"Let me see the doll," Mouse says.

I hold it aloft before putting it on my dresser. "Don't touch it, Mouse. This doll is to look at not to play with."

"What kind of doll can't be played with?"

"This one. It's a storybook doll," I answer.

"Why can't I play with it?"

Now I understand why Columbia often tells me "You're too young to understand." I feel that way now about Mouse. "Just leave it alone. Okay?" I grab a deck of cards and Jaylynn and I go outside and sit in the shade of our cottonwood tree. The limbs now spread over our entire front yard.

As I deal Columbia flounces by. "Playing cards, I see. Old Maid I suppose. A good game for you children."

"No," I say, "we're playing Canasta." Feeling generous I add, "You want to join us."

"Jaylynn, did you know I'll be graduating from high school in nine months?" Columbia asks.

"Who cares? Graduation is stupid," I say.

"That's because you're a snot-nosed kid in grade school," Columbia says. "Sorry, Jaylynn, I meant Rebel, not you."

"We're pre-freshman. In the eighth grade this year," Jaylynn says. "Our last year at Cherokee K-8."

"You're more mature than some people I could mention." Columbia crinkles her nose at me. "Graduation is an important rite of passage."

"Yeah, yeah, yeah," I add. "Graduation will be just another one of your boring events I'll have to attend. If I have to hear the Crippled Trio sing, *You'll Never Walk Alone* one more time I'll scream."

"The Triple Trio is an elite woman's music group. I'm sure we'll sing at graduation. For graduation we wear robes and c —"

"Big deal. I'm not going," I say.

"You have to go," Jaylynn says.

"You should listen to Jaylynn, Rebel. She has more sense than you."

"Telephone, Columbia," Mother calls from the front door. "It's Bobby."

"I'm coming. I'm coming." Columbia runs toward the house.

"Bobby and Columbia sitting in a tree, k-i-s-s-i-n-g," I holler, then I turn to Jaylynn. "Why did you side with Columbia and say I should go to her graduation? I thought you were my friend."

"I think it would be exciting, and she's your sister."

"I know I'll have to go, but I'm sure it will be boring with a capital B."

* * *

The following May as Columbia's graduation approaches, I hear Daddy telling his boss on the telephone, "I can't be out of town the last week in May. Columbia's graduating from high school." Sheesh. Graduation must be a big deal.

"Mother! Where are you?" Columbia yells as she bursts into the house. "Our caps and gowns arrived today."

"Let me see them," I say.

"You can look, but don't touch." Columbia places a large blue box on the sofa, removes the lid and reveals a sparkling white gown and a hat with a flat cardboard top. Columbia swats my outstretched hands. "I don't want your grimy paws on my graduation gown."

"What a weird hat." I snatch the flattop hat and put it on. The pointed cap extends halfway down my nose forming a white beak. "I feel like a bird with a book on my head." I prance around the room flapping my arms like wings.

"Give me that. You'll stretch it out of shape." Columbia yanks the hat off my head and inspects it for damage. "Where's my tassel? If you've lost my tassel, I'm going to —"

"Calm down, your tassel's right here."

"Columbia," Mother calls from her sewing niche. "Bring the gown here."

"Coming." Columbia flounces off with her nose in the air. I follow. At Mother's command, Columbia slips on her unfinished graduation dress and fastens her gown over it.

"I never dreamed the gown would be so short." Mother steps back to view Columbia from across the room. "Your dress will need a four-inch hem. Stand on this footstool so I can pin in the hem."

Columbia fidgets on the footstool, squirming like an earthworm on the sidewalk after a rainstorm. "Hurry up. I want to see how I look."

"Hold still. Ouch!" Mother sucks a drop of blood off her index finger.

"What happened?" Columbia screeches.

"I stuck myself with a pin."

"Are you bleeding? Let me see." Columbia jumps off the footstool.

"It's nothing. Get back on the footstool." Mother extends her pricked finger toward Columbia with a drop of blood as bright as a ruby on it.

"You're bleeding!" Columbia shoves the hem of her graduation gown toward Mother. "Look! There's blood on my gown."

Mother peers through the bottom half of her bifocals in vain to find the offending blood stain. Columbia' points to a speck the size of a gnat's eyelash. It might be dirt or a fabric flaw, but more likely it's just Columbia's imagination. For once in my life, I keep my mouth shut. I tiptoe from the room before Columbia starts crying. Sheesh.

* * *

Commencement is held in Schoenfeld's City Auditorium. A brick sweatbox with windows lining the sides. The stage is at one end. The floor area is primarily for the band and the graduates. There are three rows of folding chairs on the floor for the public. The rest of the public seating is up steep steps, too steep for Grandma and Grandpa to climb, so Daddy takes Mouse and me to the auditorium at six o'clock to save chairs on the floor. We place programs on nine seats on the first row and sit to guard them.

Columbia left an hour ago for the high school moaning, "This is the last time my class will all be together."

Sheesh! You would think it was the end of the world.

Mouse and I watch the stuffy auditorium fill with people. Finally, Mother, Daddy, Amherst and our grandparents arrive. Aunt Bessie, Uncle Waylon, and Wanda appear soon after them. Aunt Bessie and Wanda sit with us. Uncle Waylon climbs to the top of the auditorium to take his place in the KDOG radio booth. The temperature rises in the auditorium with the addition of each warm body. By eight o'clock the auditorium is a standing-room-only inferno.

"If you think it's hot down here," Aunt Bessie says, "you should be with Waylon in the KDOG booth. I sat there once during a basketball game. I almost passed out from heat prostration."

"There isn't any oxygen up there," Wanda says. "I was panting like a dog. Daddy told me to stop because people listening to the radio could hear me breathing. That's why we're sitting with you tonight. At least I won't sweat out my undies sitting here."

Grandma, who is sitting beside Wanda says nothing. If I'd mentioned sweating or my undies in public, Grandma would have given me a tongue lashing or a piercing glare that warned of impending annihilation.

"How did Waylon handle the heat?" Grandma says. "He's always been sensitive to temperature extremes."

"He was sweating like a pig in a slaughterhouse," Wanda says. "Sweat dripped off his forehead into his microphone and shorted it out. I had to run out to the car to get another mic."

"KDOG was off the air ten minutes," Aunt Bessie says. "*The National Anthem* and the prayer by Father Jordan for the safety of the players weren't aired. The next day the Catholics bombarded KDOG with telephone calls accusing Waylon of favoring the Protestants."

"Waylon doesn't favor religion, period," Mother says.

"Hearing a few words from the 'good book' might do him some good," Aunt Bessie says.

"Is Uncle Waylon a heathen?" Mouse asks.

"Shh, Mouse," Mother says. "Don't interrupt adults when they are talking."

"Just because Waylon doesn't attend church doesn't mean he's a heathen," Grandma says. "I rarely attend church now."

"Why don't you come to church, Grandma?" I ask.

"Rebel, don't ask adults personal questions," Mother says.

"The steps are difficult for me," Grandma says.

"Waylon wouldn't have any trouble climbing the steps," Mother says. "It's kneeling and praying for forgiveness that would be difficult for him."

"That and the fact he is hung over most Sunday mornings," Aunt Bessie adds.

"Imbibing of spirits is good for men," Grandma says. "Keeps them healthy."

"In that case, Waylon should be healthier than a horse," Aunt Bessie says.

"I wish Daddy would go to church," Wanda says. "Maybe he wouldn't drink so much then."

"Wanda, honey, this is adult talk." Grandma smiles at Wanda. "Please, don't interrupt."

"Mom," Mother says, "since it's difficult for you to attend church, if you ever want spiritual guidance or to take communion, Pastor Rozell makes home visits."

"I have no need to see Pastor Rozell," Grandma says. "God and I have our own agreement. I refuse to forgive people who have wronged me until they admit the error of their ways. God expects no less. He doesn't forgive until you ask. You're familiar with the story of the prodigal son, aren't you Bonnie?"

"Yes," Mother says.

"I know it too," I say. "We read it in Sunday School. The father was so happy to see his son he rushed down the road to greet him."

"Before he repented," Mother says.

"Maybe so, but the bottom line is, the girl, uh, I mean the son, repented and admitted he was wrong. And as for you young lady," Grandma points a gnarled finger at me; "you should not interrupt your elders."

"Wanda did and you didn't say anything to her," I say.

"Rebel!" Mother says. "Don't argue with your grandmother."

"You need to nip Rebel's sassy behavior in the bud," Grandma says, "before she's completely out of hand."

"You ladies calm down," Grandpa says. "The procession has started."

Grandpa whispers something to Mother, and Daddy put his arm around her shoulder. Mother pulls a handkerchief from her purse and dabs her eyes. Aunt Bessie shakes her head and mouths the words, "I'm sorry."

Sorry for what? I'm mulling over their comments when a multitude of flashbulbs sparkle like stars throughout the auditorium filling the air with an odd smell. We stand for the graduates as they march by like royalty. I pull my damp dress away from the back of my legs and pray the ceremony will be short or, like Wanda, I will be sweating out my undies tonight. The heat is stifling. Before the graduates sit, three girls faint, and the tuba player collapses into the kettle drums.

An hour into the ceremony I wonder why people make such a big fuss over graduation. It's nothing but a bunch of boring speeches. Sheesh. At nine-thirty the graduates, all one hundred and twenty-two stand, and as their names are called, they walk across the stage to receive their diploma from the president of the school board. At eleven o'clock, the butt-paralyzing event is over.

"I never thought I'd live to see a grandchild graduate from high school," Grandpa says. "That was really nice. I'm so proud of Columbia."

Nice is not a word I'll ever use to describe a graduation ceremony. The only nice thing about this monumentally boring event is that it's over.

As we shuffle outside Grandma says, "It was hotter than Billy Goat hell in there. I hope it's cooler next year."

"Next year?" I ask. "No way. I'm not sitting through another graduation come hell or high water."

"Watch your mouth," Grandma says.

"Me either," says Wanda.

"Of course, you will," Mother says. "Next year Amherst graduates. She'll be giving one of the speeches if she remains first in her class."

Oh brother. I'm doomed. I've less than a year to convince Amherst to give a short speech. And I mean short. Even if it's only five minutes, that's four minutes too long.

"It's hard to believe Columbia will be going way to college this fall," Mother says.

"I can believe it," Daddy says. "She better go. I've sent checks to Bethany College for her dorm deposit and tuition. They won't refund that money."

"Columbia and Amherst will both do well in college," Grandma says. "They have focus. They know what they want to do. It's Rebel I worry about."

"Rebel's young," Grandpa says. "She'll figure out what she wants to do long before she goes to college."

"I certainly hope so," Grandma say. "If not, I hope I'm not around to see her go to hell in a handbasket like some family members have."

"Shhh, Rose." Grandpa helps Grandma into our car. "Don't spoil a happy occasion by thinking about past hurts."

Their conversation is perplexing, but I dwell on the fact that when Columbia goes to college, I'll get her bedroom and several hours of bathroom time will become available. I plan to claim the bathroom time. I'll be a freshman this fall. In the past year my opinion of boys has changed. I'll need time to primp.

Chapter 19
In the Heat of the Game

It's a known fact; Kansas is the flattest state in the Union, smack dab in the middle of the Great Plains. Early explorers called the Plains a vast desert, but it's not like the sandy Sahara. The Great Plains are miles of wide-open country with few trees. The land is good for growing wheat and raising cattle, but the wind always is blowing. In winter, the wind is cold and filled with stinging snowflakes. The sun creeps above the horizon at about eight in the morning and is gone by five in the afternoon.

Spring lasts all of two days, then comes the broiling summers. From June to September, rain is scarce, and the Kansas plains have sixteen hours of sunshine and twenty-four hours of a nonstop hot wind. These days are perfect days for swimming, but the pool is three miles from our house and Mother doesn't drive. Columbia and Amherst take the Bel Air to work and rarely will take the FAB4 to the pool. Our other option for entertainment is to walk four blocks to Ritterbush's Grocery to buy a Coke or a Popsicle and walk home slurping them. This simple pleasure has two drawbacks. One, my paltry allowance, and two, Mother requires me to take Mouse, because she says, "Mouse will be bored if you're not here to play with her." Phooey.

Mouse doesn't talk much when she's with the FAB4, but she remembers every word we say because I've heard her blab our secrets. At age ten, Mouse has mastered the fine art of extortion. She had a great role model: me. If I don't buy Mouse a Popsicle, every word we say will be reported to Mother or become common knowledge in the entire neighborhood before sunset. For the price of a Popsicle, she keeps her mouth shut, but that means I can only afford two trips a week to Ritterbush's.

Bored, and out of money in August, I knock on Columbia's bedroom door. Amherst is busy painting Columbia's fingernails.

"How about a game of Monopoly?" I ask.

"Go away." Columbia blows on her fingernails. "I have a date tonight."

"Is that all you think about? Playing kissey-face with Bobby," I ask.

"When you're older, you'll understand the importance of having a man in your life."

"You've got to be kidding. Bobby's not a man. He doesn't have enough whiskers for a good shave."

"Yes, he does," Columbia says. "You're just too young to understand."

"I understand more than you think," I say.

"You might fool Rebel, but not me," Amherst says. "Those aren't whisker burns on your neck."

"Yeah, what are those red marks?" I ask. "They don't look like mosquito bites either."

Columbia blushes as red as the marks on her neck. "You're too young to understand, Rebel."

"No, I'm not. I know all about hickeys. That's why you're wearing a turtleneck sweater when it's so hot you could fry an egg on the sidewalk. I bet Mother would like to know about those hickeys."

"Pipe down, Rebel, before the whole world hears you." Columbia brushes her straight hair making it gleam. "I'm not playing a stupid game with you and your puny attempts of blackmail won't work either. I know all about you and Jaylynn sneaking out last week after dark to spy on Jimmy and his friends camping in his backyard. Perhaps I should tell Mother about this."

I say nothing. Columbia has me whipped.

"Just one game of Monopoly please," I beg. "I'll let you be the banker, Amherst."

"Count me out," Amherst says. "Go play with Mouse."

"Last year the three of us played Monopoly all the time," I say. "How about a game for old time's sake?"

"Are you nuts?" Columbia says. "College students do not play Monopoly with children."

"You're not in college yet."

"I will be in three weeks."

"Big deal," Amherst says. "Last year you bragged about being a mighty senior. Now you're lowly freshman at the bottom of a big heap of upperclassmen."

"You're jealous," Columbia says. "No matter how smart you are, I'll always be one step ahead of you."

"You're not smart enough to get any scholarships. I'll get gobs of them," Amherst says.

I leave them to their one-upmanship fight. I have no fire power. I flip on the TV and wait for it to warm up. We're 120 miles away from the nearest TV stations. Daddy erected a fifty-foot TV antenna beside our house, which allows us to receive the stations. Sometimes the pictures are full of snow when the wind blows the antenna in the wrong direction. Summer programming consists of news, old movies, and black and white test patterns when the stations are experiencing technical difficulties, which is often. An old *Our Gang* comedy is on now. One I haven't seen, but they are all pretty much the same. I watch Spanky and Darla goof around until Alfalfa starts to sing, then I snap off the TV.

"I'm going to visit Grandma and Grandpa," I shout.

"Good riddance," Columbia and Amherst reply.

"What's Mouse doing?" Mother calls from her bedroom where she's reading.

"Playing with her dolls."

"Tell Mom and Dad I'll be over to see them this evening," Mother says.

"Okay." I push open the back screen door.

Dressed in blue shorts and a halter top, both of which Mother made, I walk across our well-groomed yard, and along the edge of our vegetable garden toward no-man's-land, our alley. Six-foot tall scratchy weeds threaten to close the alley this summer. The city's mowing crew tries to keep them cut, but their puny tractor finds it nigh onto impossible to chop through the jungle of rag weed, marijuana, goldenrod, sunflowers, and pig weed. Grandma and Grandpa are often outside sitting in blue metal lawn chairs, bobbing in a slow syncopated rhythm, but not today.

They must be on their screened-in porch. In books a screened-in porch is always described as a shady area stretching across the back of a house that faces a lake or mountain scene. Gentle breezes waft through the screens as the heroine swings in a hammock sipping icy mint juleps. My grandparents' porch is nothing like that.

Their porch is a small wart on the north side of a towering three-story apartment building. The porch is more dismal than shady. The screened wall faces north, and since our summer breezes come from the South, there's not a chance for a puff of air. My grandparents don't drink alcohol, so there are no frosty mint juleps, but glasses of Hawaiian Punch, which they call "bug juice," are always available.

I pull open the screen door and see Grandma sitting on a pillow-ticking fabric cushion in a wicker barrel chair reading the latest issue of *Reader's Digest.* She waves a fan with a flower design by her face in a distracted manner. Her wispy, snow-white hair doesn't even twitch as the fan slices through the sticky air.

"Hi, Grandma. How you doin'?" I've been on the porch less than ten seconds and already I feel sweat trickling down my back.

"Sit down, Rebel." Grandma motions toward a metal folding chair with her fan.

"Sure is hot today isn't it, Grandma?"

"Hot as Billy Goat hell." Grandma closes the magazine.

This is as close as Grandma ever comes to swearing. "How can summer be as hot as Billy Goat hell, Grandma? In the winter you tell me it's as cold as Billy Goat hell. Which is it, hot or cold in Billy Goat hell?"

"Hmmm, that's a good question, Rebel." Grandma eyes my skimpy outfit. "My goodness girl, you don't have on enough clothes to flag a train."

Why would anyone want to flag a train, and besides we live miles away from the train track? Grandma must be crazy with the heat. "I came to play cribbage with Grandpa. You wanna watch?"

"Sure. You want a glass of bug-juice?" She pushes herself up from her chair, puts her fan on the table, and hobbles toward the kitchen.

"Yes, please. With lots of ice. And tell Grandpa I'm here."

I grab her fan and flap it in front of my face until she returns.

"Here's your bug juice."

I rise and take the glass of juice from her hand.

"Grandpa will be right out. He's watching the last inning of the White Sox game." Grandma returns to her wicker chair.

I take a big swig of the bug-juice which forms a pink moustache on my lip. I wipe it and beads of sweat off my face. I finish my bug-juice before Grandpa enters the porch carrying the cribbage board and a deck of cards.

Due to the intense heat and humidity, Grandpa's usually well-ironed slacks are rumpled. Instead of wearing a crisp sports shirt, he only has on his white undershirt which clings to his moist, pale skin. His snow-white hair is plastered to his damp forehead.

"Think you can beat me today?" Grandpa smiles.

"I'm going to try."

We cut for the deal. I lose. Grandpa shuffles and deals. "Terrible! Doesn't make much difference what I do with this hand?"

"Your lead, "Grandpa says. "Might as well play 'em like you got 'em, even though I know you don't."

I play a jack. He matches it. "Two points for my side." Grandpa pegs his points.

During the rest of this hand the best I can do is peg 'three of a kind' for six points. "I count first. Let's see, I have 15-2, 15-4, a pair makes six, and Jack of nobs is seven." I peg my points.

"Read 'em and weep." Grandpa lays his cards on the table: two Jacks, a ten, and a five. Ugh. And I cut him a queen which increased his hand to sixteen points.

"I'd like a good hand like that." I shuffle the cards.

"Two sevens and two eights in the crib, that's another twelve points," Grandpa says. "It's a poor dealer that can't deal herself a good hand."

I ponder his saying as I shuffle and reshuffle the cards.

Don't wear the spots off them," Grandpa says.

"Okay." I deal the cards. "I have a good hand this time, Grandpa, just you wait and see." I show my hand to Grandma, who shakes her head in disbelief.

"Your turn to cut, Grandpa." He cuts the deck and with a dramatic flair.

"Well, what do you know? A five," I say. Grandma shakes her head again, this time in amazement. I have a killer hand. After playing the hand, I spread my cards on the table. "Read 'em and weep, Grandpa." One game follows another until the cards blur before my eyes.

"Want to play another game?" Grandpa shuffles the cards for the umpteenth time.

Good grief. I've played cribbage in this sweat box for three hours and drunken half a gallon of bug juice. My damp shorts cling to my moist underpants. My sweaty legs are stuck to the metal folding chair. When I stand, they'll make a disgusting sound, similar to one Uncle Waylon makes after eating beans and drinking beer.

"Rebel, supper!" Mother's voice calls across the alley.

"No more cribbage today, Grandpa. I have to go home, besides I'm too hot and sweaty."

Grandma gasps and slumps over onto the table.

"Grandma, are you all right?" I wave a cardboard fan over her body.

She clears her throat, pulls herself erect, inhales deeply, and with great dignity says, "My dear Rebel, when will you ever learn that horses sweat, men perspire, but women glow."

"Jumpin' Jehoshaphat, Grandma, I thought you'd had a heart attack!"

"Ladies should not use such language," Grandma says.

Some days I can't win. This is one of them. When I stand, my legs break their vacuum seal from the metal chair. Schwuuuck. "I'm way past glowing, Grandma. I'm so hot I'm gonna burst into flames." I flap my knees together and twitch from side to side trying in vain to get my damp shorts out of my crotch.

"What's the matter with you?" Grandma says. "Fidgeting like that in public."

"My shorts are stuck in my —"

"Not another word. Ladies do not mention such things in public."

"Now Rose, calm down," Grandpa says. "It's a hot day and she's a child."

"But she won't always be one," Grandma says. "She needs to learn now how to behave so we don't have a repeat of what happened years ago."

"Plenty of time for that," Grandpa says.

"What happened years ago?" I ask.

"Nothing you need to know about. Just see that you mind your manners," Grandma says.

Perplexed and sweaty, I push open the screen door and inhale the fragrant scent of basswood trees in bloom. "I almost forgot to tell you, Mother said she'd be over after supper."

Grandma calls, "Don't rush off in the heat of the day without your blankets."

Why would I want a blanket on a day that's either hotter or colder than Billy Goat hell? And what I am supposed to do with this blanket, flag down that train she was talking about earlier?

With a mighty "Arrrgh" and a futile swat at a swarm of mosquitoes, I disappear into the bug infested weeds in the alley and another afternoon of summer slips away.

* * *

The Friday before school starts, once again I'm playing cribbage with Grandpa. I look at my cards and assume my best poker face. I hold three fives and a Jack of spades, the makings of a perfect cribbage hand. The odds of this happening are at least one in a zillion. Grandpa's played cribbage for sixty years, and he's never had a perfect twenty-nine-point hand. My hands are shaking. I put my cards on the table and wipe my sweaty palms on my shorts. To get the coveted twenty-nine points, I must cut the deck to reveal the remaining five. Sheesh!

"Grandma, come here," I call.

"You don't need Grandma's help," Grandpa says. "You're an excellent player."

"I want Grandma to see my hand."

When her cane taps across the linoleum floor in the kitchen, I rise and offer my arm to steady her as she steps down onto the porch. I show her my hand.

"Ooo-weee," she says.

"Wish me luck." I place my hand on the deck. I run my thumb along the edge of the cards and concentrate. Forty cards. I need to find that five of spades. I close my eyes and concentrate on the five of spades and make a thin cut. Grandpa reaches for the top card. I hold my breath.

"Did you want the six of clubs?" Grandpa says.

"Nooooo."

"Good, because you didn't get that." Grandpa lays the cut card face up beside the deck.

"Hot damn! The five of spades." I quickly cover my mouth. "Oops, sorry Grandma."

Grandma shakes her head in disbelief, too stunned to reprimand me for swearing. "I swan to man, Rebel. You could charm the bees out of the trees."

After the hand is finished, I peg my twenty-nine points. Not only do I win, but I skunk Grandpa, beating him by more than thirty points. "Wow, that's the first time I've ever done that."

"That's my girl. A first-rate cribbage player. I've taught you everything I know." Grandpa smiles and pats my hand.

"Do you want to play another game?" I'm high on winning, excited at the thought of another game.

"No, I'm beat."

"Okay, Grandpa. I'll see you tomorrow. Maybe I'll let you win."

I run home dodging grasshoppers that fly among the tall weeds. Nasty things, grasshoppers, ugly, and they spit brown juice. A crow caws overhead and perches on a telephone pole. Grandma says a crow flying over you means a death is coming soon. She's superstitious. She also believes putting an umbrella on a bed is bad luck, and so is making a rocking chair rock when no one is in it.

That night I dream of playing cribbage. A white crow sits at the table opposite me. When I deal the cards, the crow flies away, and sirens screech in the background. I awake with a start in the middle of the night. The sirens are real, not part of my dream.

I look out my bedroom window across the alley. Red lights swirl through the darkness. Two silhouettes are pushing a gurney toward an ambulance. My heart pounds. Six couples live in that apartment building. Everyone is old. I pray the ambulance isn't taking one of my grandparents. My mouth is dry. Tears fill my eyes when our back door squeaks open.

Moments later Mother enters the room I share with Mouse, "He's gone." Tears stream down her face. "Your grandpa died in his sleep."

I slump onto my bed. Dead. How can Grandpa be dead?

Grandpa will be buried in St. Louis. Columbia can't attend his funeral as she's just started college and Amherst can't miss the beginning of her senior year. Grandma and Mother take the train to St. Louis, and Mouse and I ride with Daddy across most of Kansas and all of Missouri. I wish that interstate system was finished. This trip lasts forever. Daddy usually entertains us by playing roadside bingo which requires us to search the landscape for weird items, but not on this trip. Even being able to ride shot gun in the front seat does not make the trip better.

Aunt Lily, Cousin Pansy, Mother, and Grandma meet us at the cemetery. Everyone is wearing black clothes, except Pansy who wears her usual purple. Aunt Lily and Grandma have real flower corsages, composed of Lily of the Valley and white roses. After a short grave-side service, Grandpa's casket is lowered into the ground.

Tears streak my face as I approach the open grave. I grab a handful of dirt and sprinkle it into the grave, a symbolic goodbye. My mouth is dry. I'm unable to say goodbye. After tossing in the dirt, I run to our car and sit in the back seat. I wipe away my tears leaving muddy streaks on my cheeks. The thought of Grandpa in a box underground frightens me. I know his spirit is in heaven, but I can't see heaven.

Grandma decides to stay in Saint Louis with Aunt Lily for a few days, so Mother rides home with us. After stopping for a late supper in Marysville, Kansas, Mouse falls asleep. I slump against a back window and watch the sunset. When the evening star appears, I think Starlight, star bright, first star I saw tonight. I wish I may, I wish I might, have the wish I wish tonight. I wish… wish… There's no point wishing. My wish won't come true. Where are you Grandpa? Is heaven on that star or beyond the stars?

In the front seat, Mother and Daddy quietly discuss how long Grandma can live by herself. "I don't want her in a nursing home if she can manage in her apartment," Mother says.

"I agree," replies Daddy, "but that means more work for you. Waylon should take some responsibility, she's his mother too."

"It will be better if he doesn't interfere. You know how Mom is. She'd always side with him."

"I know," Daddy replies. "It was just a suggestion."

We ride in silence for miles, and then Daddy says, "I'm going to miss your dad. He's been like a father to me."

"But not as much as I will," Mother says. "Are you girls sleeping?"

I'm not, but I don't feel like talking so I say nothing.

"Dad always protected me," Mother says. "When Mom attacked me or criticized the girls, especially, Rebel, Dad always came to my defense." Mother sniffs, and Daddy pats her shoulder.

Mother's right. Grandma finds fault with me more than she does my sisters. I've lost track of how many times she's told me, 'Ladies don't do this or ladies don't do that or I better watch my Ps and Qs.'

"Dad told me once that Rebel is the spittin' image of her," Mother says.

"Really?" Daddy dims the headlights as we drive into Schoenfeld. "What do you remember about her?"

"Not much. I was young when she left," Mother says.

I wonder who the her is they're talking about. I don't look like anyone in my family.

"I don't think Mom ever wanted me." Mother says. "She's always favored Waylon which I can understand, but now that Dad's gone, I have no one to defend me."

Daddy is silent. I'm sure he wants to say 'sheesh,' because that's what I'm thinking. Sheesh. Why wouldn't Grandma want her own daughter?

Chapter 20
Drama: Comedy and Tragedy

Schoenfeld High School is in the center of town. Eighth grade students from Cherokee, Pawnee, Apache, and Sioux Grade School in Schoenfeld, along with kids from several rural grade schools make up the Freshman class. All total more than 500 students attend the high school.

On Monday, when I walk into Schoenfeld High School, the students rush to their lockers and First Period classes. I was at Grandpa's funeral last week, so I am totally lost. Kids push by me as I search for room 34. I arrive at my English class after the tardy bell. Not a good way to start the year.

Instead of reading American literature, Mrs. Fletcher assigns sentences for us to diagram. Despite groans from most of the students, I don't mind the assignment. Diagramming is mindless work; drawing little lines and putting words on them keeps me from thinking about Grandpa.

The highlight of the day is lunch. Schoenfeld High School has a cafeteria, the perfect place for the FAB4 to scope out boys. Within a few weeks we decide all the guys in our class are immature dorks or dipsticks, but there are plenty of cute upperclassmen to dream about.

We have a ten-block walk home now. We pass J.M. McDonald's and J.C Penney's which allow us to window shop. Two jewelry stores display items none of us can afford or need, the Rialto Movie Theater and Snyder's Florist. We pass both the Rexall Drug store that has a soda fountain and several small tables, and the Dairy Queen (DQ) that has a larger seating area, and a huge parking lot which will be great when I'm old enough to drive.

Today we're stopping at the DQ. The prime table by the window is filled with upperclassmen. We're relegated to a table along the back wall. I can spend about fifteen minutes here as Mother wants me home forty minutes after school's dismissed. I begged Mother to give me an hour to walk home, but she said, "You see your friends all day at school. You don't need to spend thirty minutes lollygagging with them at the DQ." This puts a real crimp in my social life.

My only chance to be with kids after school, especially boys, is to join an activity. Sports are only for boys which is okay with me. I'm about as coordinated as a three-legged woman on a tight rope. Other options are special music groups, but no boys are in them. Chess club is mostly boys, but they're super nerds. Latin club would be a real bore, and I don't want to join the Home Economics Club and sit around after school with a bunch of girls discussing canning, sewing, and diapering a baby.

So today when Mrs. Fletcher our English teacher says, "Are any of you interested in forming a Drama Club? We'd meet after a school, study theater, and perform a play later this fall."

My hand shoots into the air. The limelight is calling me. Several others raise their hands, including Paul, the boy I hope will ask me to a Sock Hop at the YMCA. When Steve, Jaylynn's current love interest raises his hand, so does Jaylynn.

"Twenty students," Mrs. Fletcher says. "Great. We'll have a fine production."

"What play will we do?" "Will we wear costumes and makeup?" "When will we practice?"

"Everyone, calm down. We'll practice after school for an hour on Monday, Tuesday, and Thursday. Of course, there will be costumes and makeup. It wouldn't be a play without them."

"I don't want to memorize lines," Jimmy says. "What can I do?"

Jimmy not wanting to be on the stage stuns me. He's been a bad actor his entire life.

"Well," Mrs. Fletcher says, "a play needs production people to build and paint sets, others to operate the lights, find costumes, and put makeup on the actors."

"I don't want to put lipstick on people," Jimmy says, "unless it's Lucy." He smooches his lips to make a kissing noise.

"Yuck! Fat chance," Lucy says. "I'd rather die than have you touch my lips."

I nod to Lucy and rub my lips. Jimmy's kiss years ago still lingers, not a pleasant memory.

"I'm not going to wear lipstick," a couple of guys holler. "Only sissies do that."

Mrs. Fletcher claps her hands. "Quiet class." She points to papers on her desk. "Your parents must sign a permission slip before you can tryout on Thursday after school. There are thirteen roles in the play *Harvey.* Those who aren't selected for the cast will be on a backstage crew."

I take a form, inhale the smell of fresh mimeograph ink and grab three copies of *Harvey.* The FAB4 reads the play aloud as we walk home. "I don't care what part I get. I'll even be the rabbit, but I have to be on the stage," I say.

"I'm more interested in debate," Shirley says.

"I'd rather be backstage," adds Jaylynn. "I'd be scared to speak in front of an audience."

"I think I'll stick with my dancing," Wanda says.

"Not me. I hope I get the part of Myrtle Mae. She's so dramatic and gets to kiss her boyfriend. If Paul gets the boyfriend role, I'll have to practice kissing him three times a week." I sigh. "It's tough to be an actress, but acting is in my blood."

"Who's an actor in our family?" Wanda asks.

"No one. I'm going to be the first!"

Despite the fact I'm supercharged about Drama Club, I forget to have Mother sign my permission slip. On Wednesday night, I drift to sleep, mumbling, "Get Mother to sign the permission slip at breakfast."

The next morning Mouse has knots in her shoestrings that I have to untangle. Daddy wants to leave earlier than usual since big wigs from the State Department of Roads office in Topeka are visiting, Mother burns the toast, and I have to eat oatmeal. Nothing like a bowl of library paste to start the morning. Thankfully she did not toss raisins in this glop.

"If you're coming, come on." Daddy places his empty coffee cup in his saucer.

"Wait for me." Amherst scurries around the living room gathering her stuff. "The Bel Air has a flat tire. I'll have to ride with you."

I grab my books and homework. The doorbell rings. "I'll get it!"

Jaylynn is outside waiting to ride with us. We get in the back seat and Amherst hops in the front. "Did your mom sign your permission slip last night?" Jaylynn asks.

"Oh, no. I forgot." I fan the pages of my textbooks looking for the permission slip.

"What are you looking for?" Amherst asks.

"My permission slip so I can be in a school play."

"What makes you think you can be an actress?" Amherst says.

"I don't think I can, I know I can. Fame is in my future." I pull the permission slip from my spiral notebook. "Here, Daddy. Sign this." I thrust it over the seat.

"What is it?"

"Rebel thinks she's going to be the next Audrey Hepburn," Amherst says.

"Did you ask your mother about this?" Daddy asks.

"No, I forgot, but she won't care. It's an after-school activity. Teachers will be there."

"My mom and dad are letting me do it," Jaylynn says.

"All right." Daddy stops the car near school and scribbles his name on the paper.

"Thanks, Daddy." I grab the paper. We exit the car; Daddy drives away, and Amherst walks quickly not wanting to be seen with lowly freshman since she is a senior. "That was close. If Daddy hadn't signed the permission slip, I would have forged his name," I say to Jaylynn.

"Really? You better call your mom and let her know you're staying after school today," Jaylynn says.

"I'll call her before class starts. There's always a line to use the office phone after school." Jaylynn hangs her jacket in our locker while I call home. Not sure if Mother would have signed the permission slip, I say, "Mother, I have to stay after school for about an hour today. I forgot to tell you. Mrs. Fletcher wants me to help with a special project. Okay?" I hold my breath. Silence. "Mother, did you hear me?"

"I'm shooing Mouse out the door. She dawdles every morning."

"I did, too, when Mighty Munson was my teacher." The old chant we sang about that terrible teacher springs to mind. Mighty Matson was her name. She drove her pupils all insane.

"What was it you wanted, Rebel?"

"I need to stay after school for an hour and help Mrs. Fletcher. Is that all right?"

"Of course."

"Thanks, Mother. Bye." I dash to my locker, not wanting to be tardy and receive detention time today. I hope God doesn't keep a record of white lies. The stage is calling me.

***

"Mother!" I fling open the front door Friday afternoon. "Where are you?"

"In the kitchen. Take off your shoes. I'm mopping the floor."

"Do I smell cookies?" I place my shoes by the front door.

"Yes, molasses crinkles."

I grab a cookie off the cooling rack. "Guess what, Mother?"

"Don't talk with food in your mouth." She pushes the mop under the kitchen table.

I swallow my mouthful of cookie and gush, "I'm going to be in *Harvey*, the school play. I wanted to play Myrtle Mae, one of the leads, but Mrs. Fletcher chose me to play the rabbit, Harvey. She's directing the play. We practice three afternoons after school, and in April we'll have four performances. Isn't that exciting? Tickets are only $2 each and…

"I wish you'd asked me before trying out. I don't relish telling your grandma about this." Mother sighs and shakes her head.

"Why? She likes our school programs. She and Grandpa always came to them."

"This is different. Your grandpa took immense pleasure in your activities. He told me many times to let you girls experience life and try new things. But your grandma's not like him. She has rigid rules on what's proper behavior for young ladies. Acting isn't on that list. Don't tell her about the play. Let me break it to her tomorrow."

"Okay." Phooey! No point my telling Amherst, she has Senioritis. All she cares about is graduation this spring. Columbia is away at college, and Mouse is too young to understand how important this is. "No one cares about anything I do."

"Now, Rebel, you know that's not true," Mother places the mop in the bucket. "Your father and I take pride in everything all you girls have accomplished."

"I wish Grandpa was still alive. He'd be excited that I was in a play."

"I wish he was alive too," Mother says.

"My middle name is Rose, to honor Grandma, but I don't think she cares about that or anything I do. She likes Wanda and my sisters better than me." Tears well in my eyes despite trying to blink them away.

"Come here, Rebel."

I walk toward Mother's outstretched arms. She engulfs me in a hug. "Your grandmother is an unhappy woman. She refuses to look on the bright side of life and dwells on past hurts. She's not going to change at her age. We have to accept that's how she is. I know she's hard on you. I wish I could change that, but I can't."

I feel Mother's tears on my cheeks. I don't know if she is crying for my pain or hers. Grandpa was our buddy, our defender, the calming voice of sanity, and now he's gone.

The next afternoon I stop by Grandma's house on the way home from school. As I enter the back porch, Mother and Grandmother are in a heated conversation in the kitchen. I know better than to eavesdrop, but how else am I supposed to get any information?

"Letting Rebel act in a play is the first step toward a no-account life. First the stage and then heaven knows what," Grandma says. "Next her painted face will be plastered all over town."

"Rebel's playing the rabbit in *Harvey.* No one will see her face when she's on stage."

"All the same," Grandma says, "you know what I think about such things and why."

"That was a long time ago. Times have changed. Students have been in school plays for years. It's not risqué."

"Women who perform for others gain a bad reputation. The stage is for fallen women and those of ill repute. Mark my words, nothing good will come of this," Grandma says.

"Rebel has no desire to become an actress. This is a high school play, not Broadway."

"Don't be impudent, Bonnie. I suppose you'll watch Rebel perform, but I won't. I refuse to condone an activity I think is shameless."

"Suit yourself. I wish Dad was still alive. He'd go."

"Your father was a good provider, had a heart of gold, but was ignorant about what was right and proper," Grandma says.

"I suppose you're referring to me."

"Not necessarily, but if the shoe fits, wear it."

"I've done everything you've ever asked," Mother says. "Isn't that enough?"

"I suppose so," Grandma says. "But it's different. You're not

Waylon."

"Thank goodness. I have no desire to be like him."

"Watch what you say about my son," Grandma says. "Adjusting to a little sister was difficult for him. He'd ruled the roost for years. I encouraged him to accept you. I can't help it if you two can't agree on anything."

"You could have tried harder," Mother says. "Dad did."

Grandma must have stood because I hear her cane tap across the linoleum kitchen floor and go into her carpeted bedroom. I wait. The cane soon taps on the kitchen floor again. "I have something for you. I wanted to burn it years ago, but your father said you should have it. I promised to give it to you, so I'm honoring my word even though he's dead. Here, take it. I'm glad to be rid of it."

Silence.

I can't see what Grandma gives Mother, but I sense tension in their silence. My knees hurt and my calf muscles are cramped from crouching behind a chair on the porch. I long to stand and peek from my hiding place to see into the kitchen, but if they see me, I'll suffer a double whammy. First a stern command from Mother to go home, and then a tongue lashing from Grandma for eavesdropping.

"This letter was sent to your address, but it was for me," Mother says. "You opened my mail and read it! Why didn't you give it to me? It's several years old. They've probably moved. I'll never find them."

Seconds later, Mother barges onto the porch. Tears glisten in her eyes. She shouts over her shoulder, "It wasn't my fault. It happened more than thirty years ago. Can't you ever forgive?"

"She was no damn good. Didn't deserve my forgiveness," Grandma hollers. "And she never asked to be forgiven."

Mother shoves the porch door open and slams it shut in a very unladylike manner. I hear her stomp down the steps and run toward our house. Grandma's cane taps her progress away from the kitchen toward the living room.

Their explosive conversation leaves me shaking. Common sense overrules my curiosity. Neither Grandma nor Mother have seen or heard me. It's best I leave it that way. I open the porch door, hoping it won't squeak and walk home slowly, deep in thought.

When home I call, "Mother, where are you?"

She answers from behind her closed bedroom door. "What do you want, Rebel?"

"Nothing. I just wondered where you were."

"I'm reorganizing my cedar chest. Do you want to see my doll?"

"Yes," Mouse hollers.

Only nine, she's still enthralled with Mother's antique bisque doll. I no longer play with dolls, but say 'yes,' so I can see what Mother is doing. Kneeling by her cedar chest, she removes a manila envelope. A folded paper flutters to the floor. I pick it up before Mother notices. She's occupied taking a small envelope from her pocket, which must be the letter Grandma gave her. I am dying to know who wrote it. "New York, five years ago. I wonder where they are now?"

"Who?" I ask.

Mother tucks the letter inside the large envelope. Her tears are gone, but her cheeks are still moist. I sit beside her in a heavy silence. Waiting. Waiting for answers. Waiting for I don't know what. Just waiting.

"Let me see the doll," Mouse says. "She's so pretty."

I unfold the paper I hold. It's an ornate marriage license for Henry Rothberg and Bonnie Jacobs. That's Daddy's name, but Bonnie Jacobs isn't Mother's. Her maiden name is Cassidy, like Grandma and Grandpa's. "Is this your marriage license?"

"Let me have that." Mother takes the paper from me and in one fluid motion folds it and shoves it inside the manila envelope. "Do you want to pick out a dress for the doll?"

"No! Who is Bonnie Jacobs?"

"Layovers to catch meddlers and you're the first meddler I caught." Mother hands a blue wool coat and bonnet to Mouse. "Here, put these on the doll, and then I'll put her away." Hmm. More layovers to catch meddlers. Anything I find interesting is always a closed subject. Phooey.

* * *

As for *Harvey*, it is a great success. Columbia even came home from college to see me perform. She owes it to me. I sat through years of her music concerts and that awful graduation last May.

I couldn't see the audience through the eye holes in the rabbit costume, but when I removed the rabbit's head piece for the curtain call, I saw Aunt Bessie, Mother, Daddy, and my three sisters on the second row. As promised, Grandma wasn't there, but I'm sure Grandpa was there in spirit.

Chapter 21
A Spirited Graduation

In a mere eight months I'll be the first member of the FAB4 to get a Driver's License. Hurrah! Today, I'm trying to memorize historical dates about people long dead for my freshman final exams. Amherst is in the next room mumbling words and phrases over and over.

I push open her door. "Amherst, knock it off. You're driving me crazy. My history exam's tomorrow and you know what a stickler Mrs. Terminie is for dates."

"My valedictorian's speech is more important than your test," Amherst says. "The auditorium will be filled with people waiting to hear every word I say."

I don't argue with her, but I know that's not true, because I for one don't care. "So, what's this great speech about?"

"Setting goals. Achieving them against all odds and encouraging people to make the world a better place." Amherst stands in front of her mirror to recite her speech, again.

"Sounds boring. How long is it?" I pick at the ragged cuticles on my fingers. Despite Grandma's warning that swallowing bits of fingernails will perforate my stomach and kill me, I can't stop the nasty habit of nail-biting, but now I spit out the fingernails. Not very ladylike behavior, for which she had reprimanded me, but if her prophecy about fingernails puncturing my stomach is true, this spitting behavior will spare my intestines.

"Twenty-five minutes." She crosses out several words and scribbles new ones on a note card.

"What about giving a short speech like Winston Churchill did? You know the one where he said never, never, never, ever give up or give in or give out or whatever. Seems like that says it all and you could be done in fifteen seconds."

"Shows what you know. I'm allowed twenty minutes, and I plan to use every second of it and then some. So, bug off."

She starts her speech again. I plug my ears and leave. September cannot arrive soon enough. This fall when Amherst and Columbia both leave for college, Mouse will move into Amherst's room, and I will get Columbia's room. Mother envisions redecorating the larger bedroom

Mouse and I have occupied for years into a guest room. Columbia and Amherst will share it when they come home from college. Sounds like a good plan to me. They've had rooms of their own for years. It is time for them to share a space.

Jaylynn has a teen phone line. My odds of having one are slim, but I plan to launch my campaign for one as soon as Columbia and Amherst are gone. Currently there is no way I can have a private conversation. Our only phone is in the living room. Sheesh! Thankfully it is not a party line. Daddy's job with the Roads Department is important enough for us to have a private line. Poor Shirley is on a party line with Crazy Floyd that operates the garbage service. More times than not she can't even make a phone call since the Fly-By-Night phone line has so many people calling to complain. Wanda is on a party line with Miss Pentstemon who is super nosy.

Despite the drone of Amherst's speech, I memorize what I'm sure is the date of every political event from Columbus to Eisenhower. I make the high school Honor Roll all four quarters, so I receive a pin at the Academic Awards Banquet. Columbia hasn't finished her freshman year at college, and Amherst is at graduation rehearsal, so neither of them attend my awards banquet. This is the curse of being a third-born child.

This week is the dreaded graduation. Amherst spends the day fidgeting like a four-year-old waiting to use the bathroom. At 4 o'clock she put her cap and gown in the Bel Air and leaves for the auditorium. At 6 o'clock, Daddy takes Columbia, Mouse, and me to the auditorium to save seats.

As Daddy nears the auditorium, Columbia says, "Look, there's Bobby and some of my old gang." She waves to her former classmates.

"All right, girls," Daddy says. "Your mother wants you to save eight seats. Be sure several are on the front row, so your grandma doesn't have to climb any stairs."

"Sure." Columbia jumps out of the car before Daddy comes to a full stop and strolls toward her friends.

"The auditorium is over here, Columbia," I yell as Daddy drives away.

"I'll be there in a second."

"Yeah, I bet." Columbia wears Bobby Benson's high school ring on her left ring finger, held in place with a glob of foam and tape. They've been going steady since their graduation last year. Columbia is so sweet when she's around him, I wanted to barf. She never says a mean word if he is near but lambasts me after he's gone. Generally, because I've been spying on them when they sit on our porch swing after dark, but how else am I suppose to obtain lessons on kissing?

Columbia and Bobby are holding hands now. Mouse and I are on our own. Inside the muggy auditorium, a few seats are still available on the first row. We hang programs on four seats and are deciding on other nearby seats when Columbia runs into the auditorium.

"Save these over here." Columbia points to chairs on the other side of the aisle.

"You save those," I snap. "Mouse and I will save these."

"I'm not going to sit here by myself for an hour," Columbia says. "I want to talk with my friends. I haven't seen them for almost a year. You can save these seats Rebel, and Mouse can save those down there."

"So, it's all right if we sit by ourselves for an hour, but you can't," I snarl. "You have all summer to see your friends. You came early to save seats, so save them."

"You can't order me around. I'm older than you. I'm going outside."

"You better be here when Mother and Daddy arrive," Mouse said, "or I'm telling them you ran off to be with your friends."

"Mouse, you're as bad as Rebel." Columbia pulls a small lipstick case with a built-in mirror from her purse. "Mouse is a good name for you. You're always squealing on someone. Eek eek eek, just like a mouse."

"No, I'm not." Mouse sniffs back tears. "But you're supposed to help Rebel and me."

"Big deal." Columbia hangs programs on two chair backs and scampers off.

Minutes later Shirley arrives with her younger sister Beth to save seats. They place jackets and programs on six seats two rows behind me.

"I'll sit with you, Shirley. Beth, go sit with Mouse to keep her company?" I say.

"So, what's going to happen tonight?" Shirley asks.

I grab a program off one of the chairs and explain all the boring details. "Amherst is giving one of the speeches. I've already heard it 100 times, Boooooring."

"Is this seat taken?" A woman holding a squirming baby asks.

"Afraid so." I replace the program on the chair in front of me. The woman climbs upward toward vacant chairs. "Maybe I should have given her that seat."

"Then where would you sit?" Shirley asks.

"Anyplace but in this auditorium."

We amuse ourselves by smiling at cute boys walking up the stairs. "If Paul comes by here, I'll let him have my seat, and then I'll have to sit on his lap."

"Ha! Your mom would have a fit," Shirley says.

"Yeah, but it's a nice thought."

"Here comes Columbia, with your grandma. You better get back to your row," Shirley says.

Grandma is using Columbia's arm for support as they walk to the seats Mouse and I saved. "It sure was lucky I went out for fresh air when I did, Grandma, because I was there to help you," Columbia says.

Mouse and I glare at Columbia. "Liar, liar pants on fire," Mouse whispers to me.

Aunt Bessie, Wanda, and Mother and Daddy arrive a few minutes later.

"We had to park four blocks away," Mother says. "I'm glad we left early."

"Rebel, before the procession starts, will you take this jug of water to Waylon?" Aunt Bessie asked. "He's in the sound booth at the top of these stairs. It's hot and stuffy up there."

I carry the jug up the stairs as the drone of Pomp and Circumstances begins. I knock on the small door at the top of the auditorium.

"Come in and be quick about it. I'm going on the air in a minute," Uncle Waylon calls.

"Aunt Bessie asked me to bring you this." I turn to leave.

"Sit down, Red. Keep me company. Boring as hell up here." Uncle Waylon fills his glass from the jug. "Hotter than hell up here too."

Uncle Waylon motions to me to sit then leans toward the microphone. "This is Waylon Cassidy of KDOG-AM live at the 1960 Schoenfeld High School graduation. The graduates are seated and now Miss Amherst Rothberg, my niece, will give the valedictorian address. Listen closely; I might quiz you about it on the Morning Show tomorrow." He flips a couple of switches and leans back in his chair. "I don't have anything to do until after the choir sings." He drinks half of the liquid in his glass and wipes his brow with a paper napkin. "Your older sisters have their lives planned. What about you, Red, what do you want to do?"

"I'm not sure. I've several years to decide." Beads of sweat trickle down my back.

"You're not planning to be in show business, are you?" He tops off his glass with more ice and liquid from the jug.

"I don't know. I liked being in *Harvey* this year."

"The call of the stage ruined your mother's life and mine," he said.

"When was Mother in a play?" Maybe this is why Grandma dislikes me being on the stage. Perhaps Mother embarrassed her family on the stage.

"Until your mother came along, I ruled the roost. Spoiled rotten some folks said, but I liked being an only child. She should have stayed in Chicago."

"Who should have stayed in Chicago?" Uncle Waylon is making less sense than usual. The heat and lack of moving air in the small sound booth is stifling. I'm so hot and thirsty that without thinking I grab Uncle Waylon's glass and take several big swallows. "Aaack. What is this? Poison?" My throat burns, my stomach heaves. "I think I'm going to vomit."

"Geez Louise, Rebel, that's gin and tonic," Uncle Waylon says. "Come here. Let me smell your breath. Don't breathe on anyone; they'll know you've been drinking. Here, eat this Life Saver, now go back to your seat and keep your mouth shut."

I walk back to my seat in the dark. If that's what alcohol tastes like, I have no desire to try more. My head is spinning, and not just from the gin. Who was Uncle Waylon talking about that should have stayed in Chicago? Mother is right; booze often does the talking for Waylon.

The rest of the evening continues as a monumental bore except the choir sang *Somewhere over the Rainbow* instead of *You'll Never Walk Alone.* No one is more surprised than Daddy when Amherst received a full ride scholarship to the University of Kansas.

After the ceremony, Columbia rushes to rejoin her former high school friends. I hear them talking about college and how juvenile high school is. She certainly sang a different tune about high school last year. As we near her, she yells to Mother, "There's not enough room for all of us in our car. I'll ride with Bobby." She flounces away before Mother can reply.

Columbia has on a floral print, v-necked sleeveless dress she sewed for herself this week. I plan to scope out her neck when she arrives home. She might fool Mother, but I know what she and Bobby plan to do.

The rest of us cram into our 1958 Buick for the short ride home. Daddy bought the Buick new last year before Columbia graduated from high school. He said, "With Columbia in college next year and Amherst the year after, I better buy a car now while I still have some money." While we were at the graduation, Jaylynn and her family arranged the food Mother and Mrs. Birdfoot prepared this afternoon. Our living room is now decorated with balloons and a 'Congratulations' banner to honor Amherst and Charlie's graduation.

"When will Shirley and her family arrive?" Jaylynn asks me.

"You mean, when will Charlie Birdfoot get here?" I ask.

Jaylynn blushes.

"Soon. Shirley was seated behind us at the auditorium."

A few minutes later, Shirley and her family arrive.

"Congratulations, Charlie," Jaylynn says. "I bought you something."

"Thanks." Charlie opens a box and shows everyone a gold pen and pencil set. "It's really nice. I'll use it at college next year."

"Do you really like it?" Jaylynn asks.

"Sure. Have fun in high school next year kid." Charlie grabs a sandwich and crosses the room to talk to Uncle Waylon.

"I don't think Charlie remembers me," Jaylynn moans.

"My brother's a jerk," Shirley says. "Forget him."

Columbia and Bobby arrive forty-five minutes later. She is flushed, and Bobby has a lipstick smear on his collar. Mother gives Columbia one of those 'we'll talk about this later looks.' I smirk. It's nice not be on the receiving end of a reprimand.

Columbia tilts her head to one side to hide her neck. "Seems chilly in here," she says.

"Your neck is red. Must be moon burn," I say. "Let me see."

"Get away from me." Columbia rushes to her bedroom and returns wearing a sweater buttoned up to her neck despite the muggy night.

After we eat cake and ice cream, Amherst and Charlie leave to meet friends at an all-night party at the YMCA.

"Is Amherst dating Charlie?" Jaylynn asks.

"No way," Shirley says. "Charlie's stuck up. Amherst isn't his type. No offense to your sister, Rebel."

"No offense taken," I reply.

"I think he's nice." Jaylynn sighs.

"That's because you don't live with him. All he's talked about for months is getting a football scholarship and being a BMOC this fall."

"What's that?" I ask.

"Big man on campus," Shirley replies.

"I suppose he'll forget completely about me," Jaylynn says.

"Lucky you," Shirley said. "You were right about gradation, Rebel. Long and boring."

"It's been an exhausting day. I'm out past my bedtime," Grandma says. "I need to go home before I turn into a pumpkin."

"Columbia and I will take you home," Bobby says.

"That's kind of you to offer, Bobby," Mother said, "but your Studebaker will be hard for mom to get in and out of. Henry will take her home."

Columbia's plan to be alone with Bobby again is foiled. She walks him to his car. I turn on the porch light. Mouse pulls back the living room curtain to watch them smooch. The FAB4 join Mouse. Usually Mother says, 'get away from the window. Give Columbia some privacy,' but tonight she says nothing.

Chapter 22
Summer Revelation

The week after Amherst graduated, Daddy left for a two-week trip to inspect road construction in southeast Kansas. Today as we get ready for church, Amherst and Columbia are fighting over who will drive us to church. Amherst is winning as she has the keys.

As usual, Columbia says, "I'm the oldest, so I should drive."

"I've never had an accident like you have," Amherst snaps.

"Just fork over the keys and let me drive," Columbia snarls.

"You girls stop that!" Mother says. "Columbia, you may drive to church, and Amherst will drive us home. Now everyone get in the car."

"I'll ride shotgun," I plop onto the front seat.

"No dice," says Amherst.

"You always sit up front. I'll be driving next year, so I should sit up front to observe how Columbia shifts the car."

"You driving next year!" Amherst groans. "Spare me."

"Hope I'm not around then. The roads won't be safe," Columbia says.

"Enough of this!" Mother says. "I'll sit up front. Now, let's go before we are late."

I slouch in the back seat, jammed between Amherst and Mouse. Columbia turns the key in the ignition. The motor whines and whines. Columbia keeps trying until the car is silent.

"Guess the battery is dead," Columbia says.

"Great," Amherst says. "Now we have to walk to church."

"I'll call Bobby and see if we can get a ride with him," Columbia says.

"We are not begging for a ride," Mother says. "Start walking."

"My hair will be a windblown mess if I have to walk," Columbia moans.

"Fat chance of that happening. You used half a can of hair spray on it this morning," I say. "There was none left for me."

"Big deal. Your hair is always a mess. Nothing can tame those frizzy curls," Columbia hisses.

"Girls! We are on our way to church," Mother says. "Try to act like young Christian ladies."

Despite our brisk walking, we arrive fifteen minutes late. I skip Sunday school, go directly to the sanctuary, and sit on a hard pew. The ceiling in the sanctuary is high, making it a bit cooler than outside. Paper fans on wooden sticks are in each pew by the hymnals. The windows of the church are open, but the heavy curtains hang limp. There's not a hint of the usual prairie wind. If Pastor Rozell has one of his long sermons, I might collapse with heat prostration, or disintegrate as Columbia would say. I open my purse, see what I want and pop it in my mouth.

Mother and my sisters soon join me. The organ blares to life, and we all sing. "So, I'll cling to the old rugged cross and exchange it someday for a crown. Ahhhh-men." I finish the hymn with gusto; singing is the best part of the worship service.

I sink onto the wooden pew, cross my legs and slip my hands under my butt to serve as a cushion. Seconds later, Mother taps my knee and points to the floor, her subtle way of reminding me young ladies do not cross their legs at the knees.

For heaven's sakes, its 1960. What difference does it make what I do with my legs? But I move the offending leg; church is not the place to challenge Mother.

Five minutes into the sermon, I sigh with boredom. Mother frowns and then focuses her gaze on my bulging cheek.

Uh-oh. I'm in trouble now. I stare at Pastor Rozell and feign interest in his sermon. He's saying something about the wages of sin being death.

"Rebel," Mother hisses. "Take that gum out of your mouth. Ladies don't chew gum in public."

"It's not gum. It's a chaw of tobacco." I suck a dribble of brown juice into my mouth.

Mother gasps, her eyes narrow to slits. The muscles in her jaw throb. I turn away, fearful that her gaze will turn me to stone. Today Pastor Rozell's sermon is short. After the benediction, I try to hurry from the church.

"Not so fast young lady," Mother's hand is like a claw on my shirt collar.

Columbia and Amherst usually walk home on the opposite side of the street rather than be seen in my presence, but today I feel their breath on my neck. They never miss a chance to eavesdrop on my misfortune.

"Gum I could forgive, but tobacco!" Mother's quick steps kept pace with her angry words. "What in the world possessed you to chew tobacco in the first place? And in church, no less. The saints preserve us. I ought to jerk you bald-headed for a stunt like this. Rebel, you're enough to try the patience of Job."

Behind me my older sisters chuckle.

"Sorry," I mumble. Hmmm. If Mother jerks me bald, maybe my hair would grow back brown and straight, that would be nice.

"Where in the world did you get that nasty stuff?" She demands.

I mull over whether to lie or tell the truth. Since I'm already in a heap of trouble, I figure telling the truth is best. "The guys building the house around the corner gave it to me."

"What?" Mother snaps. "I can't believe my ears. How many times have I warned you about talking to strangers?" She shifts her lecture from my unladylike behavior to the snares awaiting young ladies who talk to strangers, especially men. "And taking gifts from them, what were you thinking? It might have been poisoned."

"Too bad it wasn't," says Columbia.

"Yeah, that would have been a blessing," Amherst adds.

While Mother continues her sermon, I concentrate on saving enough saliva to spit a stream of tobacco juice two feet away like the construction guys do. "Pit-too." My effort falls a good six inches short.

"Stop that! Spit that horrid stuff out, right now." Whomp! The palm of Mother's hand sends a shock through my shoulder blade.

I gasp, gag, and sputter, "I can't. I swallowed it."

Columbia and Amherst convulse with laughter.

"What's funny?" Mouse asks.

"Nothing," Mother snarls. "And as for you, Rebel, I hope it makes you sick." Mother shakes her head and groans, "What am I going to do with you, Rebel? It's a poor house indeed that can't raise ladies." Mother and my sisters march into our house.

I sit on the steps and ponder where this 'poor house' proverb originated. My guess is from Grandma. Grandma! Ye gods. If she finds out I was chewing tobacco in church, she'll hang me out to dry.

* * *

After lunch on Sunday, my sisters and I always spend time with

Grandma. Today we had a light lunch of BLTs and potato salad since Daddy is gone. Columbia and Amherst gobble their lunch and rush out the back door and across the alley to Grandma's.

I am left to wash and dry the dishes, my punishment. An hour later, the kitchen clean to Mother's satisfaction, I push open the screen door and am greeted by two smirking faces.

"Grandma wants to talk to you," Amherst sneers.

"You're both rat finks. Bleah!" I push past them with my tongue out.

"I'm telling Mother you stuck out your tongue." Columbia flounces into the house.

"So, what else is new?" I holler. "Tattletale, tattletale, hanging on a bull's tail."

Instead of entering Grandma's back porch, I walk to her front door. I grab the metal doorknocker. It is cool to my touch, but warm and damp before I have the courage to use it.

"Come in. The door's unlocked," Grandma calls.

"Hello, Grandma." I step inside her apartment. "I can't stay long. I promised Mother I'd do the ironing for her this week. There are a lot of blouses, so I better go. See you next week. Bye."

Grandma hobbles toward me and extends the handle of her cane like a hook. I back into the hall.

"Not so fast, young lady." Grandma's cane prevents me from closing the door.

Behind me a door in the hallway creaks open. A green eye peers from a two-inch-slit. Mrs.Fangmeyer, Grandma's nosy neighbor.

"Hello, Mrs. Fangmeyer." I turn and speak to the eye. "Nice day for spying, isn't it?" Her door slams shut.

Grandma looks down the hall to make sure no one else is gawking, and then jerks me inside her apartment using her cane as a crook. I'm a lamb being pulled to the slaughter.

"What's this I hear about you chewing tobacco in church?" She points to the sofa with her cane and plops into a nearby wing-back chair.

I wish Grandpa were alive. I need his moral support. I slump in the corner of the sofa, hoping to make myself invisible.

"Sit up straight, Rebel."

I do as I am told.

"Amherst and Columbia told me you had tobacco —"

"They are no-good rat finks."

"Don't interrupt," Grandma says.

"Sorry, Grandma, but I don't know why everyone's making such a big deal out of a little bit of tobacco. It's not like I used the collection plate as a spittoon."

"Land sakes, I should hope not!" Huffs Grandma. "Rebel, I don't know what's to become of you. If you don't start minding your P's and Q's you'll turn out just like my sister."

"Aunt Lily? What's wrong with her? Outside of the fact, she's been married four times to men who were all no damn good."

Grandma arches her eyebrows.

"Pardon my French, but those were your exact words to describe her no-account husbands."

"I'm not referring to Lily." Grandma leans forward. Her gnarled finger emphasizes each word she says. "You remind me of my younger sister."

My mouth gapes in a very unladylike manner. Astonishment silences me. For my entire life, all fifteen years of it, I believed Grandma only had one sister, the formidable Aunt Lily. "A younger sister? You've never mentioned her. Is she dead or alive? Where does she live? What's her name?"

"That doesn't matter. What's important for you to know is that her behavior was shameful, just like yours. Decent folks shunned her." Grandma leans back in her chair. Tears fill her eyes, but she blinks them away. "She was such a pretty girl."

"What did she do?" I cross and then uncross my legs. Pull my cotton pedal pushers over my knees. Scratch my nose and then cross my legs again, this time at the ankles.

"Stop squirming. Ladies don't fidget."

"Sorry, Grandma." I will myself to relax. "Well, what did she do? Huh?"

"Don't say 'huh.' You sound like a donkey." Grandma rubs her swollen, arthritic knuckles, pulls a lace handkerchief from her sleeve and dabs the corner of one eye. "She did things ladies didn't do in 1914."

I lean forward, wide-eyed, expecting to hear a sordid tale, but she says nothing. The silence is suffocating, and eternal. Asking personal questions is impolite, but I forge ahead. "What things, Grandma? Did she swear? Smoke? Dye her hair? Take a drink in public?"

"She might have. I don't know." She strokes her chin, then her voice becomes stern, "Of course, no lady would ever do those things. You know that don't you, Rebel?"

I nod. "Yeah, sure, but if she didn't drink, smoke, swear, or dye her hair, what did she do?" What's left but s-e-x? This ought to be good!

Grandma exhales. Her rigid posture dissolves and she slumps to half her size. She gazes at me, but her focus is on past events. She squints, as if to sharpen every detail about her long-lost sister. "I'm not saying another word about her. No one in my family has uttered her name since that dreadful day almost forty years ago, and I don't intend to break our vow of silence. Don't ask again, Rebel. Just let this be a lesson to you."

She presses her lips into a tight line and pulls herself erect. There is no way to pry information from Grandma once she's sets her jaw like that.

After a game of Scrabble, which I lose, I walk home contemplating Grandma's warning: "Let this be a lesson to you." What lesson am I supposed to learn from this? I have no idea what her sister, my great-aunt did. I didn't even know she existed until an hour ago.

After supper as Mother washes the dishes and I dry, I say, "Grandma told me today she has a younger sister."

"Hmm." Mother grabs a Brillo pad and scrubs a skillet.

"Did you know that?"

"Uh-huh."

"Come on, Mother," I beg. "Tell me about her. What's the big mystery?"

"No mystery. Her name was Daisy."

"So, another flower name?"

"Yes. You know your grandma's maiden name was Lafleur. Your Aunt Lily, Grandma Rose, and their sister Daisy were called the three little Lafleur girls of Francisville."

"Yeah, but Grandma never said there were three LaFleur girls. Aunt Lily named her daughter, Pansy. Why didn't Grandma give you a flower name?"

"My middle name is Rose," Mother replies.

"Yeah, but she could have named you Marigold, Dahlia, or even Tulip."

"Tulip! What an imagination you have, Rebel. I'm happy being Bonnie Rose."

"So, what did Daisy do that caused such a fuss?"

"It all happened a long time ago. Just forget about —"

"No, I want to know about Daisy. Did you know Aunt Daisy? Was she married? Did she have children? Where does she live? Come on; tell me what she did, puh-lease."

"Rebel, quit whining. And don't interrupt, that's not polite."

"I know. I'm sorry." I wait. Mother is as tight-lipped as Grandma. I can't hold my tongue. "Tell me about Aunt Daisy, I promise I won't interrupt this time."

"I don't know the details. All I know is that Daisy was disowned. I heard Aunt Lily call her a black sheep once. It's all ancient history. Just forget about it, Rebel."

Forget about it? Mother must be joking. Our family has a mystery. This is big news! Despite my continued pleas, Mother says nothing.

Later that night, I confront Columbia and Amherst. "Did you know Grandma has a younger sister named Daisy?"

"Grandma had a couple of siblings that died when they were young," Columbia says. "That happened a lot back then."

"What about you, Amherst? Do you know anything about this younger sister?"

"No. Who told you she had one?" She runs a comb through her wet hair flicking drops of water on me.

"Grandma. And Mother told me the sister was named Daisy. And guess what? She was disowned."

"Disowned? Why?" Amherst puts down the comb and squeezes Clearasil onto her fingertips and applies it to her forehead. "Pimples are a curse. No one would know if you had pimples, Rebel, with all those freckles on your face."

"Gee thanks. Don't complain, Amherst. Pimples will go away after a while, but I'll have these nasty freckles for the rest of my life. So, do you know anything about this Aunt Daisy or not?"

"Nope and I don't care," Amherst says.

"Close the door on your way out," Columbia says.

I'm dismissed. I go to my room and flop on the bed. My family has an actual mystery, maybe not an exciting murder mystery like in *And Then There Were None*, the book I am currently reading, but a mystery none the less, and Amherst and Columbia don't even care. That figures. All Columbia thinks about is Bobby, and Amherst just worries about pimples.

Mother has told me, 'Two can keep a secret if one of them is dead.' Since Grandma, Aunt Lily, Mother and probably Uncle Waylon and Cousin Pansy all know about Daisy, one of them should be itching to blab. I wonder who? I drift to sleep imagining what my Great Aunt Daisy did that made her a black sheep.

Chapter 23
First Date

My incessant begging this summer results in Mother increasing the time I can 'lollygag' after school with my friends this year from ten to thirty minutes. Every afternoon the FAB4 stops at the DQ or Rexall's to discuss the events of the day. Boys first, school activities second, and homework last, if at all. Today we're stopping at the DQ.

"I'm going to try out to be a cheerleader," Jaylynn says.

"That's great," I say. "I'll vote for you."

"Me too," says Shirley.

"I'm trying out too," Wanda says. "All those years of dancing Daddy paid for might finally be useful."

"Uncle Waylon will be happy to hear that. He hated going to your dance recitals," I say.

"I hope you make it, Wanda. Just promise me you won't get stuck up," Shirley says.

"Wanda would never do that," I say. "She's like her Mom, my Aunt Bessie. She doesn't have a mean bone in her body."

"Wanda, maybe you can teach me how to do the splits without killing myself," Jaylynn says.

"Jaylynn," Shirley says, "do you think you'll like being around a bunch of snotty girls?"

"Marlene Klienmeyer is sure to be elected. She's the most popular girl in our class, but I can't stand her," I say.

"Me either," said Shirley.

"Me three," adds Wanda.

"Her nose is permanently in the air. It's a wonder she doesn't drown when it rains," I say.

"Her older brother Matt is really nice," Wanda says. "He's always hanging around my locker. I think he has a crush on me."

"Is he cute?" I ask.

"Has he asked you out?" Shirley whispers.

"Yes, he's cute, and no he hasn't asked me out, but Sally Meeks asked me if I thought Matt was cute, and then I saw her talking to Matt at lunch. I think Matt is trying to find out if I'm interested," says

Wanda.

Shirley waves her hands in the air, closes her eyes as if in a trance and hums. "I see a hot date in your future."

"What's with the mumbo-jumbo?" Jaylynn asks.

"I'm communicating with the Great Spirit," Shirley says. "I'm part Cherokee, you know."

"You and your Great Spirit," I say. "If you're part Indian, I'm the Queen of France."

"Well, your highness, where's your crown? My grandmother is a full-bloodied Cherokee. Sylvia Eagle Birdfoot. Her father was Chief Running Hawk."

"Really?" Jaylynn says.

"I didn't know that," says Wanda.

"Does she live on a reservation?" I ask.

"No." Shirley frowns. "She lives in an apartment in Wichita."

"Well, you learn something new every day," I say. "Do you know how to do a rain dance?"

"Sure, watch." Shirley stands and does an imitation of Chubby Checker doing the twist.

"Very funny," I say.

"Well, you ask a stupid question —" Shirley says.

"I know, I know. You get a stupid answer," I respond.

"Rebel, why don't you and Shirley try out to be cheerleaders?" Jaylynn says. "I'm sure you'd be elected. It would be really cool for all of us to be together."

"Count me out," Shirley says. "After years of attending Charlie's games, I have no desire to see another football game. Ever!"

"Yeah, but being a cheerleader is not like sitting in the stadium with your parents. The cheerleaders lead the team onto the field and stand near the team bench during the game. That gives you plenty of opportunity to be close to the football players," Jaylynn says.

"Sorry, not interested." Shirley leisurely licks her chocolate cone.

"It's not my thing either, Jaylynn. I'm trying out for the school play. Paul is too. I saw his name on the audition list. The play's a murder mystery. In one scene the detective kisses the female lead. If Paul and I get the leads, he'll have to kiss me, and then I'll be the first member of the Kisser—."

"A stage kiss isn't a real kiss," Shirley says. "The guy that kisses you has to be your boyfriend."

"That's right," Jaylynn says.

"We never made that stipulation." I scowl.

"Yes, we did," Shirley says. "You're getting snippy because you don't stand a snowball's chance in hell of ever becoming a member."

"I'm not snippy, but you keep changing the rules. My chances are as good as yours."

"What are you talking about?" Wanda says.

"The Kissers Klub," Jaylynn said. "You can't be a member unless a boy kisses you."

"Why am I the last to know about this?" Wanda asks.

"Because you didn't walk home with us yesterday. You had a dental appointment. You're part of the FAB4 so you're in," I say, "but there are rules. And Shirley makes new ones every day."

"I do not! We all agreed on the rules yesterday."

"Humph! So you say."

"What are the rules?" Wanda asks.

"The kiss has to be on the lips," Jaylynn says.

"And the guy is supposed to be your boyfriend," Shirley says, "or at least you're on a date with him, not a stage kiss."

"And whoever gets kissed first, has to share the details with the rest of us," I add.

"To give us pointers," Shirley says.

"I have a possibility next Friday," Jaylynn says. "Steve wants me to meet him at the YMCA dance after the football game."

"When did he ask you?" I pop the last bit of my chocolate-dipped cone into my mouth.

"Today, after 5th period. I was at my locker getting my English book, and someone put their arm over my head and closed the locker door. I turned around to see who did it and looked right into his big brown eyes. His lips were less than four inches from mine. I about died."

"Oh my gosh!" Shirley says.

"What did he say?" Wanda asks.

"Yeah, tell us everything." I wipe my sticky fingers with a napkin. "He said, 'Hey kid, you want to meet me at the dance this Friday?'"

"That was it?" I shake my head.

"Yes."

"That's not very romantic," Shirley says.

"He's a junior, isn't he?" I ask.

"Yes."

"Oooo, an upperclassman," says Wanda. "Watch out."

"Does he have a car?" Shirley asks.

"I don't know," Jaylynn replies.

I have bleak prospects for a date or kiss. "Jimmy's my biology lab partner," I say. "Yuck. I wish teachers wouldn't do everything alphabetically. I always get stuck by him."

"Could be worse," Shirley says. "I got Nancy Brandt. Not only is she dumb, she's bossy. I'll probably do all the work, and she'll take all the credit."

"Ye gods, it's almost four. I need to go home." I stand and gather my books.

We walk home waving at guys crusin' the strip. None stop to ask if we want a ride, which is good because that saves us making up stupid excuses, like 'we enjoy the fresh air' or 'we we're breaking in a new pair of shoes.' We have to refuse a ride because none of us are allowed to ride with teenage drivers, especially boys. Sheesh! I'll never get a kiss at this rate.

* * *

The next week the good news is Jaylynn and Wanda are elected cheerleaders, and I have the lead in the school play. The bad news is Paul did not get the male lead, and after two weeks the Kissers Klub still has no members.

"Steve met me at the YMCA dance like we planned," Jaylynn says, "but told me he doesn't like to dance." She shakes her head and sighs.

"Bummer," I say.

"What did you do all night?" Wanda asks.

"He suggested we sit in the balcony overlooking the dance floor, but the chaperones had blocked the stairs. So, we spent most of the evening standing around."

"Did you dance at all?" Asks Shirley.

"Twice to slow dances. That was the only time Steve held my hand," Jaylynn says.

"Has he called you?" I ask.

"Yes, but only to talk about a chemistry assignment. I hope he asks me to the Homecoming Dance."

"I already have a date for Homecoming," Shirley says.

"Who?" Wanda and I ask.

"Since when?" Jaylynn asks.

"Last night Jerry Wunderkin called me. He's in my history class and a second-string football player," Shirley says. "If we get serious, I'll be forced to go to football games again. Crap. After my brother Charlie graduated, I thought I'd be spared football games, but I wouldn't miss the opportunity to see Jerry running around in tight pants."

"If Steve would only ask me to the Homecoming dance, I'd—" Jaylynn sighs.

"Is that all you can think about?" I ask.

"If you wait for him to call, you'll be an old maid," Shirley says. "Call him and ask for help with an algebra problem, then you can casually mention the Homecoming dance and that you'd like to go. That will give him the opportunity to ask you."

"I can't do that," Jaylynn says.

"Why not?" Wanda asks.

"Because I'm the best student in algebra. Everyone knows I don't need help."

"Well, you sure need help on getting a date," Shirley says.

"I'm doomed with this red hair and freckles. No one will ask me," I say. "Paul is ga-ga over Tricia Jones. I don't know what he sees in her."

"That's obvious," Jaylynn says. "It's her 36 Cs. She struts around in her cheerleading sweater, which is two sizes too small, and rolls up her skirt so it will be above her knees."

"Those boobs are fake," Shirley says. "I've seen her in the shower after gym class. She's flatter than an ironing board."

"No kidding. I don't believe it," I gasp.

"Trust me. I saw her stuffing her bra with tissues," Shirley says.

"Hot dog," Wanda says. "I can't wait to tell the other girls on the cheerleading squad."

"We can call her Tricia Tissues." Jaylynn giggles.

"I'm going to Homecoming with Jimmy," Wanda says.

"What? You must be nuts to go with Jimmy Randall," I say.

"He's not so bad," Wanda replies.

We all looked at Wanda as if she's lost her mind.

"All right, he's a bit dorky, but Mom and Dad know him, so they didn't make a big deal about me having a date," Wanda says.

"From what I hear," Jaylynn says, "he's a sloppy kisser, isn't that right, Rebel?"

"That was years ago. Do you have to remind me?"

"My dad's picking us up after the dance," Wanda says. "I plan to invite Jimmy to sit on our porch when we get home. I hope the evening is a bit chilly so he can keep me warm."

"Hoping to get a smooch?" Shirley asks.

"Take the bulb out of your porch light," I say. "That spotlight makes it as bright as day at midnight."

"Good idea."

Outside the autumn air is crisp as we walk home. Oaks, cottonwood, and elm trees ablaze with red and gold leaves have an azure sky for a background. While Wanda and Shirley talk about Homecoming and hoped for kisses, and Jaylynn bemoans the fact she has no date, I'm quiet. I kick dry leaves off the sidewalk. My chance of having a date for Homecoming is slim and none. Shirley has a date. Steve will probably ask Jaylynn if she drops a couple of hints. I'd sooner die an old maid than go with Jimmy, but all the same I'm jealous of Wanda. I never should have started the Kissers Klub.

* * *

The next afternoon the FAB4 meets at Rexall's. Not as many students stop here after school because there's only counter service and two small tables, but we like the privacy. The soda counter has a variety of syrups to add to their fountain Cokes. Today I'm having a chocolate Coke. Shirley arrived first and snagged the table in the back for us. When I arrive, Jaylynn is gushing about Steve's call.

"He said he called about the algebra assignment, but Mr. Morris didn't give us an assignment yesterday. So, I said, 'My gosh, I thought we didn't have any homework. I must be losing my mind. I'm so busy making decorations for the Homecoming Dance with the other cheerleaders. I'd forget my head if it wasn't attached.'"

"That was a sneaky way to bring up the dance," Shirley says.

"And then Steve said, 'How about you and me going together?'"

"What are you going to wear?" Wanda asks. "My mom's going to buy me the blue, pullover sweater and blue plaid, pleated skirt I saw at J.M. McDonald's Department Store. The sweater is really soft, made with angora."

"Oooh that sounds gorgeous," says Shirley. "I looked in every store in town and finally found a red wool dress with a full circle skirt at Montgomery Ward that I like. With some black heels it should look really good. The dress has a scooped neck. I don't know what I'll wear at the neck. Maybe a necklace or a scarf. Or just a circle pin on the shoulder. What do you think?"

"The circle pin, definitely. They're all the rage." I say. "But be sure you put it on your left shoulder?"

"What difference does that make?" Shirley asks.

"Columbia says if you wear the pin on your right shoulder, it means you're not a virgin."

"Really? I didn't know that," the others say.

"Marlene Kleinmeyer wears hers on the right," Jaylynn says. "Do you think she's gone all the way with her latest boyfriend?"

"I doubt it," I say. "She's so dumb she doesn't know her right shoulder from her left."

"Mom and I might go shopping for clothes in Salina this weekend," Jaylynn says. "I'm so tall nothing here fits me."

"Did I tell you I got the lead in the school play? I must have 200 lines to memorize," I say.

"Really. That's nice. Good for you."

My big news can't compete with Homecoming and dates.

Jerry and I are meeting after the football game," Shirley says. "He's driving his parents' car. He can't take me to the game, because he's on the varsity team now. But he'll take me home after the dance. Maybe we can double date, Jaylynn."

"That would be great. I'll ask Steve about it."

"It's lover's lane for you two and a porch swing for me," Wanda says. "We better synchronize our watches, so we'll know who gets kissed first."

"I don't plan to check my watch if Steve's kissing me," Jaylynn says.

"You better," I say, "or you'll turn into a pumpkin at ten o'clock when your curfew hits."

"Mom said I could stay out until eleven," Jaylynn says.

"So did my folks," Shirley adds. "We really should double date. It would be a blast."

"I not going to the game," I say.

"What?"

"Why not?"

"Because everyone will be wearing their fancy clothes to the game and meeting their date afterwards, and I'll be standing on the corner in my Pep Club outfit like an idiot waiting for Daddy to come pick me up. I might as well wear a sign that says, 'I don't have a date for the dance.'" I sniff back tears. "Wanda, your dad was right when he told me years ago 'better dead than red.' I'm cursed. A fifth wheel. I don't fit in anyplace."

"You got the lead in the school play," Jaylynn says.

"Big deal. Paul only has a small part. I'll be co-starring with Larry Wilson, he and Alfred E. Newman could be twins."

"It could be worse," Wanda says.

"How?"

"I don't know, but people always say that it could be worse," Wanda says.

"Gee thanks. I don't see how my life can get worse. I'm covered with freckles. I wear hand-me-down clothes. My hair is impossible. I'll never have a date. I'm going home." I grab my books and leave more than half of my chocolate Coke on the table. As I go out the door, I hear Shirley say, "Do you think Rebel would go on a blind date? We could ask Skip to take her to the dance." Criminy, now I'm a charity case!

I turn right at the first corner and walk a block south, taking a back street home instead of the main drag. I kick stones like I did years ago. For the first time in months I think about Grandma's sister, my great Aunt Daisy. She was disowned, a black sheep. Maybe she didn't do anything terribly wrong, perhaps she was just different. Was being different years ago grounds for expulsion from polite society? If so, I might follow in her footsteps and be branded a black sheep.

I contemplate visiting Grandma before going home, but she won't have a sympathetic ear to my lack of a date, and I don't dare mention I'm in another play. I sniff back tears as I enter our home. Mouse is watching the Mickey Mouse Club. I hear Spin and Marty talking. Mother is not in the kitchen. I walk along the back hall to my room unnoticed.

At the beginning of the school year, after moving into Columbia's bedroom, Mother and Daddy surprised me with a teen phone line. I rarely receive calls until after supper when a member of the FAB4 calls to yak or to discuss homework. I toss my books on the bed and flop down beside them. I'm startled when my yellow Princess phone lights up and makes a muted ring.

"Hello," I wipe tears from my cheeks.

"Uh, is... uh, is this Rebel?" A male voice says.

"Yes. Who's this?"

"Paul. Paul Eisner. Uh, I tried out for a part in the play with you. Remember?"

Do I remember? Ha! That's all I've thought about for days. "Yeah. You were good. I think you should have gotten the lead."

"I wish I had. But playing the murderer is okay. Um, so what are you doing next week?"

"The usual, I guess. School, homework, church."

"Um, you have any plans for the Homecoming Dance?"

"Well, nothing definite."

"You want to go with me? I mean if you're not doing anything else."

Thankfully Paul can't see me jumping up and down mouthing, 'Yes! Yes! Yes!' I take a deep breath to calm my racing heart. "That would be great. You want to meet at the dance?"

"We could, but my older brother Ronnie has a car. He said I could tag along with him and his girl. You want to do that?"

Boy do I. I know what Mother will say about me having a date with a boy who has a car. Well, he doesn't really have a car, but his brother does. Sheesh! She'll have a fit if I'm riding in car with two boys.

"Rebel, are you home?" Mother calls from the kitchen. "I just finished folding your grandma's laundry. I want you to take it back to her before supper?"

I lick my lips, imagining how Paul's lips might feel on mine. "I have to go, Paul. Mother wants me to run an errand. I'll talk to you at lunch tomorrow, okay?"

"Sure."

"Bye. See you soon."

Mother is cooking chicken and dumplings for supper, one of my favorites. I'll wait until after we eat to ask Mother about riding with Paul and his brother. No point ruining my dinner.

* * *

Paul's family farms south of town. After Mother learns that Paul attends St. Mark's Lutheran church in the country, she reluctantly says I can ride with him and his brother, but only if they both come into the house so she and Daddy can meet them. I hope Mouse has forgotten all the mean tricks we played on Columbia when she brought Bobby into the house for inspection. I do not need her giving Paul the third degree.

The dance is less than a week away and I have no idea what to wear. My friends all have new outfits. I know a store-bought dress for me is out of the question since Daddy's paying Columbia and Amherst's expenses at college. I push my dresses back and forth across my closet rod searching for a possibility. Nothing.

"Mother can you make me a new dress for the Homecoming Dance this weekend?"

"Can't you wear your blue dress with the plaid collar? It looks nice, and it still fits."

"Mother, everyone has seen that dress a zillion times," I moan.

"That blue dress is very nice. You wear it to church every Sunday. If it's good enough for God, it should be good enough for Paul."

"That dress was Columbia's. She wore it for years, and I've worn it for more than a year. God probably wouldn't recognize me if I wasn't wearing it."

"God judges your heart, not your clothes."

"Good, because if He judged my clothes, He'd feel sorry for me because I always have to wear hand-me-downs."

"You're right, Rebel. This is a special occasion for you. You should have something new. Look through my pattern box and select one you like but choose a simple pattern. I'm busy this week and don't have much time to sew. Friday is Mouse's Halloween party at school. I'm her room mother, so I have to make cookies, plan games, and be at the school most of Friday."

"Thank you, thank you, thank you Mother." I race to her sewing nook to find a pattern.

What a week. Jaylynn, Wanda and the other cheerleaders are busy making decorations. The sophomore class is required to decorate the school gym where the dance will be held, so our class works until 9 p.m. Thursday night hanging crepe paper streamers and balloons, and arranging sunflowers, corn stalks and pumpkins in the gym. The guys roll in a huge Conestoga wagon, our school emblem. Inside are speakers that will blast our dance music. A small table holds a turntable and stacks of 45s are nearby. Mr. Genzlinger, the assistant football coach, will spin the records. I hope there are plenty of slow dances so Paul will have to hold me.

Friday is a perfect fall day. The humidity is low, the sky is a deep aqua, and the air is heavy with the sweet smell of rotting leaves. I turn on the radio as I dress for school. I don't put any stock in horoscopes, but most mornings Uncle Waylon reads them on KDOG.

"Those of you lucky enough to be the sign of Aquarius," Uncle Waylon says, "you have a four-star day. Romance is in the air. Tonight, have fun. So, you guys and gals going to the Homecoming Dance tonight with an Aquarius might get lucky. I know my niece Rebel, who's an Aquarius, is excited she has a date. I don't know who the unlucky guy is, but forewarned is forearmed: Rebel, like all red-haired girls is a handful, beware young man."

Uncle Waylon clears his throat and continues. "My daughter Wanda has her first big date tonight with Jimmy Randall, one of the boys in our neighborhood. I know he's a good kid, but Jimmy, don't forget I've got my eye on you boy. And now, here's Walter with the sports report for tonight's big game."

Ye gods, humiliation in the first degree. Now I understand why Columbia and Amherst hated to have their names mentioned on the radio by Uncle Waylon. Mother had no luck getting Uncle Waylon to stop talking about them on his radio, but I'm going to beg her to try again. I hope Paul didn't listen to the radio this morning.

Friday after school, the FAB4 walk home quickly so we can prepare for our big dates. We agree to meet Saturday morning at Wanda's house since she doesn't have a sibling to horn in on our discussion. We want to share the details of our first big date undisturbed.

I wash my hair, roll it onto huge brush rollers and pray that after it's dry, I can comb it into a soft pageboy like Sandra Dee's. Mother finished my dress on Thursday. It is a lovely shade of teal wool. She calls it blue, but I think it looks green. The dress has a slim skirt, long sleeves, and a high round neck. I have black-patent leather princess heels, but no jewelry to wear. I search for Columbia's circle pin in her jewelry box, but it's gone. She must have taken it to college. Mother offers me her pearl necklace. The iridescent pearls look right at home on my ocean-colored dress.

I apply makeup, what little I am allowed to wear: lipstick and mascara. I look quite svelte, except for my hair. The rollers have not softened my curls. I look like a long-haired Little Orphan Annie. As for keeping Mouse under wraps when Paul arrives, I give her a quarter and promise her another quarter when I received my allowance if she stays in her room.

I wait in my room so I can make a grand entrance. After hearing Mother and Daddy talking to Paul, Ronnie, and his date Judy, I enter the living room.Paul smiles. I feel my face flush.

Thankfully, Mother doesn't ask any prying questions. Of course, Daddy is ready with his camera. He uses a roll of film taking photos of Paul and me, Judy and Ronnie, then all of us alone and then together. Every combination of posed people was worth two or three snapshots.

At 7:15 we escape. Paul opens the back door of Ronnie's car. I wave to Mother and Daddy on the porch, and slide across the back seat of the car.

Judy and Ronnie have been dating for more than a year. She slides across the front seat to sit by him. I sit in the middle of the backseat. Paul enters the car, shuts the door and slides over beside me. I move a bit, thinking he doesn't have enough room. He slides closer and takes my hand.

This is what I've dreamed about, but now that it is happening, I'm nervous. Is my hand sweaty? Should I squeeze it? What will he do next? Surely, he won't try anything with his brother in the front seat that would be so embarrassing. Is Paul one of those guys who wants to see how far a girl will go? Sheesh. I wish I had talked to Columbia about dating instead of teasing her.

Parking is limited near the football stadium, but Ronnie finds a place two blocks away in Pawnee Park. The small park has a few benches scattered among the trees, and a statue of a young Pawnee girl that commemorates the Pawnee Morning Star sacrifices. A rather grisly sacrifice of a young girl in a religious ritual.

"If we hurry, we won't miss the kickoff." Ronnie grabs Judy's hand. They run toward the stadium.

"Do you care if you miss the kickoff?" Paul asks.

"Not really. You can go ahead if you want. I can't run in these shoes."

"No, I want to be with you."

I'm glad the evening is cool, or I'd be sweating like a pig. Oops, sorry Grandma, I'd be glowing as bright as Lady Liberty's torch.

Paul takes my hand as we walk toward a bench surrounded by pine trees. "I don't see how you walk in those high heels," Paul says. "Let's sit so you can rest your feet."

We sit. He slips his arm around my shoulder and pulls me close. In the background the high school band is playing our fight song. When the crowd shouts 'Hurrah Pioneers win tonight' at the end of the song, there will be a drum roll, then everyone yells, 'Kick Off.'

We sit in silence listening to the music. I should have worn more Chap Stick. My tongue is dry, unable to moisten my lips. I miss the drum roll because my heart's beating so loudly, and because Paul's lips are on mine!

"I've wanted to do that for a long time," Paul says. "I don't care what your uncle said about you on the radio this morning; I think you're hot."

"You heard what Uncle Waylon said and you still wanted to go with me?"

"Yeah. I'm not some unlucky guy like he said. I'm the luckiest guy in Schoenfeld tonight."

My smile is smothered by another kiss.

* * *

Saturday morning Aunt Bessie greets me with a hug. "How's my favorite niece? That dress your mother made you for the dance sure was pretty. Matched your eyes perfectly. I bet you were the prettiest girl at the dance with the exception of my Wanda of course."

"Thanks, Aunt Bessie. Mother loaned me her pearls to wear with it."

"Wow. Wish I could have seen you and your date."

"She looked really pretty," Wanda says.

"Don't worry, Aunt Bessie. Daddy took lots of pictures. I'll show them to you next week. Is Uncle Waylon here?"

"No, he's with the Sewage and Water boys hoisting a few at the Pink Chicken. I don't suppose he'll be home until after supper."

I know Aunt Bessie dislikes being around Uncle Waylon after a day of drinking, and I don't blame her one little bit. I've seen Uncle Waylon drunk on more than one occasion; it isn't pretty.

"Why don't you and Wanda come to our house for supper? We could play Crazy 8s afterwards."

"That would be nice. Let me call your mother and ask what I can bring."

I'm not to invite guests to the house without asking first, but Mother never scolds me for asking Aunt Bessie. She knows why I often invite Aunt Bessie and Wanda to join us on Saturday night. We never mention Uncle's Waylon's drinking. Mother and Bessie are like sisters, kindred spirits like Anne of Green Gables would have said.

"Where are Jaylynn and Shirley?" Wanda asks.

Before I can respond, the doorbell rings. We all grab Cokes from the fridge, go to Wanda's room and close the door. Even though we're all talking at once, screams of surprise follow my announcement. They all struck out. I'm the first full-fledged member of the Kissers Klub!

Chapter 24
Spring Flowers

This year Aunt Lily and Pansy decide to make their annual pilgrimage to Schoenfeld the week I'll be starring in a play and celebrating my sixteenth birthday. Daddy, Wanda, Mouse, and I meet them at the train station while Mother and Aunt Bessie help Grandma prepare lunch.

When we arrive at Grandma's, her table is set for five with her finest china and crystal. "I've planned a quiet lady's lunch so we may talk without interruptions. My dear sister Lily, you sit here." Grandma points to a chair with a sweeping gesture. "Pansy, this place is for you. Bessie, sit by Lily, and Bonnie, you sit next to her. Adults only for lunch," she says as she looks at me.

Usually being treated as a kid bothers me, but not today. A two-hour lunch under Grandma's watchful eye means my manners would be scrutinized. Any infraction would bring a rebuke, and later Mother would receive an earful about my behavior. My exclusion means an enjoyable afternoon for Mother, and me.

"Come on girls, let's go," Daddy says. "I hear Burger Barn calling."

"See you at our house after awhile, Pansy," Mouse says. "I helped get the guest room ready."

The three of us rush toward the front door.

"Ladies don't run, Rebel," Grandma says, "unless the house is on fire."

I slow my pace. Wanda and Mouse continue their race to the door. Why me? Why does she always pick on me?

"Henry before you leave," Pansy says, "would you please bring me my small case from the car. I can't be without it."

"I'll get it," I say. Happy to be outside, I pop open the trunk and pick up a small gray Samsonite overnight case. The size is no indication of its weight. I re-enter Grandma's apartment, slowly.

"Tomorrow night we could —" Mother says.

"Sorry it took so long," I gasp.

"Rebel don't interrupt your mother," Grandma says.

"Sorry, Mother. Sorry Grandma." I extend the case toward Pansy. "Here."

"Thanks Cousin Rebel." Pansy clutches the case to her breast before carefully placing it by her feet. The bottles inside clink against each other.

"It fell over in the trunk. I hope nothing is broken."

Pansy opens the case and looks at a jumble of bottles and jars. "It's a little mixed up. No damage done. You and Mouse can help me straighten it later, okay?" Pansy smiles at me.

Pansy might be an old maid, but not a nasty one like Miss Penstemon on our corner. Old lady Penstemon is as mean as a hungry snake on hot pavement.

"I'd be happy to help you, Cousin Pansy. Perhaps you can give me some makeup tips."

Grandma frowns. "Now what were you saying, Bonnie, before you were so rudely interrupted?"

"I'm sure Pansy will enjoy staying at our house. Mouse and Rebel have been looking forward to her visit."

"We always stay under the same roof," Aunt Lily says.

"The girls will be disappointed if Pansy doesn't stay at our house," Mother says.

"Pansy's never spent a night away from me," Aunt Lily says. "I'm not sure she should."

"Pansy's thirty-seven," Aunt Bessie whispers to Mother. "Seems to me she's been a mama's girl long enough."

"I agree," mumbles Mother. "Talk about tied to the apron strings."

"Bet Aunt Lily refuses to keep scissors in the house," Aunt Bessie says. "Afraid Pansy would cut those apron strings and leave." Mother and Aunt Bessie stifle a laugh.

"My apartment can't accommodate two guests comfortably," Grandma says to Lily. "I thought it would be nice for just you and me to be together, like when we were growing up. Remember how everyone in the neighborhood called us the LaFleur girls. Lily and Rose, the prettiest girls on Garden Street."

"You're forgetting about Daisy, the weed of Garden Street," Aunt Lily says."

"I haven't forgotten anything, I have a very sharp memory," Grandma says. "If I don't mention someone, it's because I prefer not to."

"Suit yourself," Aunt Lily says, "but the truth finds a way of escaping your mouth when you least expect it, just like a belch."

Grandma clenches her jaw, which I know means this topic is off limits, but Aunt Lily continues to tread on thin ice.

"An ounce of prevention is worth a pound of cure, Rosy," Aunt Lily says. "From what you tell me about Rebel's shenanigans, she'd benefit from hearing about what happens to people who defy their family and polite society."

"I'll thank you to keep your opinions to yourself," Grandma says. "When I need your advice, Lily, I'll ask for it."

Sheesh, Grandma and her sister have been together less than ten minutes and already they are at each others' throat. This might be a long four-day visit.

"Our lunch is getting cold," Grandma says. "Henry, you and Rebel need to skedaddle."

"I'm sure Pansy will be fine staying across the alley with Bonnie and her family," Aunt Bessie says. "Bonnie's raising four fine daughters. Mouse plays the violin and draws exceptionally well, and she's only ten. Columbia and Amherst are excelling in college, and Rebel's on the honor roll and has the lead in the school play this weekend."

Mother and I gasp and hold our breath. Theater is a sore subject around Grandma. Aunt Bessie should know that. Instead of giving a sermon about only fallen women being on the stage, Grandma says, "Our soup is getting cold. Let's continue with lunch. We're having a wonderful cheese soufflé and I don't want it to fall. You may leave Rebel."

I turn to leave, thankful I'll not be lectured, but Pansy grabs my hand. "Rebel, when is your stage performance?"

"Tonight, tomorrow, and Sunday afternoon."

"I'd love to see your play."

"That would be great, Pansy."

"We're going tomorrow night," Aunt Bessie says. "You could join us."

"I don't think Pansy should go out at night in the wilds of Kansas without a proper escort," Aunt Lily says.

"Waylon will be with us. I'm sure he can protect her," Bessie replies.

"It's not an issue of Waylon being there," Aunt Lily says. "I've never permitted Pansy go to the theater, and I don't think now is the time to start. I have no intention of seeing Rebel on the stage and neither should Pansy."

"Well, that's the first sensible thing you've said in years, Lily," Grandma says. "I never attended Rebel's theater productions either and I don't plan to start now."

"Ladies should not make spectacles of themselves," Aunt Lily says.

"Absolutely not." Grandma agrees.

Aunt Lily and Grandma nod their heads at each other. Their last words on the subject. I sense a double whammy coming my way. If Grandma and Aunt Lilly team up against me, even Mother's support will not save me.

But Aunt Bessie ignores their nod. "What about the matinee on Sunday? If we went to that performance, Pansy wouldn't be out after dark?"

"That would be such fun," Pansy says. "What do you think, Mama? Would that be all right?"

"We'll see." Aunt Lily scowls at Bessie.

"Great idea, Bessie," Mother says. "We could all go to church at eleven, have a nice lunch at Nell's, then go to the play. After the play, we're celebrating Rebel's s birthday."

"Count Waylon out for church," Aunt Bessie says. "The only way I'll ever get him into church is at his funeral, but —"

"I'm sure Waylon, worships the Almighty in his own way," Grandma says.

"— but I'm sure Waylon will join us for lunch at Nell's Restaurant," Aunt Bessie says. "Nell serves a really nice Sunday dinner."

"We'll see," says Aunt Lily.

Grandma clears her throat and stares at me. I flee before her eyes drill holes through me. "See you later Pansy," I call over my shoulder.

* * *

Saturday morning after play practice, I collapsed on my bed, exhausted from doing the second act three times. Mouse enters my room with a sigh.

"What's wrong, Mouse? What did you do with Pansy this morning?"

"Well, first we all took a ride. Daddy drove all around in Schoenfeld." Mouse snuggles beside me on the bed. "We stopped in Pawnee Park.

I wanted to see the Morning Star statue, but Aunt Lily said it was too windy, and Grandma said her knees were too stiff to walk that far, so Pansy, Daddy and I went. He took a photo of Pansy and me by the statue."

I smile. My first kiss months ago in Pawnee Park floods my memory. Since then, Paul has kissed me numerous times, but that first kiss is still special. "What did you do after that?"

"Daddy drove by the new Piggly Wiggly grocery store. He told everyone to go on in, and he'd stay in the car and read the newspaper. I should have stayed with him and listened to the radio, but I went in hoping Mother would buy me a Forever Yours candy bar, but she didn't. Grandma, Mother, and Aunt Lily walked up and down every aisle a zillion times and bought nothing! Pansy bought an avocado and a cucumber. I asked Pansy why she was buying vegetables, and Grandma told me it wasn't polite to ask personal questions. Aunt Lily said it was some of Pansy's damn foolishness, and then Grandma told Aunt Lily not to swear. Then Aunt Lily got steamed and said she would say whatever she damn well pleased and that Grandma ought to mind her Ps and Qs and respect her elders. Grandma got huffy and hobbled off to the car. I went with her. About thirty minutes later, Aunt Lily and Pansy exited the store." Mouse sighs deeply.

"Geez. Why did Pansy buy vegetables?" I ask.

She said, "Going to make a mask." How do you make a mask out of vegetables, and why would anyone want one?"

"She means a facial mask, Mouse. I've read about it in *Seventeen.* You put cucumber slices on your eyes and mash the avocado on your face. It's supposed to make your skin soft and smooth."

"You'd look like a green monster if you did that. Aunt Lily is right, sounds like damn foolishness to me."

"Mouse, you better not let Mother or Grandma hear you say 'damn,' or you'll be grounded until Easter."

"I sure hope Pansy can come to my play Sunday afternoon."

"We drove by the high school," Mouse says.

"You did. Why?"

"I don't know. Mother suggested it. Pansy asked if that was where your play was and before Mother could answer, Grandma told Aunt Lily, she was dead set against you being on stage. Grandma said you are out of control, more like you-know-who every day."

"Who's you-know-who?" Mouse asks.

"Beats me. Sometimes I think Grandma is losing her mind, rambling on about stuff that makes no sense. Aunt Lily is no better."

"Do you think we will be weird sisters like that when we get old?"

"I hope not."

"Me too."

* * *

That night, the opening night of the play, Paul holds my hand backstage before the curtain rises to calm my nerves. I don't forget any of my lines, and the audience laughs in all the right places.

After the final curtain, when the house lights are turned on, I see Jaylynn, Shirley, and Wanda on the front row. The stage manager arrives on stage with bouquets of flowers and presents them to several actors and actresses. With two sisters in college, and frugal no-nonsense parents, I know there will be no bouquet for me. I'm fine with that. Just being on the stage is the best gift Mother can give me. I know she takes a lot of guff from Grandma every time I'm in a play.

"Rebel Rothberg," the stage manager calls. "Rebel?"

Someone nudges me. I walk forward to claim a bouquet of miniature, yellow roses. I bow to the audience. I'm anxious to go off stage and open the card. Finally, the applause dies and the curtain is drawn. I fumble with the small envelope and pull out the card, "To the most beautiful red-haired girl in the play. Paul." I look backstage and see Paul walking toward me. He hugs me and whispers, 'I love you.' I want this moment to never end.

* * *

Much like *Chicken Little* who ran around screaming "the sky is falling, the sky is falling," I feel the world must be coming to an end because Sunday morning Aunt Lily decides to allow Pansy to attend my play. It's our final performance and we receive three curtain calls. Pansy is clapping wildly on the second row. I've never seen her this animated.

I come down from the stage to talk to my family. "Mother, can Paul come to my birthday celebration?"

"I think it's best he doesn't join us when Aunt Lily and Pansy are here."

"Okay. Let me tell him good-bye. I'll meet you in the parking lot."

Paul is backstage being very friendly with Marlene Klienmeyer. Marlene releases Paul's hand when she sees me. I tell Paul goodbye, and he brushes his lips on my cheek, a peck similar to the one Mother gives me at bedtime.

"See you later, Paul," Marlene twitches her butt toward the door.

"Call me later, will you Paul?" I ask.

"Sure."

"Me too," Marlene says.

I don't hear Paul's answer, but I don't like the smirk on Marlene's face. I'll call the FAB4 later to see if Marlene has broken up with her boyfriend and is scouting for a new one. She's like a black widow spider, devouring one boy after another. I don't want Paul to be one of her victims, but I can't compete with Marlene. Despite Jaylynn and the other cheerleaders telling Marlene that virgins wear their circle pin on the left shoulder, she keeps hers on the right.

Boys! If Marlene takes my boyfriend by 'going all the way' she can. I have no intention of doing that. If that's what it takes to become a Black Sheep, like my mysterious Aunt Daisy, I'll remain a little lamb. I sniff back tears on the way to the car. I don't think Paul is that kind of a guy, but according to Wanda's Aunt Mary Jo, all boys want is s-e-x. Sheesh.

* * *

Despite Grandma's difficulty walking, she and Aunt Lily have decorated our dining room with balloons and a Happy Birthday banner while we were at the play. Grandma is seated in her favorite wingback chair when we arrive. The sturdy chair arms allowed her to push herself upright without help. Across one arm is draped a beautiful, crocheted afghan made of colorful granny squares.

"This is for you Redcliff Rose," Grandma says. "It took me eight months to make it with these crippled fingers." Her gnarled, swollen hands extend the afghan toward me. "I can't crochet any more. This is the last afghan I'll ever make."

"Oh Grandma, it's so beautiful. I'll treasure it forever." I clutch the afghan to my chest. Lavender, Grandma's favorite scent, permeates every fiber of the wool. I've grown to love that aroma too.

Tears welled in Grandma's eyes as she pulls a small box from her purse. "This is for you too." She hands me a gift wrapped in gold foil. I know it has taken her a great deal of effort to wrap it.

"Must be something special. Mother always tells me 'Precious things come in small packages.'" I tug on the tape. It refuses to budge.

"Here," Mouse says. "Use the scissors."

I remove the paper to reveal a leather box scarred by age.

"Let me see it," Mouse says.

"Hold your horses." I open the lid. Nestled inside the purple velvet lining is an oval, antique, gold locket. An elaborate engraving of roses covers the front of the locket. An "R" is obvious within the scroll work. "It's gorgeous!" I remove the locket and open it. Inside is an old photo of two girls tinted with faint colors. What might have been a third face is scratched and covered with dark ink. "Who are the little girls?"

"Let me see it." Mouse says.

I extend my hand toward her. "Look, but don't touch."

"Wow. What a tiny picture. That's neat. I wish I could paint that well."

"You will someday, Mouse. Just keep drawing."

"That is Lily and me," Grandma says. "My grandmother Rose Matilda gave it to me when I was about your age. The locket has been passed from a grandmother to a granddaughter for more than 150 years."

"I'm surprised you gave it to Rebel," Mother says.

"The locket should be given to a girl named Rose," Grandma says.

"I know," Mother says, "but I figured you would give it to Wanda."

"Well, you figured wrong," Grandma replies. "Rose Matilda was Rebel's great-great-grandmother the same as Wanda's, but Rebel's middle name is Rose, so she should have it."

"What's this dark spot on the photo?" Mouse asks.

"Let me see that locket," Aunt Lily snaps.

"No need for you to see it, Lily," Grandma says. "Rebel, I want you to take care of this locket. It's valuable. It might not be worth much money, but the family connection is priceless."

"I will, Grandma. I'll only wear it on special occasions."

"May I try it on," Mouse asks.

"All right, but just this once. Your name isn't Rose, so you can't have it."

"I don't want it. I just want to try it on." I fasten the locket on Mouse.

"Come here, Mouse," Aunt Lily says sweetly. Aunt Lily takes off her glasses and squints at the smudged photo. "Well, I'll be. You scratched out the little weed. I remember when this photo was taken, do you, Rose?"

"Of course, Lily. I'm not feeble-minded yet," Grandma says. "It was at her fifth birthday party."

"What a party that was," Lily says. "Pony rides, magicians, food galore. Nothing was too good for the little weed. She was spoiled rotten. Spare the rod and spoil the child."

"Who are you talking about?" I ask.

"Nobody," Grandma says. "Just take care of the locket, Rebel."

"Let me take the locket off you, Mouse," Mother says. Mouse stands quietly as Mother removes the locket. She holds it in the palm of her hand and stares at the photo. Her face has a wistful look, the same thoughtful pose she has when she looks at things in her cedar chest. She studies the picture, rubbing it gently with her forefinger. "Here, Rebel. Put it back in the box. Your Grandma's right, this is very special. You must take care of it."

* * *

Later that evening, I hear Mother and Daddy talking as they put the leftovers from my birthday celebration in the refrigerator. "Even though my middle name is Rose, I knew I would never get that locket, but I never dreamed she'd give it to Rebel."

"Maybe she's had a change of heart after all these years," Daddy suggests.

"I doubt it," Mother replies. "Henry, you know how headstrong Mom and Aunt Lily are. The whole family is stubborn and pigheaded. Forgive and forget, that's my motto, but that doesn't happen in Mom's family. They're blue-ribbon grudge holders."

I go to my bedroom and contemplate what Mother said about grudges. She's right. Grandma is like a bulldog chasing a defenseless bunny. Once she chomps onto something, she has no intention of letting go. The same seems to be true for Aunt Lily. As I reach for the phone to call the FAB4 to discuss Paul and Marlene, it lights up and rings.

"Hello."

"Hey, Rebel, how you doing? Did you have a nice birthday?" Paul asks.

"Yes, it was nice. My Grandma gave me a gorgeous antique locket. If we go to the movies on Friday, I'll wear it so you can see it. It's very special, only girls in the family named Rose can have it."

"Uh… I don't know about going to the movie on Friday. You're really special, and I like you, but —"

"—but what?"

"I don't think we should spend so much time together."

"What! We only go out once a week. It's Marlene, isn't it?"

"What makes you say that?"

"I saw her hanging all over you this afternoon."

"She was just being friendly."

"A bit too friendly if you ask me. I thought we were going steady."

"We were, uh we are. That's what I want to talk about. I think—

"—If you don't want to go out with me anymore just say it," I snap.

"Can't we just be friends, Rebel?"

"I don't think so. Good-bye, Paul." With a shaking hand I place the receiver back on the phone.

There's no point to call the FAB4 now. There's nothing to discuss. Paul and I are over, a done deal, finished, history. I stare at the yellow roses in the vase on my dresser. The words 'I love you,' on the card pierce my heart, a broken heart.

Chapter 25
Stripping Gears

Before school the next morning I tell the FAB4 about Paul's telephone call. Jaylynn and Wanda promise not to speak to Marlene at cheerleading practice unless it is absolutely necessary. I appreciate that.

"Paul is not worthy of you," Wanda says.

"Let's TP his house this weekend," Shirley suggests.

"Great idea, but how will we get there?" Jaylynn says. "He lives in the country and none of us drive."

"My dad would probably take us," Wanda says.

"Yeah, I'm sure Uncle Waylon would, but it's not necessary."

Within hours everyone in high school knows Paul and I are no longer dating. It doesn't take a brain surgeon to figure that out. Marlene is hanging on Paul's arm like snot under a baby's nose. In math class Paul sits across the aisle from me. He says, "Hi," I turn the other way and talk to Skip.

Jimmy calls me several nights later. "Paul's not the guy for you. I'm your man. Want to go to a movie on Friday?"

"I'm busy on Friday." That was dumb. I should tell him I'm busy for the rest of my life. I'll become a crabby old maid like Miss Penstemon before I'll lower myself to be seen with Jimmy in public.

"What about Saturday night? The drive-in is showing *King Kong vs. Godzilla.*"

"I'm not allowed to go to the drive-in." Dumb again. I need to tell him to bug off and leave me alone.

"Okay, we'll go to the Rialto Theater in town. They're showing an Elvis movie. I don't like The Pelvis, but I'd suffer through it to be with you."

What a line. "Sorry. I have plans on Saturday night."

"You sure? They have the best popcorn in town. I'll buy you a big bag."

Now there's a real selling point. Daddy makes great caramel popcorn, the best. No popcorn on the planet is better than his. "Thank you, but I told you I had other plans."

"Well, you can't blame a guy for trying. See you around Red."

"Bye, Jimmy."

Mother overhears my conversation and says, "What are your plans for this weekend? I haven't heard you mention anything?"

"My plan is not to go out with Jimmy. That's my plan."

Mother chuckles. "Very clever, but why not? Jimmy's a nice boy. In church every Sunday."

I shake my head. Mother has no idea what Jimmy is really like. True, Jimmy is in church every Sunday, but I expect Jack the Ripper was a church member too. I don't think Jimmy is a crazed slasher, just a dork, and I don't want to be seen with him.

Despite being dumped by Paul, boys remain an important part of my life. I hope someone will ask me to the Spring Sock Hop, but what looms as a huge milestone on the horizon is getting my driver's license. I am the first of the FAB4 to get my learner's permit. I'm anxious to get my driver's license so I can cruise the strip with the FAB4 in the Bel Air. The car has been sitting idle behind the garage for six months, ever since Columbia and Amherst left for college.

This week, for the umpteenth time Daddy says to Mother, "I want you to learn to drive. Then when I'm traveling, you won't have to walk every place."

Mother replies, "I'd lose my girlish figure if I drove every place. Walking is great exercise."

Daddy sighs. "I'd feel better if you knew how to drive."

"But I wouldn't. You know how my mom is. She's a world class worrier. Name a situation and she can detail a half dozen horrible scenarios that might happen. She gave me plenty of grief when Columbia and Amherst drove the Bel Air. I don't need to add more fuel to her fire by learning to drive."

"Okay, but if you ever change your mind —"

"You'll be the first to know, I promise."

Daddy starts the Chevy Bel Air and takes it for a short spin once a month so the oil will not turn to sludge. The rest of the time it sits behind the garage. Although more than ten years old, the red two-door convertible with a white top is in excellent condition. The white cloth interior has no rips and the radio works. On more than one occasion, I've taken the car keys off the hook by the back door, unlocked the car, sat behind the huge steering wheel, and imagined myself pulling into the DQ with the radio blaring. If that doesn't turn a few heads, nothing will.

The high school uses a Ford Falcon for drivers' education which has an automatic transmission, but the Bel Air has a stick shift on the column. If I ever hope to drive Mother on errands, to church meetings, and, more importantly, cruise up and down the main drag on Friday night, I must master manual shifting.

"Daddy, I'm ready to learn how to drive the Bel Air." I wave my learner's permit by him.

"When the school year is over, "I'll teach you."

"But that's months from now. Why can't I start now?"

"Because I said so," Daddy replies.

Mother sighs and muffles a belch. She will soon be asking for a 7-Up to settle her stomach.

"Please, Daddy. I'm on the honor roll. I promise to be careful. Puh-lease."

I feel Daddy is ready to yield, when Mother says, "Rebel, your father said he would teach you in June. Quit beating a dead horse. Now bring me a 7-Up."

"Phooey." I stomp off to my bedroom. Time to form a plan.

Daddy is going out of town next week and on Thursday afternoon Mother attends the Lutheran Women's Missionary League at church. If I hurry, I can be home after school by 4:00. She won't arrive home until at least 5:30. This gives me plenty of time to start the car and practice shifting gears.

Despite my better judgment the next morning I tell my plan to the FAB4 and swear them to secrecy. Shirley and Jaylynn would never break a confidence, but occasionally Wanda has slipped up and blabbed something to her mom or dad. I do not need Aunt Bessie finking me out to my mom or worse yet, Uncle Waylon snooping around. Recently Uncle Waylon has stopped taunting me about redheads being nothing but trouble, and I have no intention of rekindling that fire.

The lilac hedge behind our garage hides the Bel Air from Grandma's watchful eyes. I rush home after school and grab the car keys from the hook by the back door and go outside. Mouse follows me.

"What are you going to do?"She asks.

"Nothing that concerns you. Go back in the house and mind your own business."

"You're going to start the car, aren't you?" Mouse says. "If you don't let me go with you, I'll tell Mother as soon as she gets home."

"Sheesh, Mouse. You are a certified rat fink."

"Takes one to know one." Years of teaching Mouse how to spy on Columbia and Amherst have returned to haunt me. "All right, come on, but you have to promise not to tell, ever. Promise?"

Mouse crosses her heart and zips her lips. I unlock the door, climb in and pop the lock on the passenger side.

"Wow, these seats are hot," Mouse says.

"What did you expect? The car's been parked in the sun with the windows rolled up for ages." I stick the key in the ignition and crank the engine. It roars to life.

"Away we go!" Mouse calls.

I floor the gas pedal and try shifting gears. Despite pushing, pulling and jerking, neither the gear stick nor the car move. Then I remember to push down the clutch. I slide forward on the seat to be closer to the steering wheel, push the clutch to the floor, grab the stick shift and push the lever up. After the grinding noise stops, the car motor revs louder.

"Why aren't we moving?" Mouse asks.

"Shut up! I'm trying to remember what to do next." I let out the clutch. The car jerks forward; the engine dies.

"Wasn't much of a ride," Mouse says.

"Be quiet! I can't concentrate with all your yapping." I start the car again, push in the clutch, shift into a gear, floor the accelerator, let out the clutch, the car makes two quick jumps forward and smashes into the clothesline pole. "Sheesh! Now look what you made me do." I open the car door.

"I didn't do anything. Where are you going?" Mouse asks.

"To check for damage." I do a quick inspection of the bumper. "The car's fine, no dents. Get out here. I need your help."

"What can I do?" Mouse asks.

"We have to push the car back to where it was and straighten the pole. That way Mother will never know."

"Do I look like Superman? I can't push the car back."

"You'll have to try, Mouse. I don't know how to put the car in reverse."

"Your goose is cooked," Mouse says. "You're a goner. Grounded for life. No phone privileges, no TV, no desserts, no nothing from now until hell freezes over, and all the little devils go ice skating."

"Gee thanks. Now get out of the car and help me."

"All right, but I don't think this is going to work," Mouse grumbles.

"Do you have a better idea?"

"No."

"Then shut up and push." Mouse and I push on the car with our hands, our hips, and our butts. The car doesn't move. "This isn't going to work."

"I told you so," Mouse says.

"Will you shut up so I can concentrate? I have to figure out where reverse is on the shifter." I start the car, push in the clutch, locate a different gear, release the clutch, and the car bounces against the clothesline pole again, bending it more. "H-E double toothpicks! Where the heck is reverse?"

"You're dead meat. Road kill," Mouse says. "And don't swear."

"I'm not swearing. I'm stating facts vehemently." I jerk the gear shift again with no luck.

"Look! Here comes Uncle Waylon and Wanda. I wonder what they want?" Mouse yells.

"Sheesh and double sheesh. That's all I need. I might as well invite Grandma to join us then they can all string me up right here. Nice knowing you, Mouse." I rest my head on the steering wheel and pray to become invisible.

"Hey, Rebel." Uncle Waylon's voice booms through the closed car window. "Taking the old Chevy for a spin? You didn't get very far. You need some help?"

I get out of the car and push pass Uncle Waylon. Wanda runs when she saw me coming. "Wait, Wanda! I want to talk to you. I'm never telling you another secret again as long as I live." I grab the hood of her jacket. "You blabbed, didn't you?"

"I'm sorry. I had to. I was afraid you'd kill yourself," Wanda says. "I didn't tell my mom, because I knew she'd have a fit and tell your mom."

"Well, gee thanks. Telling your dad wasn't very smart either."

"Yes, it was," Wanda says. "I showed him those old Thanksgiving photos of him and Mary Jo and I said, 'if you tell Mom, I'll show her these photos.'"

"Good idea, but do you think he'll keep his word?"

"Yes. He's already in hot water with Mom because he's spending too many nights and too much money at the Pink Chicken. He offered me $10 for the photos, but I refused."

"What are you guys talking about?" Mouse asks.

"Go away! This is none of your business." Mouse looks hurt and glares at me. I cannot afford to have her mad at me. No telling what she might do. "Mouse, I need your help. I want you to be my secret agent."

"And do what?" Mouse asks.

"Go to Grandma's house and see what she's doing. Think of something to keep her in the living room until I come and get you. I don't want her to see what's going on in our backyard."

"What's in it for me?" Mouse asks.

"My eternal gratitude," I say.

"What's that mean?"

"You get no money," Uncle Waylon says. "Now get going, Mouse, and do as you're told. Once in a while, you gotta do things for family without expecting anything in return."

"Okay. I'll be your secret agent. I won't tell Grandma a thing." Mouse marches toward the alley singing Secret Agent Man.

Uncle Waylon's comment about helping family is out of character for him. He never does anything without expecting something in return. Money. Beer. Or a political favor. I don't know if he has just given his life to Jesus or if seeing the photos of Mary Jo caused this transformation, but I don't care. He's here to help, and I need all the help I can get.

"What were you trying to do, Red?" Uncle Waylon asks.

I ignore him calling me Red. I can't afford to look a gift horse in the mouth. "I was practicing shifting gears, and suddenly everything went to hell in a hand basket. Mother will be home in an hour, and I'll never see daylight until we land on the moon if this car isn't back where it belongs."

"Red, you've got yourself in a real mess here. I know what that's like. Been in a mess or two myself. More than once your Daddy helped me out and kept his mouth shut, so I owe him one."

"Thanks Uncle Waylon. You're the best."

Within thirty seconds he has the car parked behind the garage, Next Wanda, Uncle Waylon and I push the clothesline pole vertical.

"There, everything looks good as new," Waylon says. "Rebel, don't get any ideas in that red-haired head of yours. I'm not coming to your rescue every time you mess up. This was a one- time deal. I still say you are a heap of trouble, just like your mother, and her mother too."

"Okay. Thanks again Uncle Waylon. I'll be eternally grateful."

"Yeah. Yeah. Yeah."

He and Wanda leave, and I walk across the alley to fetch Mouse. That night, after I say my prayers, thanking God that Uncle Waylon helped me, I reflect on his final comment: You are a heap of trouble, just like your mother, and her mother too. He often picks on Mother and me saying we are nothing but trouble, but I've never heard him say a bad word about Grandma, his mother. Grandma makes no bones about the fact that Waylon is her favorite child. She spoils him rotten. Why in the world would he say such a thing? I fall asleep mulling over possible reasons. None make any sense.

* * *

On the first Sunday of summer vacation, with me riding shotgun and Mouse in the backseat, Daddy backs the Bel Air onto the street. As he drives toward the old airport, he smoothly shifts gears and explains the function of the clutch and how the gear positions make the letter "H" on the column. I don't care how the car functions; I just want to drive. At the airport we change positions.

I slide the bench seat forward to reach the pedals, which jams Daddy's knees into his chest. After adjusting the rearview mirror, I turn the key and the car springs to life. I floor the accelerator; the car doesn't move. I turn the steering wheel from side to side. "Daddy, we're not moving."

"Of course not. Did you listen to anything I said?" Daddy does not wait for my answer. "Push in the clutch, and as you release it, give the car a little gas."

I do as instructed, more or less. I pop the clutch; the Bel Air leaps forward and dies.

"That's what happened in the backyard when Rebel —"

"Shut up, Mouse." I check the rearview mirror. Mouse has her hands clamped over her mouth.

"You have to let the clutch out slowly and smoothly." Daddy sighs and mumbles, "Why me Lord? Why me?"

After several more attempts, I have the car rolling at ten miles per hour. Soon I am going thirty-five miles an hour, more or less in a straight line down the crumbling runway. The engine roars, and so does Daddy. Shift into second! Put in the clutch! Slow down! Don't slam on the brakes!"

I follow his commands in order. The Bel Air makes a long growling noise, followed by an ominous clang. I stomp on the brakes and our bodies fly forward. Daddy grabs his knees, "Ouch."

Mouse flies off the back seat and knocks off Daddy's hat. "I'm flying!" She calls.

"Pipe down, Mouse. You told me to stop, Daddy, so I stopped."

Daddy checks his watch. "We've been here half an hour. That's long enough for your first lesson."

"Please, Daddy. Let me try one more time."

"I guess I can afford another gray hair or two," he says. "Try to remember what I told you."

This time I release the clutch slowly. The car hops along the runway like a scared bunny but does not stall. When the engine starts to whine, I step on the clutch, but do not push it to the floor. The car growls in displeasure and pain.

"Push in the clutch! You'll rip the gears out of the car." Daddy braces his hands on the dash for another sudden stop, but I find second gear. We kept rolling.

"Whee!" says Mouse. "You're driving, Rebel. You're really driving."

When we reach the end of the runway, I stop the car, remembering to push in the clutch first.

"Good stop." Daddy opens his car door and comes around to the driver's side. "Scoot over, Rebel, I'll drive home."

Daddy's kind words help my confidence. On the first Friday in July, I pass the driving test with flying colors and leave the courthouse with my driver's license. Look out Schoenfeld, the FAB4 has wheels.

Chapter 26
Surprised Parties

Paul and I have the leads in *Life with Father*, the Junior Class play which will be performed in May. A year ago, I would have been thrilled to star with Paul, but now having to play the lovey-dovey wife to the guy who had dumped me for Marlene stretches my acting skills. Marlene now has fresh meat to grind, Stewart Watson. Rumor has it she found Paul unwilling, uneducated, and unable or maybe all three. I don't care. Paul calls me occasionally, but one of Grandma's sayings, 'Fool me once, shame on you. Fool me twice, shame on me,' keeps me from dating him again. He thinks that since we are the co-stars, we should practice our lines together, alone. Our scenes together include several hugs and stage kisses. I set him straight about practicing kisses at the first rehearsal. No way, José.

"Opening night is Friday, Mother. Are Columbia and Amherst coming home?" I ask.

"Columbia is practice teaching now. Her weekends are devoted to writing lesson plans and grading papers. She must do well practice teaching or she won't graduate from Bethany college this June."

"I suppose you'll make me go her stinking graduation. It's not fair. My play is far more entertaining."

"Columbia's the first of you girls to graduate from college. It's special. You have to be there."

"She's the oldest. Of course, she would be the first." I snort my disgust. "I'm the first person in this family to ever have leads in the school plays. Doesn't that count for anything?"

"Yes, Rebel, it does. But —"

"I suppose Amherst won't be here either."

"She's studying for her Dental College Admission Test. Not everyone who passes is accepted. She wants to score high to insure she gets into dental school next fall."

"I went to all their stuff. Why don't they come to see me perform?" Tears well in my eyes, surprising me.

"Because, life is not fair, Rebel. I wish I could make it fair, but I can't." Mother pulls me close and hugs me. "Columbia and Amherst aren't able to attend because of their obligations and distance from home, not because they don't want to see you perform."

"What about Daddy?" I sniff back more tears. "Will he be here for opening night?"

"He's in Wichita for meetings and won't be home until Saturday afternoon. Your Aunt Bessie, Wanda, Mouse and I will be there on opening night, and I'll come again with your father on Saturday night."

Usually only Aunt Bessie, Mother, Daddy, and Mouse attend my performances. I understand why, but today I'm not in an accepting mood. "All right, so what's Grandma's excuse? She never comes to see the plays. She won't even let me talk about a play in her house. Why's she so mean to me? She's always picking on me." I can't control my tears. Mother pulls a handkerchief from her apron pocket. I wipe my tears, and I blow my nose.

"You know you're my special little Rebel. Always will be. I know it hurts you that Grandma doesn't see your plays, but she's a stubborn old lady. I can't change her. She ignored me when I was little. Never showed me any affection. She thinks the sun rises and sets on Waylon. Nothing I do is good enough. I'm always compared to Waylon, and I never measure up. I've been a thorn in her side for forty-one years. I can't change the past, and she won't forgive or forget it."

My eyes are wide with surprise. Grandma never liked Mother! Uncle Waylon's her favorite that's obvious. What does Grandma need to forgive or forget? Mother's forty-four years old, but she said, 'Grandma didn't like her for the past forty-one years.' What could a three-year-old child do to enrage a parent to such an extent they could never be forgiven?

Mother's body quivers as she holds me. "What's the matter?"

She calms herself before speaking. "Nothing. Rebel, don't be upset with your sisters. If you hold onto your anger, it will seep into every aspect of your life and make you miserable. That's why forgiveness is so important."

"What happened to you forty years ago?" I ask.

"I'll tell you someday, but not today. When you're older, it might make more sense."

Thankfully, Mother did not say the dreaded 'you're too young to understand.' "Have you told Columbia and Amherst whatever this secret is?"

"No. They aren't as intuitive as you are. You feel things more deeply than they do and can sense the feelings of others." Mother's voice quivers.

I want to ask more questions, but this isn't the time. "Well, aren't we a pair to draw to? A couple of cry babies. I'm sorry I'm so crabby, Mother. I don't know what's wrong with me. Just different, I suppose. You're always telling me 'you'll just have to be different.'"

"Yes, but I mean that in a good way. I don't want you to be like Columbia, Amherst, Mouse, or anyone else. I want you to be you, and to be happy about who you are."

"Really? But I don't know who I am?"

"Someday you will. Learning about yourself takes time."

"I know one thing. I have a horrid geometry test tomorrow, and I hate geometry. When will I ever use Euclidean theorems? Who cares about how many degrees in an obtuse angle? I'll be glad when this year is over, and I don't have to take any more math."

Mother smiles. "And your father will be too."

* * *

Life with Father is performed flawlessly on opening night. The applause is thunderous when the curtain drops. I'm so excited I let Paul hug me but turn my face away when he tries to kiss me. After a curtain call, the house lights come on and the drama coach presents a dozen, long-stemmed yellow roses to me. I smile and bow.

When the curtain closes, I read the attached card. To my favorite red-haired girl. Forgive me. Love Paul. I haven't said a civil word to Paul, outside of our lines for months, and now this. I look across the backstage area. Paul smiles. I return his smile. Mother's comment that it takes time to know yourself, is my second thought. My first thought however is to kiss Paul. He is happy to oblige.

* * *

On Saturday, Daddy isn't home by 5:00 p.m. "Mother, I need to leave now for school so I can get on my makeup and costume. When will Daddy be here? How will you get to the play if he isn't here by seven o'clock?"

"Mouse and I will stay home if your father isn't here to take us."

"I hope Daddy can make it." I grab my purse and leave. "See you after ten. And yes, I'll drive carefully."

Before the play starts, the drama coach comes backstage. "The play is sold out. Two extra rows of chairs have been set up near the stage."

We have three curtain calls, which I'm sure is a record. I know it is for me. Before the curtain closes, the drama coach is on stage with a dozen long-stemmed red roses.

"Will someone turn up the house lights?" The drama coach walks toward the apron of the dark theater. "It's wonderful to have so many parents, students, family members, and Schoenfeld residents attending tonight. I know Schoenfeld is a long way from Broadway, but I think the kids did a great job tonight, don't you?" There is more applause.

"Flowers are only presented on opening night, but these just arrived. Will someone turn on the house lights! What are you kids doing backstage without a chaperone? Not turning on the lights, that's for sure." The audience laughs. "Lights, please." The house lights flicker on.

"Rebel, come here." The Drama coach motions for me to come down stage.

I look at the cast members standing on either side of me. "What's up?" I whisper. They shake their heads and shrug their shoulders. I walk to the edge of the stage.

"Rebel, these are for you. I've been asked to read the card." He hands me the roses and pulls a small card from the envelope. "To a special daughter, sister and niece who is the best actress in our family. Love Daddy, Mother, Columbia, Amherst, Mouse, Aunt Bessie, Wanda, and Uncle Waylon."

This is the second time in my life I am struck speechless. The other time happened years ago when I grabbed an electric fence when picking plums with Jaylynn. I smile and bow to the audience, and I see all my family seated on the front row chairs, including Columbia, Amherst, and Uncle Waylon. The flashbulbs from Daddy's camera blind me, which is how I explain my tears.

Chapter 27
All that Glitters

Tonight, Jaylynn and I are going stag to a dance at the YMCA. Mother and I agree not to tell Grandma because she believes young ladies should not go out in the evening unescorted. Paul and Steve, Jaylynn's long-time steady, are both at an out-of-town basketball game.

"Let's go Jaylynn." I pull on Paul's Letter Jacket he earned for his track participation last year. We don't have class rings yet, so wearing his jacket will let guys at the dance know I'm going steady. I grab my purse, open the door and stare into the face of Vera Arpkey, one of Mother's neighborhood friends.

"Don't rush off girls," Mrs. Arpkey says. "I brought you a present, Rebel. Jaylynn you're going to love it." Mrs. Arpkey hands me a huge box. Inside is a puce, vinyl Eisenhower-style jacket trimmed with fur that looks like it was skinned from that raccoon that was tossed out in our alley years ago. "Isn't it gorgeous?" Vera sighs, obviously proud of her purchase.

The collar is stiff, made from fur no self-respecting animal would be caught dead or alive in. I catch a glimpse of Mother's pursed lips and slight shake of her head, her subtle warning me to control my tongue.

"Well, it's certainly uh… well it's uh… unique. That's for sure."

"No, it's not. The store had two of them. I bought the other one for me," Vera gushes. "It's in the car. I'll go get it." She waddles outside and returns wearing an identical jacket.

Jaylynn rolls her eyes and coughs to stifle a laugh.

"Go ahead, put on your coat," Vera says.

I take off Paul's Letter Jacket and button the puce coat over my sweater. The color clashes with my copper-colored hair and blue pleated skirt. "What do you think, Jaylynn?" The fur collar scratches my neck.

"Striking. Very festive," says Jaylynn.

"We make quite a dashing pair." Vera stands beside me. "Look, we're twins."

Good grief, twins? Mrs. Arpkey must be nuts. I'm seventeen, well almost seventeen, and she's fifty, if she's a day. Plus, she weighs a hundred pounds more than I do.

"The two of us should paint the town red next Friday night. What do you say?" Vera asks.

Vera and Buck Arpkey's idea of a night out is the early bird special at Nell's Café and a couple of polkas at Witkowski's Ballroom. I bet Vera hasn't been out past ten o'clock since she went to the Wayne Newton concert in St. Louis five years ago, which she has never stopped talking about. I'd rather suffer the tortures of the damned than be seen in public in this hideous jacket.

I think about saying, "Sorry, Mrs. Arpkey, I had a bad check up at the dentist last week, and I need to spend three hours flossing every night until I enter college," but I know Mother would have a hard time defending that answer. This is the first time in my life I'm happy Mother micro-manages my social life, wanting to know where I am every minute from the 3:20 p.m. dismissal bell at school until my curfew at 11:00 p.m.

"That's a great idea Mrs. Arpkey, but you know Mother. She's very strict. You're such a swinger, I don't know if I could keep up with your pace." I try to look crestfallen.

Vera giggles. "You're right. I do live a pretty wild life. I'd hate to be charged with contributing to the delinquency of a minor. Especially with the daughter of my best friend." Mother smiles, first at Vera and then at me. "We'll have a hot time on the old town when you're older."

"I'm sure that will be fun for Rebel." Mother winks at me.

"Thanks for the coat. I hate to rush off Mrs., Arpkey, but Jaylynn and I want to get to the YMCA dance before all the chairs are taken." I take off the puce coat.

"Aren't you going to wear your new coat?" Mrs. Arpkey asks.

"Uh… I would, but there are no hangers at the Y. Everyone just throws their coats in a pile on the floor in the gym. I'd hate to ruin the coat before I have a chance to wear it."

"That's very sensible. Guess I'll see you in the coat this Sunday at church," Vera Arpkey says.

"I'm sure you will," Mother replies before I can respond.

"Come on, Jaylynn. Let's go." I push her toward the front door.

"You girls drive carefully. Don't do anything I wouldn't do." Mrs. Arpkey giggles again.

"We won't."

"Be home by eleven o'clock," Mother says.

"Sure, sure." I pull the door shut and escape into the frosty night. "Sheesh. Did you ever see such a monstrosity, Jaylynn?"

"No. What are you going to do with it?"

"I don't know, but wearing it is not an option. Hey, I should have worn it tonight. Maybe someone would take it by mistake."

"That coat? You've got to be kidding."

"Well, it would be a mistake if they took it." We laugh.

Sunday Mother makes me wear the coat to church. "Do it once. It won't kill you, and it will make Mrs. Arpkey happy."

The church is collecting coats for Lutheran World Relief. I plan to put the coat in the box after the service, but Mother says, "Those poor starving children in Africa suffer enough with hunger. You don't need to add insult to injury by donating that coat to them."

* * *

The Junior Prom is in three-weeks and none of the FAB4 have dates. Jaylynn recently started dating Shirley's older brother Charlie who's a senior in college. He can't attend the prom as only high school students are allowed. The faculty and sponsors are afraid older kids might spike the punch. The FAB4 made a pact, if we don't get dates soon, we will not go stag, that would be too embarrassing.

Thursday afternoon, the FAB4 are cruising the strip with the top down on the Bel Air. The warm air feels wonderful after being cooped up in school all day. My hair is blowing wild and free. Jaylynn is trying to hold her page boy in place. Wanda's soft curls frame her face so she looks like a blonde Annette Funicello. Wind does not phase her hair style. Being part Cherokee, Shirley has straight, black hair which waves in the wind like a horse's mane.

The DQ parking lot is empty when I pull into it. Arriving before the seniors means we can nab the front table by the window which allows us to see what is happening on Main Street as well as everyone who enters the DQ.

"Someone save this table for us." Jaylynn and Wanda walk toward the restroom.

"I'll save it," I say. "Running a comb through my hair won't make it look any better than it does now." Shirley sits beside me, which means

Jaylynn and Wanda will have to sit with their backs to the window.

A revving engine and an extra loud muffler, a glasspack, means Jimmy and his gang have arrived in his beat-up Thunderbird convertible. The car is a two-seater. Leroy and Allen, who are on the basketball team with Jimmy, are sitting on the back of the car with their feet inside. The rag top convertible they sit on is shredded. Skip rides up front with Jimmy. Jimmy's dad bought the T-bird several years ago. It was a total wreck and doesn't look much better than that today. The T-Bird belonged to the bank president. When it was stolen, a police chase ensued and ended when the thief wrapped the thunderbird around a telephone pole. Jimmy's dad bought the T-bird from the junk yard and had it hauled to their garage. Jimmy, his dad, and several men in the neighborhood work on the car most weekends. Even Daddy has helped a few times. Several weeks ago, Jimmy tooled to my house in the T-bird and asked if I wanted to go for a spin. I told him 'no way.' The driver's seat, what's left of it, was covered with a worn bath towel. The passenger side bucket seat is gone, replaced by a folding chair. The outside is a mishmash of scratches, Bondo, primer, and splotches of its once glorious canary-yellow paint.

I'm not a snob. I don't care if people see me in a beat-up car, but I don't want to be seen with Jimmy. He is one of the most popular kids in our class, plays a mean trumpet in the jazz band, and is a basketball starter. Most girls say he's a hunk and I'm crazy to ignore him, but to me, he's still the snot-nosed kid who made my life a living hell in grade school.

"Here comes trouble." I take a bite off my strawberry Dilly Bar.

The bell on the DQ door jingles as Jimmy, Skip, Leroy, and Allen enter. "How you girls doing?" Jimmy flips a chair around and straddles it, resting his arms on the chair back which puts his face a mere six inches from me. His friends pull extra chairs to the table. "Where's the rest of your pack?" Jimmy asks. "Never two without four."

"Here they come." Skip points toward Jaylynn and Wanda who are at the counter placing their orders. "Think I'll get me a little something." Skip pulls his billfold from his jeans and walks to the counter.

"A little is all you'll ever get," Leroy hollers. "You gotta be cool like me to get any."

"Who would be dumb enough to give you any?" Shirley says.

"You, maybe. Want to go to the prom with me, Shirl?" Leroy smiles.

I look at Shirley and shake my head. "Sure, be glad to," Shirley says. "How are we going to get there? You don't have a car."

"I'll work out the details. Don't worry. If my parents won't let me borrow their car, maybe we can double date with one of your friends. You got a date for the prom, Rebel?"

"Yep, she's taken," Jimmy says. "Red's going with me."

"Since when?" I mumble through a mouthful of ice cream.

"Since right now. Or are you waiting for Paul to ask you?" Jimmy sneers.

"Paul and Rebel are history, not that it's any of your business," Shirley says.

"I know, but what goes around, comes around, and around and around," Jimmy says. "He'll be back. Red, go with me. It will save you the embarrassment of being stood up by Paul on prom night."

"Such a romantic invite, how can I say no?" I wrap a napkin around the wooden stick of my Dilly Bar.

Jaylynn and Wanda arrive carrying drinks and an order of onion rings. Skip gives Wanda his chair and pulls more chairs to the table.

"Get your mitts off my onion rings." Jaylynn playfully swats Skip's hand away from her crunchy treat.

"Big news, Jaylynn," Jimmy yells. "Red's going to the prom with me."

"I am not!"

"You said you couldn't say 'no,' so I figured you mean yes." Jimmy grins his all-American smile. "If you don't want to go with me, just say 'no.' Bet you can't. All your friends have dates."

"They do?" I look at my friends faces to see if Jimmy is lying, he's not. Jaylynn and Wanda hang their heads.

"Great, maybe Jaylynn and I can double with you in Rebel's car," Skip says.

Jaylynn stares at her onion rings, not willing to meet my glare.

"Jaylynn, are you really going with Skip? I can't believe this. I suppose next Allen will ask Wanda." I reach for an onion ring.

"Sure, why not?" Allen says. "I was going to call you tonight, Wanda, but might as well ask you now. If your parents will let you go out with a senior, I'd like to take you to the prom?"

"Sure," Wanda replies. "I'll ask my dad. He never tells me 'no.'"

"Order up! Number 57." A tray of food is placed on the counter.

"That's me." Skip leaves to pick up his order.

"Bummer, you all have dates. Where does that leave me?" I take another onion ring.

"Go buy your own onion rings," Jaylynn says.

"I don't have any money."

"All the FAB4 but you have a date. Guess you're stuck going with me, Rebel," Jimmy says. "Let me give you a ring to seal the deal."

"I'm not interested in wearing your class ring or anyone's."

"Hey Skip, buy me an order of onion rings," Jimmy shouts. "I need a ring for Red."

Minutes later I sport a crispy onion ring on my index finger which I nibbled off.

Sheesh! I'm actually going to the Junior Prom with Jimmy. Wait until the news reaches Marlene, Darla Jo, and Tricia. Despite my dislike of Jimmy, he's a hunk. Those girls have been throwing themselves at Jimmy for years. He's always polite but has no interest in them which has made them lose their cool on more than one occasion. Tomorrow when the news that Jimmy is taking me to the prom hits the rumor mill, I plan to tell Marlene, Darla Jo, and Tricia Tissues, "Eat your hearts out."

* * *

For Prom Mother makes me a lime green, floor length sleeveless cotton sheath with a slit up the left side, just to my knee. Nothing racy. I ask to have my white leather pumps that I've worn to church for the last two years dyed to match my dress, which many of the girls are doing, but Mother says, "That's too expensive, plus no one will see your shoes." The dress has a scooped neckline. Mother offers me her pearls again, but I want something flashy to wear.

The FAB4 stage a private modeling of our gowns at Jaylynn's house. Jaylynn shoes are dyed to match her heavenly blue halter dress. The top is satin, and the ballerina-length skirt is made of oceans of blue chiffon. We all agree she looks like Marilyn Monroe. Pearl drop earrings and a pearl pendant necklace complete her ensemble. She looks gorgeous. Skip is one lucky guy.

Next Shirley models a brilliant orange dress with cap sleeves. Her dress has a high neckline in front but is low cut in the back. "I bought it at Penney's on sale," she says. "I plan to curl my hair and piled it on top of my head and let it cascade down in ringlets. If my Grandma Birdfoot was here, she'd make me to wear it in two long braids like she does for special occasions."

"Your gorgeous black hair looks great no matter how you style it," I say.

"Yeah, but I'm not sure Prom is the place to be Pocahontas," Jaylynn says.

"Show us your dress Wanda," I say.

As usual, Aunt Bessie spent a fortune on Wanda's dress. She slips into a pink satin, floor-length formal gown with spaghetti straps. "We bought it at a shop in the Plaza in Kansas City." Her shoes are pink, spiked heels with rhinestone shoe clips. Sparkling pink rhinestone earrings and a matching necklace make her look like she's just stepped out of *Seventeen* magazine.

"Stunning," says Shirley.

"We are definitely the FAB4," Wanda declares.

A week before prom we're all ready, except I'm still searching for the right necklace. I check out the costume jewelry in J.C. Penney', J.M. Mc Donalds, Sears, and Woolworth's, but nothing appeals to me except a gorgeous rhinestone necklace in the window of Duitsman Jewelry.

"I don't know what kind of jewelry to wear," I moan to Mother. "Everything in the stores looks cheap, except for a necklace at Duitsman's but it is expensive. Wanda has two jewelry boxes filled with trinkets. I'm going to go check her stash."

"Be home before supper," Mother says. "Remind Bessie the neighborhood ladies are playing pinochle tomorrow at the Randall's. One o'clock in the afternoon."

"Okay." It's a warm Spring day. The sky is deep blue. Crocuses, tulips and iris bloom in several yards. The grass has changed from brown to a minty green in the last few weeks. Soon the lilacs and peonies will be blooming. I climb the steps to Wanda's house and holler through the screen door. "Hello. Hello! Anybody home?"

"Geez, Red, your screaming could wake the dead. I'm trying to take a nap." Uncle Waylon motions for me to come in.

"Sorry. I didn't expect you to be home. I thought you usually hung around the Pink Chicken on Saturday afternoon."

"Not today. Your Aunt Bessie thinks I'm spending too much time there, so I decided to oblige her and stay home. And what does she do? Leaves to run errands. I can't win."

"Is Wanda here? I want to borrow some of her jewelry for the Prom."

"Nope, gone too. Not sure when they'll be back. So, Red, I hear you got yourself a date to the Prom."

"Yes." I have no desire to discuss my dates or lack there of with Uncle Waylon. "I'll come back later. Or better yet, have Wanda call me when she gets home. See you later Uncle Waylon." I walk toward the front door.

"Don't rush off. Sit down. Talk a spell. I don't get to spend time with my favorite niece often."

"You sure are spreading it deep today, Uncle Waylon. Might as well save my watch, the boots are gone?" I hold my hand above my head, indicating that his fake compliments aren't impressing me.

"That ain't no bull. You are my favorite niece. Columbia and Amherst were half grown when we moved to Schoenfeld, and Mouse was a baby. You're my Wanda's age. You two are thicker than thieves. You're like a sister to her. Always have been."

"Hmmph."

"Get me another beer, would you Red? And while you're in there, get yourself a Coke."

If I drink my Coke quickly, I can be out of here in fifteen minutes. I give him a Schlitz, and sit. Uncle Waylon continues yakking. He's in one of his beer-induced reflective moods and talking about being a big shot radio announcer in Chicago. I've heard these stories numerous times. With him two sheets to the wind, and no one else in the house, now is the time for me to ask a few questions.

"What was my mother like when she was my age?" I ask.

"Nothing is worse than being cursed with a mousey little kid as a stepsister."

"What stepsister? What are you talking about?"

"Nothing, I already said too much." He drains his beer and crushes the can between his fists. "Thank God she wasn't a red head." Uncle Waylon's head nods, drowsy from the beer.

"Uncle Waylon, wake up. Like it or not, red hair makes you stand out like a movie star. The Scottish kings all had red hair. Red hair is a mark of distinction."

"Ha! Not in this family," Uncle Waylon slurs. "It's de-stink-shun that's for sure.'

"What do you mean? I'm the only one in this family with red hair."

"Shows how much you know." Waylon pops open the new can of Schlitz.

"So who else had red hair? Huh? Did Aunt Daisy have red hair?"

Uncle Waylon snaps upright in his recliner. "Who told you about her…? I mean where do you come up with such nonsense? I only have one aunt, Aunt Lily, you know that."

"Grandma mentioned a younger sister once, and Mother told me her name was Daisy. I've never seen a picture of her. I thought maybe she had red hair."

Waylon scowls, clenches his teeth and squints. "Your mother is full of hot air. Doesn't know what she's talking about most of the time." He takes a big swig of his beer, belches, then mumbles something about blood being thicker than water, and secrets were just that, secrets "Now, go peddle your papers."

I guzzle my Coke, put the empty bottle in the kitchen and walk toward the door.

"And tell your mother to keep her trap shut,"

I have no intention of telling Mother anything about this conversation. Curiosity is powerful. I know what happened to the cat that indulged its curiosity. I have no desire to rattle Mother's cage, but I want to know about Aunt Daisy. Years of clues flood my mind. Old pictures in Mother's cedar chest, the letter Grandma gave Mother after Grandpa died. Grandma's refusal to see my plays, ugly comments about my red curly hair, and Uncle Waylon's reaction to my questions about Aunt Daisy. He knows something. I'm sure of it. He slipped up when he said, 'who told you about her?' He knows who *her* is.

Waylon is a first-class blabbermouth. He doesn't keep secrets. Only one person could make him keep his mouth shut: Grandma. A stern look or a harsh word from Grandma would make the devil cringe. If Uncle Waylon has been whipped into submission, Grandma is leading the conspiracy and the mystery of Aunt Daisy runs deep, to the very core of our family.

* * *

On the night of the prom, I dress, pull my hair on top of my head, and hold the mass of curls in place with bobby pins. A few tendrils escape framing my face with copper ringlets. I clip on rhinestone earrings I borrowed from Wanda. Within minutes my ear lobes already feel painfully pinched. I'm ready" I walk into the living room. Mouse, Mother, and Daddy are waiting. Daddy with his camera, of course.

"Wow, Rebel," Mouse says. "With your hair up like that you look like a movie star."

"Thanks, Mouse."

"You're right, Rebel. That dress needs a necklace. I think I have just the thing." Mother pulls a slim box from behind her back and hands it to me. Gold script letters on the box spelled Duitsman's Jewelry.

"What is it? What is it? Let me see," Mouse stands by me as I lift the lid from the box. "Wow, diamonds. Are they real?"

"I don't think so, but they look real." I take the ornate rhinestone necklace, the one I'd admired in the jewelry store window from the box. "It's perfect. I can't believe you bought it for me. I love it. Will you fasten it for me, Mother?"

Daddy snaps a picture as Mother places the necklace on me. "I can't get the clasp open." She squints and tilts her head to look through her bifocals. "Okay, now I have it. Stand still."

The necklace feels cool around my throat. When the clasp is hooked, the necklace lays flat and heavy against my skin. "I want to see." I stare at my reflection in the hall mirror. Mouse is right. I look like a movie star.

"Come here and stand still so I can take your picture." Daddy motions toward a blank wall in the living room. The doorbell rings.

"Mouse, answer the door. But wait until I'm in my room. I want to make an entrance." I hurry to my bedroom. The doorbell rings again. I apply lip gloss. Spray White Shoulders perfume on my wrists. My ear lobes are killing me, but that's a small price to pay for beauty.

"Rebel, Jimmy's here," Mother calls.

I walk into the living room and see Jimmy in a dark blue suit, crisp white shirt, and a red and blue striped tie. His blonde hair is drooping over one eye. He holds a box from Snyder's Floral.

"I didn't know what color your dress was, so I bought a white corsage. I hope that's okay. You look nice, Red. Real nice."

"Thanks." I have long since stopped asking him not to call me Red. "Mouse, get the boutonniere out of the refrigerator." Mouse scampers off to the kitchen. I open the box Jimmy hands me. Four huge gardenias are bound together with silver ribbon and a smattering of rhinestones twinkle at me. "Gardenias. They smell wonderful. Here, Jimmy. Pin them on me."

"Uh… no. I'd probably stick you. Will you do it Mrs. Rothberg?"

Mother pins the gardenias on my right shoulder. "That will keep them from being crushed when you're dancing."

"Here's your flower, Jimmy. Can I pin it on you?" Mouse asks.

"Sure kid. But don't stick yourself or me." Jimmy bows his six-foot two frame toward Mouse so she can reach his lapel.

"You ready?" Daddy snaps a photo, and we pose for several more.

"That's enough, Daddy. We'll be late for the Prom."

"What time should I have Rebel home?" Jimmy asks.

"This is a special night. See she's home by midnight," Mother replies.

"Thanks, Mother. See you later, Daddy. Bye Mouse." Jimmy takes my hand and we walk into a night of glittering stars.

His kiss at midnight is not like the one I imagine Prince Charming will give me some day, but it's much better than the sloppy kiss he gave me in grade school.

Chapter 28
Summer: What a Drag

After I finish my junior year, Mother gives me a diary. I do not want to be a slave to the pen this summer, even though I enjoy writing. This year I wrote an essay each week in English class. I toiled over those theme papers and received good grades for my effort, but I have no desire to write compositions this summer.

"Is this an assignment? Something I have to do?" I have big plans this summer. Swimming, attending the county fair, baby sitting, and hanging out with friends, especially Paul who has been calling me lately. I don't want to spend hours every day pouring over a diary.

"No. Just a suggestion. You said you wanted to know yourself better. This is one way to do it."

"What can I learn from writing about my life?"

"You might be surprised. If something upsets you, write about it," Mother says. "If something makes you happy, write about that too. Months later when you reread your diary, your words will help you determine what's important in life and what isn't."

"Okay, thanks." I put the diary on my dresser and prepare to go swimming with the FAB4. I have a modest two-piece suit this summer that is reversible, giving me two suits for the price of one. One side is white with green trim, the other hot pink with green trim. I put the pink side out, pull on a long tee shirt, and slip on my flip flops which are hot pink with a large yellow sunflower on them that covers my toes. I grab a bottle of baby oil with iodine which I mixed, and a bottle of lemon juice. I roll them into my beach towel and hurry toward the back door, as quiet as a mouse, but Mouse hears me. Caught. Rats!

"Where are you going?" She asks.

"Nowhere."

"Why do you have on your swimming suit? Mother! Rebel's going swimming. Can I go?"

"Yes. Rebel, take Mouse with you today," Mother calls.

"Oh Mother, please. She's a child. I'll be a senior in high school this fall. I don't want to babysit a sixth grader at the pool."

"You can take your sister once in a while. It won't kill you," Mother says. "My ladies' group at the church is serving cookies and punch to the residents of Shady Rest Nursing Home this afternoon and then playing games with them. Your father won't be back from Dodge City until tomorrow. You girls are on your own for supper."

"Can we go to Salvador's Pizzeria for supper?" I ask.

"Yeah, can we?" Mouse appears from her room wearing her one-piece suit, purple with a striped ruffled skirt.

"All right." Mother hands me a $5 bill. "Buy a large pizza. That way there should be some left for me to eat when I get home at eight."

"Okay, bye." The screen door snap shut behind us.

"Drive carefully!" Mother calls.

"I will." I receive this instruction every time I leave the house. I've been driving for more than two years and have never had an accident, unlike Columbia who sideswiped a car the day she got her driver's license.

"I'll ride shot gun," Mouse shouts.

"Ankle biters ride in the back seat."

"I'm not a little kid." Mouse does not move from the front seat. "Are you going to put the top down?"

"Not until you get in the backseat." The top remains up as I drive to pick up the FAB4.

Wanda and Jaylynn hop into the back seat. When I stop to pick up Shirley, her younger sister Beth sees Mouse and shouts, "Wait for me! I want to come swimming too." Shirley gets in the back seat while we wait for Beth to gather her gear.

"Put the top down," Wanda and Jaylynn shout. "The sun's out. It's a great day to cruise."

"I told Mouse she had to get in the back seat first."

"No, let her and Beth ride up front," Shirley says. "Put the top down, then Jaylynn, Wanda and I can sit on the back of the car like the Homecoming Queen does in the parade."

"Okay." Minutes later the top is down, the radio blaring, and Jaylynn, Shirley and Wanda are sitting on the folded convertible top waving to people and other cars. Their feet rest on the back seat. Most of the boys our age are working, so we only see a few guys cruisin' the strip.

While making our second pass on Main Street looking for boys, Marty Williams pulls up beside us at a stoplight. He's trouble, and I know it. Marty is four years older than we are. He dropped out of high school his junior year. He smokes and is rumored to drink three-two beer, a low-alcohol beer that eighteen-year olds can buy, with a different girl every weekend. He goes through girlfriends like rain gushing down the down spouts after a cloud burst.

"Wanna drag, Rebel?" Marty pulls a cigarette from his mouth and blows a smoke ring.

Drag racing on Main Street is common late Saturday night, but not during broad daylight. Two Saturday nights a month, Mayor "Buzzy" Wacker, the Chief of Police, Uncle Waylon, and half the police force shoot pool at the Pink Chicken. On those nights, Main Street becomes a four-lane wide drag strip. Any kid with a souped-up car who lives within thirty miles of Schoenfeld has a stripe painted on the curb to mark the precise spot their car reached 60 MPH in the zero to sixty race.

"I don't think so." I stare straight ahead.

"A pretty red-haired girl like you should be hot to trot. You're not chicken, are you?"

"No."

"I've never raced a girl," Marty says. "Winner gets a kiss."

"Do all of us get a kiss if Rebel wins?" Shirley asks.

"Sure. I've got more than enough kisses for all of you." He puckers his lips and makes kissing sounds. "I've got a real juicy one for you, Shirl."

"Same here." Shirley blows him a kiss. "What are you waiting for, Rebel. Do it."

"Go ahead, Rebel. It will be fun," Wanda adds.

"What's a drag race?" Mouse asks.

"Is that your little sister?" Marty revs his engine.

"Yeah, that's Mouse."

"Hey little Mouse, you want to fly down the street like Mighty Mouse? Come over here and get in my car." Marty's engine whines, ready to charge down the street.

"Stay in the car, Mouse!" I feel lightheaded. I know what I should do, but I love a challenge. Racing in broad daylight is foolhardy, but what can happen. Kids do this all the time. It's hot, over 100 degrees, no one is out on the street. Why not?

"The light will be green any second now. You ready to roll?" Marty shifts into first gear.

"Do it, Rebel," Jaylynn says. "It will be fun."

The instant the light turns green, I yell, "Hang on everybody." We shoot down Main Street. At 25 mph, I shift from first to second gear and floor the accelerator. We tear past the Rialto movie theater, Penney's, Sears, and J.M. McDonalds. Marty is half a block ahead of me.

"Faster, "Mouse shouts.

"Yabba Dabba Do!" Beth gives a Flintstone yell.

"Step on it, Rebel. I want that kiss," Shirley screams.

"You get a kiss no matter who wins, you idiot." Jaylynn shakes her head.

"Oh. Yeah, you're right," Shirley says. "Go for it, Rebel."

As I shift into third gear, a stop light half of block away turns amber. Marty zooms through the intersection. "Brace yourself!" I stomp on the brakes. Jaylynn and Shirley fall onto the back seat. Wanda is thrown forward. Her face slams into the back of my seat. I'm pushed into the steering wheel. Mouse and Beth slide to the floor. The tires squeal as I lay a long strip of rubber. We stop in the crosswalk in front of City Hall. A plume of smoke, smelling of burnt rubber settles over us.

"That was fun," Shirley says. "Look, Marty's made a U Turn. He's coming back for his kiss."

"If he wants to kiss me, I'm letting him." Jaylynn takes a comb from her purse and realigns her blonde page boy. "Shirley, don't tell Charlie. Promise?"

"Do you have any lipstick I can use?" Shirley adjusts her swimsuit to show a bit of cleavage.

"He won't want to kiss me, "Wanda says. "I'm a bloody mess."

We all looked at Wanda whose nose is bent at an odd angle and is streaming blood.

"I want Marty to kiss me," Mouse says. "He's dreamy."

"Me too," adds Beth. "I bet he's a hood."

"Must be," Mouse replies. "Only hoods have greasy hair and cigarettes in their shirt sleeve.

"Mouse, you will do no such thing." I pull her off the floor of the car and search the glove box, I hand Wanda a wad of DQ napkins. "Here, see if this will stop the bleeding."

"You're too young to be kissed by a man," Shirley tells Beth.

"If I don't get a kiss," Beth says, "I'm telling Mom that you kissed a guy in public."

Marty pulls to a stop beside me. "You ladies all right?"

"We'll survive." I adjust my sunglasses.

"Who wants to be first?" Marty swaggers toward the car. His jeans hang low on his hips. His black tee shirt is stretched tightly over his chest. A sliver chain hangs from a belt loop to his billfold in his back pocket. He flicks a cigarette butt onto the street and grinds it out with the toe of his boot.

"Not me," I say. "You can skip me. I'm going steady with Paul."

"I don't see a ring," Marty says.

"Not that it's any of your business, our class rings haven't arrived yet. And I don't need a ring. We trust each other."

"Trust doesn't keep you warm at night. I'll catch you on the flip side," Marty says. "Come here Blondie, you too Shirl."

While Wanda pushes bits of paper napkins up her nose, Jaylynn and Shirley get out of the Bel Air and lean against the hood. Marty pulls Jaylynn to him and plants his lips on hers. Jaylynn's arms hang limply at her side as he continues to kiss her. Finally, he releases her. "Now you've been kissed by a real man." Jaylynn falls back against the hood of the car and sighs.

Next Marty grabs Shirley tilts her backwards onto the hood of the car and holds her there in a long embrace. When he tries to pull away, Shirley's slides her arms around his neck keeping him locked in their embrace.

"I've never seen anybody kiss like this," Mouse says. "Not even Columbia and Bobby."

"Wait until Mom hears about this," Beth says. "Shirley will be grounded until Christmas."

Finally, the lip-locked pair separate. "You'll keep your mouth shut, pipsqueak if you know what's good for you." Shirley glares at Beth.

I want a kiss," Mouse says.

"Sure kid." Marty blows kisses to Mouse and Beth. "Look me up when you're legal."

"Are we going swimming or not?" A horn honks behind us. "I have to go. The light is green. We're blocking traffic." Jaylynn and

Shirley hurry into the car. I proceed slowly and carefully through the intersection, thankful that my racing has caused no more damage than a bloody nose.

* * *

Beth and Mouse are happy to play in the pool and leave the FAB4 alone. We spread our towels on lounge chairs, slather on baby oil and iodine, and slip on sunglasses so we can stealthily check out who is doing what and with whom.

"Do you think Marty will ask me out?" Shirley pulls her black straight hair into a ponytail and fastens it with a rubber band.

"No guy has ever kissed me like that," Jaylynn says. "Marty's kiss made my knees weak."

"I brought lemon juice," I say. Rumor has it that lemon juice applied to your hair while you're in the sun will lighten its color. I'm hoping to change my hair from copper to strawberry blond.

"Where does Marty work? Maybe we could swing by there on the way home," Shirley says.

"No way! I'm staying as far away from him as I can. He's nothing but trouble, Shirley. You get involved with him and you'll be PG before you're a senior," I say.

"You can't get pregnant the first time you do it," Shirley says.

"Who told you that?" I unscrew the lid of the lemon juice bottle.

"I overheard Marlene talking to Darla Jo at the DQ the other day. She said, 'you never get PG the first time you do it'."

"And you believe what Marlene says?" Jaylynn shakes her head. "How dumb can you get?"

"Two of Marlene's friends got married last year and had babies a few months later. They both swore they had only done it once. How do you explain that?" I comb lemon juice through my curls.

"I'm not planning on going all the way, but —"

"Not planning is what gets people in trouble. I never planned to drag race today, but I did. It was stupid. Nothing bad happened, but if Mother finds out, I won't be driving anywhere except to church the rest of this summer."

"Shirley, you can't be a little bit PG," Jaylynn says. "I wouldn't test Marlene's advice."

"I said I wasn't planning on doing it," Shirley snaps.

"Yeah, but Marty might be," Wanda says.

"He probably won't call anyway." Shirley hands the bottle of baby oil and iodine to Jaylynn.

"Here put some of this on my back.

"I hope he doesn't call." I massage more lemon juice into my red curls.

"Do you think that will work?" Wanda says.

"I don't know, but I'm going to give it a try."

"I don't think blondes have more fun," Jaylynn says. "I'm blonde and I haven't had a date for weeks."

Steve and Jaylynn drifted apart last spring. She sees Charlie, Shirley's older brother when he is home from college, which is not often. Wanda occasionally dates Skip Prescott. Shirley has an on again, off again relationship with Jeff, who was on the debate team with her last year. I'm lucky. I have Paul. He is steady and reliable now having sown his wild oats with Marlene a year ago.

"Boys are jerks," Shirley says. "Especially high school boys. I want a more mature man."

"Like Marty. He's a hood," Wanda says. "Rebel's right, he's trouble."

"Is your brother Charlie home from college this summer?" Jaylynn asks.

"Yeah," Shirley says. "He asked about you. Shall I tell him you're available?"

"Sure, but don't make it sound like I can't get a date," Jaylynn replies.

"What do you think? Is my hair any lighter?" I ask.

"Who told you lemon juice would lighten your hair?" Shirley asks.

"Marlene told Darla Jo, and Darla Jo told me. 'If you put lemon juice or peroxide on your hair and sit outside in the sun for a few hours you'll be changed into a Sandra Dee look alike.'"

"And now you believe what Marlene says?" Jaylynn shakes her head. "I can't believe what I'm hearing."

"Isn't she the girl that stole Paul from you?" Wanda asks.

"You told me not to believe Marlene about getting PG, and now you believe what she said about bleaching hair," Shirley says. "This makes no sense. You're crazy with the heat."

"Well, I think it's true. I saw Darla Jo last week and her hair looked just like Sandra Dee's."

"Did you check the roots?" Jaylynn says.

"It's a dye job for sure," Wanda adds. "I can tell. It's professionally done."

"How can you tell that?" I ask.

"Because it's too perfect. Normal hair has various colors and highlights. Darla Jo's hair is all one color, just like my dad's is after he comes home from the barber shop," Wanda says.

"Uncle Waylon dyes his hair?" I gasp at this revelation.

"I've never heard of a man dying his hair," Jaylynn says.

"Me either," adds Shirley.

"His hair would be totally gray if he didn't," Wanda says. "Dad says radio personalities and politicians need to look young and virile."

"I wonder what Grandma would say if she knew Uncle Waylon dyes his hair," I mumble.

"Nothing." Wanda shrugs. "Waylon's Grandma's favorite son. He can do no wrong."

You got that right, I think.

"I'd try peroxide if I were you," Wanda says.

"I'd accept I was a red head," Shirley adds. "It's unique."

"That's easy for you to say. You all have gorgeous hair. Long and thick. Full of body. You can wear your hair in lots of styles. In a French roll, a duck tail, a page boy. I can't do anything with my hair. It is an unruly red mop."

"Clairol should be sued for making people believe blondes have more fun," Jaylynn whines. "I'm living proof it's a lie."

"The ad doesn't say 'blondes have more fun,' it just asks, 'Is it true blondes have more fun?'" Shirley says.

"Same difference," Jaylynn snarls.

Wanda's bloody nose is no longer bleeding, but as the afternoon wears on a purple crescent forms under each eye. No amount of makeup will cover those bruises. Someone, be it Aunt Bessie, Uncle Waylon, Mother, or heaven forbid Grandma will see them and then like Desi says to Lucy on *I love Lucy*, 'you have some 'splainin' to do.'

Wanda keeps her head down when we stop at Salvador's for pizza. Her black eyes make me a marked woman. I don't enjoy my pizza knowing the wrath of God waits for me.

* * *

I take Shirley, Beth, and Jaylynn home first. "Good luck," they holler as I drive away.

At Wanda's house I see Uncle Waylon through the picture window reading the newspaper. "Mouse, stay in the car," I say.

"Fine with me. Wild horses couldn't make me go in there. Aunt Bessie will have a fit when she sees Wanda's face all smashed up," Mouse says.

"It's not smashed. Just bruised a little," I snap.

Wanda and I climb the steps to their front door. "Here goes nothing." Wanda pulls open the screen door. "Hi Dad." She rushes past him toward her bedroom.

"Not so fast young lady. Come back here," Uncle Waylon says.

Wanda stops dead in her tracks.

"Hi, Uncle Waylon. Is Aunt Bessie here?"

"No, she's at a prayer meeting. Trying to save heathen souls in Africa. Guess she's given up on me." Uncle Waylon chuckles.

"That's a lost cause," I mumble. "I'd stay and chat, but Mouse is waiting in the car. I need to go." I back toward the front door.

"Hold your horses, Red. You're not going anywhere. Come over here and sit down on the couch where I can see you. You too, Wanda." Uncle Waylon jerks his recliner into its upright position. "So, what's your story?"

"Story? I don't know what you're talking about." Wanda keeps her head bowed.

"What did you do today?" Uncle Waylon asks.

"We went swimming this afternoon and stopped at Salvador's for pizza on the way home," I say. "Nothing special. Got pepperoni as usual."

"Wanda, look at me," Uncle Waylon says. "Red, how did Wanda get those shiners? And watch what you say. I already know what happened."

"If you already know, why are you asking?" I ask.

"Don't get lippy with me, Red."

"I'm sorry Uncle Waylon."

"I'm fine, Daddy. Really, it's nothing," Wanda says.

"Maybe so, but you could have all been killed. Red, I thought you had more sense than to drag down Main Street in broad daylight." He glares at me.

I hang my head, ashamed. "I'm sorry Uncle Waylon. It was really stupid."

"Hmmph."

"How did you know, Daddy?" Wanda asks.

"I know everybody in this town. Can't be in politics without keeping your nose in everybody's business. Remember, I own KDOG. We have a nose for news. I wouldn't be serving the public's interest if I didn't keep abreast of what's happening in Schoenfeld. I have informers everywhere." He pauses to guzzle his beer. "Mayor Wacker called me. Said he saw you dragging with Marty Williams. He promised he wouldn't have the police arrest you, Red, if I could talk some sense into you."

My tongue cleaves to the roof of my mouth. Arrested? Silence fills the room and lingers for what seems an eternity. In these few seconds I imagine Uncle Waylon telling Mother, who would tell Daddy, and when Grandma caught wind of what happened, and I'd be confined to my quarters for the entire summer. I'm in deep do-do.

Uncle Waylon leans toward me. "Listen to me Red, and listen good, you hear?" I nod, waiting for the tongue lashing to start. "Red, the start of a drag race is the most important part. You need to rev your engine until it hits the sweet spot, about 5000 rpms. When the light turns green, drop the clutch. When you've gone about 100 feet, bury the throttle and shift into second. You need to know what you're doing before you take on more challengers. But there's never going to be next time, is there, Red?"

"No, Uncle Waylon." I sigh with relief.

"Okay. Wanda, you get some ice on that face ASAP. Red, I'll tell Bessie you had to slam on the brakes to avoid hitting old man Market's dog, Vermin. She's partial to dogs, so she won't question that. Neither will your mother. Since she and Bessie don't drive, they won't think to ask how fast you were driving. As for your dad, I'll think of something. Red, you two stick to this story and tell your friends to do the same."

"Yes, Daddy," Wanda says. "I fell off the seat and hit my face because Rebel had to stop fast so she wouldn't kill Vermin."

"Poor old Vermin. I would hate to kill him," I say. "He's such a sweet dog."

"Don't embellish this little lie, Red. You do that, it will backfire, and you'll get caught. You have to keep your lies simple," Uncle Waylon says. "I ought to know. I've told plenty of them."

I want to ask Uncle Waylon about his lies and the secrets in our family, but now is not the time. Will the time ever be right to find out about Aunt Daisy? "Yes, Uncle Waylon," I mumble.

"Apply the old KISS principle," Uncle Waylon adds. "Keep It Simple Stupid. Now go home and behave yourself, Red. I can't keep bailing you out of trouble. I've got enough of my own. And Wanda, get an ice bag and go to your room."

"Thanks Uncle Waylon. You're the best." I give him a hug.

"Yeah, yeah. I'm the best when you need me, and the worst when you don't. Now get of here, Red. Wait, bring me a beer before you go."

I oblige him and hurry out the door. "Mouse, if you blab, I'll get grounded, and you'll be stuck in the house all summer." Mouse understands the need for our little white lie. Hmmm. Is a simple white lie how a family secret begins?

* * *

The white lie saves me, but the lemon juice is a flop. I opt for peroxide the following week. Every day I inspect my hair, and not so much as one strand is a shade lighter. Certain that my social life is stunted because I'm a red head, I beg Mother to let me bleach my hair. My best argument is 'Uncle Waylon dyes his hair,' which is no surprise to her. My hair remains red.

The next week our class rings arrive. I'm hoping that I'll soon sport Paul's ring, which has a dazzling green stone in it, on my finger or on a chain around my neck.

On Friday Marty calls Shirley, but she refuses his offer to go to the drive-in. Obviously, she has more sense when it comes to boys than I do. The next Saturday none of us have dates. The FAB4 goes to the Rialto Theater to see *The Birds*. Scary! Darla Jo, the blonde bombshell, struts past us wearing a boy's class ring on a chain around her neck. I recognized the ring. Yep, the rat fink Paul has dumped me again. I swear I'll never speak to him again until hell freezes over and all the little devils go ice skating, and maybe not even then!

Chapter 29
Senior Moments

Now a senior in high school, my studies keep me occupied several hours each night, so I only have time to visit Grandma on weekends. I never go to her apartment without wishing Grandpa was alive, and we could play a game of cribbage. Grandma refuses to play cribbage, but she enjoys Scrabble.

"Your mother tells me you're acting in another theater production." Grandma opens the Scrabble game that lays on the table between us.

My eyes widen in surprise. Grandma never mentions my acting, except to berate it. "Yes. The drama teacher planned to do *Gypsy*. It's a new musical on Broadway." I pull a wooden letter tile from an old white sock which holds the Scrabble tiles. "Aha, I got an 'A.' Looks like I'll play first." I draw six more tiles from the sock.

"*Gypsy*! My goodness girl, do you know what that play is about?" Grandma shoves her hand in the sock.

"Not really, but it has some cool songs in it." I rearrange the letters on my wooden trough.

"*Gypsy* is about Gypsy Rose Lee, a stage performer. She was in burlesque years ago. Men flocked to her show. Men like those sorts of things. Decent folks don't."

"What sort of things, Grandma?" I'm having no luck combining my seven letters into a word.

"Male entertainment." Grandma clears her throat. "Some men enjoy watching cheap women on the stage, but gentlemen don't."

"You mean she was a stripper?" At last, I have a word to play.

"Yes. She called herself an exotic dancer, but she was nothing but a cheap floozy."

"Well, the school couldn't afford the royalties on *Gypsy*, so we're doing *Auntie Mame*. I have the lead." I place P-U-R-S-E on the star in the middle of the board. "Twenty points. Opening night is Thursday. We have three evening performances and one matinee. I wish you'd come."

"I can assure you that won't be happening. I don't care if other parents let their children travel the road to perdition, but your mother should be ashamed of herself permitting you to be on the stage."

"It's good clean fun, Grandma." I draw five letters from the sock. "I like pretending to be someone else and wearing costumes. *Auntie Mame* is set in the 1940s. My costumes remind me of dresses you're wearing in old family pictures."

"Instead of prancing about on-stage letting people gawk at you, you should cultivate good manners." Grandma attaches her word, S-A-N-E onto my word to earn thirteen points.

"What's wrong with my manners?" I bite my tongue. A comment like this is begging for a lecture. I connect my next word to her N. "N-O-B-L-E. Twelve points."

"Your manners are —" Grandma spelled L-I-N-K using my L. "Sixteen points. Your manners are fine," she pauses. "Most of the time."

I knew there would be a qualifying remark. "This is the last week of rehearsals. After the performances are over, I'll miss spending time with the cast members. We've had a lot of fun together." I rearrange my tiles trying to form a word. "I have terrible letters. Only one vowel."

"Take your time but hurry up." Grandma chuckles.

"All right. Here. K-E-Y. A whopping twenty points. Pretty good for a lousy play." I draw two letters from the sock. "You know what I like best about being in a play, Grandma?"

"When it's over, I should hope!"

"Well, yeah, sort of. The practices are grueling."

"Rebel, don't say 'yeah', it's 'yes.' You sound like a donkey braying. Tell me, what's so wonderful about being on the stage."

"The applause. I love the applause."

Grandma gasps and taps her finger arthritic fingers on the table. "Rebel, respecting your elders, obeying your parents, and living a circumspect life will merit you far more in life than the applause of strangers."

"But I like the applause."

"I told your mother letting you go on the stage was a big mistake, and I'm right. You're not doing this theater stuff when you go to college are you? You're still planning to go to college, aren't you?"

"This is my last play. And yes, I'm going to college. Mother and Daddy would go ballistic if I didn't."

"Well, I should think so. What do you plan to study?"

"I'm not sure. English maybe. I'd like to write plays."

"The saints preserve us."

We play in silence for several minutes. "The score is 218 to 246. In your favor, Grandma." I reach into the sock. "I just took the last four tiles."

"I have a headache, Rebel." Grandma stands. "I'm going to get an aspirin."

"I'll do it, Grandma. It's your turn to play."

"Thank you, but I'll get it. The aspirin bottle is in my dresser. I don't want you rooting around in my things." She hobbles toward the bedroom leaning heavily on her cane. "Aaaargh." A thud follows her anguished cry.

"Grandma! Are you okay?" I rush to her bedroom. She lies in a crumpled heap. "Are you all right? What should I do? Let me help you up."

"No! No! Ooooo," she moans. "My hip. I think I broke my hip."

"Don't move. I'll call Mother. No, I'll call the ambulance. No, I'll do both." My hands shake as I dial home and then for an ambulance. Within minutes Mother and Daddy are beside me and shortly thereafter we hear the wail of an ambulance siren.

After Grandma is whisked away in the ambulance, Mother, Daddy, and I hurry across the alley to our home. "Rebel, stay here with Mouse. Your father and I will go to the hospital. I'll call you later. There's leftover pot roast in the refrigerator for supper." They leave. I'm numb.

Several hours later, Mouse and I have eaten and are watching TV. "What's taking them so long at the hospital?" Mouse asks.

"I don't know. I thought Mother would have called by now to let us know what's happening." My words are prophetic. The phone rings.

"I'll get it." Mouse runs toward the house phone.

"No. Let me. I'm in charge here." I snatch the receiver from her hand. "Hello. Thank God. Uh-huh. Sure. Anything else? Okay. I'll do it." I replace the heavy black telephone receiver in its cradle on the phone base.

"Well, what's happened?" Mouse asks.

"Grandma's hip is broken. The doctor will set it tomorrow. She'll have to be in the hospital for a few days, and then she'll probably go to a nursing home for a few weeks. Mother wants me to bring some personal items for Grandma to the hospital." I walk toward the back door and remove Grandma's spare key from the windowsill. "Stay here. I'll be back in a few minutes."

"I want to come. I don't want to stay here alone. It's dark."

"All right, Mouse. Hurry up. Let's go."

I flip on our back porch light which does little to illuminate the moonless night. As we cross the alley, the streetlight in front of Grandma's apartment building casts skeletal shadows of trees across her yard. They reach like spiny fingers toward us. I fumble for the lock, insert the key and the door creaks open. I flip on the lights.

"Okay Mouse, you go to the bathroom and get her comb, toothbrush and toothpaste, and I'll search her dresser for nightgowns and underwear. We need to get her robe and slippers too." I pull open the top drawer. Lavender sachet engulfs me. The drawer holds handkerchiefs, gloves, and scarves. The second drawer contains her corset, a formidable item made of whalebone, heavy cloth, and elastic. Beneath it are hose, socks, and underwear. I grab four pairs of socks and several changes of underwear. The bottom drawer contains a variety of floral nightgowns trimmed with lace and small buttons at the neck. I pull out one and hang it over my arm. As I pull out another, a bundle of letters tied with grocery twine falls to the floor.

I stoop to pick them up. The envelopes are light blue, tissue paper thin, with red and blue chevrons around the edges. Air mail letters. I turn over the packet to look at the address. There is a small sunflower in the upper left-hand corner.

"Here's the stuff you wanted," Mouse says. "What's wrong, Rebel? You look funny. Are you sick?"

Mouse kneels beside me where I now sit. "These letters. They're all addressed to Miss Bonnie Rose Jacobs in care of Mrs. Michael Cassidy."

Big deal," Mouse says. "Put them back."

"I think these letters were written to Mother and Grandma never gave them to her."

"Let me see." Mouse takes the packet from my outstretched hand. "Mrs. Michael Cassidy, that's Grandma, but Mother's maiden name wasn't Jacobs. These letters are for somebody else. Put them back."

"No, Bonnie Rose Jacobs must be Mother. What's the chance of two women named Bonnie Rose living with Grandma?"

"I don't know." Mouse shrugs. "What difference does it make? Put them back. Let's go."

The memory of the letter Grandma gave Mother years ago after Grandpa died and addressed to Bonnie Jacobs had upset Mother. That letter must have been important because she stored it in her cedar chest. "I can't explain it, but I know these letters were sent to Mother and Grandma hid them from her."

"Why would she do that?" Mouse asks.

"Beats me. Grandma's weird sometimes." I check the postmark. March1964. Three weeks ago. The return address is hard to read. D.S. Jacobs, Vernon, France. I untie the string. Dozens of letters all addressed to Bonnie Rose Jacobs and mailed during the past twenty years fall to the floor. A few have been opened, but most are still sealed.

"This one is from someone in France. I'm going to give them to Mother." I gather the letters and retie the sting.

"I think you should put them back in the drawer. You know how Grandma feels about people who mess in her personal things." Mouse backs away from the letters as if they are toxic.

"What Grandma doesn't know won't hurt her." I find a paper bag in the kitchen and put the nightgowns and underwear in it. "Here." I extend the bag to Mouse who adds the toiletries she's gathered.

"I don't know why Grandma hid these letters, but they're addressed to Mother, so she should have them. I'm taking them to the hospital."

"I'm coming too. I'm not staying home alone when it's dark."

Daddy meets us in the hospital lobby. "Your Grandma is in room 125. Down the hall and to the left. Rebel, you handled the crisis well today. You stayed calm. That's what's important in an emergency." I smile my thanks. "Take that stuff to her room and then we'll all go home."

"Are you going to give Mother the let —?" Mouse asks.

"Later, Mouse. Later." I hurry down the hall with the grocery bag. Maybe I have ESP like Grandma says I do, because I know finding those letters is going to cause a bigger uproar than a Kansas tornado.

Chapter 30
Discoveries

Auntie Mame is a great success. Mame is the type of free spirit I want to be. She's a larger-than-life character who always makes an entrance. In one scene, Mame is leaving for a nightclub. I wore a gold lame gown, held a cigarette in a long black holder, and grab a flamboyant evening wrap as I exit the stage. The cigarette was fake, the dress bought at a secondhand shop, but the jacket was that hideous puce coat with the fake fur collar Mrs. Arpkey gave me three years ago. The collar is still scratchy. That monstrosity was perfect for Mame, but not for me. I donate it to the costume department. Good riddance.

I drive home after the cast party having a mental debate about what to do with the unopened letters hidden in my dresser. I shouldn't have taken them. That was wrong. Grandma hid them for a reason. So, if I put them back, no one would be the wiser, except for Mouse, and I could bribe her to keep quiet. Yep, that's the smart thing to do, but not giving them to Mother seems wrong. In math two negatives make a positive. Maybe two wrongs, my taking the letters and then giving them to Mother, will make a right.

At home I retrieve the letters from my dresser. Mother and Daddy are busy working the Sunday crossword puzzle in the living room. Mouse is watching the The Wonderful World of Disney.

"Mother," I say, "please don't get mad at me, but I took something from Grandma's house. I think you ought to have them."

Mother shakes her head. "Rebel, when you start a conversation like this, I know you've been up to no good, and I'll have to smooth out another mess with your grandma. What did you take? Let me see it."

I thrust the packet of letters into her waiting hand. "I found them hidden under her nightgowns. I only took them because they were addressed to you. Most of them haven't even been opened. I didn't read any of them. I thought you should have them. You've never mentioned anyone in France. Who is D. S. Jacobs? Who wrote you all these letters?"

Daddy drops the newspaper and his pencil. He puts his arm around Mother's shoulder as she clutches the letters to her chest. Tears stream down her face. She makes no attempt to wipe them away. "It's all right Bunny. It's okay. I'm here. It's okay. Calm down."

"D. S. Jacobs is Daisy Sunflower Jacobs," Mother sputters. She pulls the top letter from the stack and hands it to Daddy. "Open it. I'm too nervous. I'd probably tear it to shreds. What does she say? Read it to me, please."

I frown. "Daisy? Is she the Aunt Daisy no one ever talks about in this family?"

Mother nods 'yes.'

"Why are you crying, Mother?" Mouse forgets the Disney movie and joins Mother on the couch.

Daddy uses his pocketknife to slit open the airmail envelope which opens into a flat piece of paper. A small photo is included. He smoothes the creases to make the letter flat.

"Don't cry, Mother. I love you." Mouse snuggles against Mother.

"You told me several years ago you hardly knew Aunt Daisy. Why are you so upset about her writing you?" I ask.

"It's a long story, Rebel." Mother says.

"I'm all ears. Tell me." I pick at my nails impatient to hear this gut-wrenching secret.

Mother sighs. I'm afraid she'll say, 'you're too young to understand,' but she says, "Daisy LaFleur was the younger sister of your great-aunt Lily and your Grandma Rose. The trouble started years ago, long before I was born. Daisy wanted her parents, your great grandparents, to give her money so she could pursue her dream and they refused."

"What did she want to do?" I pull the footstool near the couch and sit. If Mother is finally going to talk about Aunt Daisy, I plan to know all the details, not a whitewashed version of the truth.

"She wanted to go to Paris and dance," Mother says.

"What's wrong with being a ballerina?" Mouse asks.

"Nothing," Mother replies.

"I always wanted to be a ballerina, but you said Grandma would have a fit."

"Your grandmother has a fit just thinking about dancing," Daddy says.

"Daisy didn't want to be a ballerina," Mother says. "She dreamed of dancing the Can-Can at the Moulin Rouge. Very risqué. Ladies did not do such things in the 1890's."

"Nah nah, nah na nah na," Mouse hums.

"Oh my gosh. That's why Grandma doesn't like dancing. Did Aunt Daisy go to Paris?" I ask.

"Maybe. These letters are from France. I don't know much about Daisy, only what little bit your grandma told me years ago."

"What did Grandma tell you?"

Mother's eyes become glassy as she remembers past events. After several minutes, which seem like an eternity to me, she says, "When Daisy's parents refused to give her any money, Daisy ran away to Chicago. There she became a famous… uh notorious would be a better word. She became an exotic dancer."

"You mean she was a stripper?" I'm sure my eyes are as large as saucers.

"You mean she took off all her clothes?" Mouse asks. "On the stage in front of God and everybody? I couldn't do that."

"I should hope not," Mother says. "When the local barbershop in Francisville displayed a poster of 'Dashing Daisy Sunflower', who wasn't wearing enough clothes to flag a train, her distinguished family was appalled."

"I bet Grandma and Aunt Lily were fit to be tied." I smile, imagining my prim Grandma having a stripper for a sister. "That's why Grandma hated my plays, isn't it? So, Daisy was on stage, a stripper. Big deal. Is this why no one mentions her name?"

"That's part of it. I was told that whenever Daisy came home to Francisville, she begged her parents for money to go to Eurpoe. Your great-grandfather said, 'I've no intention of giving money to Daisy so she can embarrass me on two continents.' Daisy was stubborn, much like you, Rebel. She vowed to go to Paris by hook or by crook. The next day she heard about a family who needed a burial plot but couldn't afford one. Daisy stole the LaFleur cemetery deed from her father's desk. Two days later that family owned the LaFleur burial plot and Daisy had the money to sail to Paris."

"Did she go to Paris?" Mouse asks. "And dance naked?"

I do a pirouette. "I knew dancing was in my soul. Aunt Daisy danced at the Moulin Rouge. Hot dang!"

"You two, calm down. Let your mother tell her story," Daddy said. "Go on Bonnie."

"By the time I was old enough to ask questions, your Grandma

Rose and Aunt Lily rarely spoke of Daisy. They told me Daisy boarded a train for New York, but for some unknown reason she got off in Louisville, Kentucky and went to the Kentucky Derby. There she met a jockey who sweet-talked her into betting all her money on a nag he was riding. He assured Daisy the horse was a winner, and she'd triple her money."

"Did it win?" I ask.

"No. Finished dead last," Mother replies.

"She lost all of her money?" Mouse asks. Mother nods.

"What a rotten deal. Poor Daisy," I moan. "What happened to her?"

"She eloped with the jockey," Mother says.

"Really? Do you know his name?" I ask.

Mother clears her throat. "Bunson Jacobs." Her stomach rumbles. "I need something to drink. My stomach feels queasy. All this talking has made my throat dry."

"I'll get it." I run toward the kitchen. "Don't say anything until I get back." Seconds later I return with a glass of ice and a bottle of 7-up.

"Thanks, Rebel. And thank you for giving me these letters. Grandma will read both of us the riot act when she finds out, but you did the right thing. Now, go get that large manila envelope from my cedar chest, please."

My knees shake as I walk into my parent's bedroom. The cedar chest sits in a corner under a window. I walk slowly, as if approaching the Holy of Holies. I've never opened Mother's cedar chest. Doing so would violate her privacy and get me in a heap of trouble. But today she is allowing me to enter her inner sanctum. I reverently lift the lid. The familiar cedar aroma wafts into the room. A brown-checked dress with a velvet collar lays across the contents like a pall. I set it aside and remove the manila envelope. "Do you want anything else?"

"Yes, that old brown dress."

I close the lid and bring the items to Mother. She puts the dress on her lap and searches the envelop for a photo. "Do you remember this?" She brushes her fingers over a sepia-toned photo as if caressing the people in it.

"Let me see." I look at the photo. "Yes. I found this on the floor when I was about ten." I stare at the photo. A lady, who I now know is

Aunt Daisy, sits on an ornate bench. Her hair is a tangled mess of curls. Beside her stands her jockey husband, Bunson Jacobs. On Aunt Daisy's lap is a smiling child in a checkered dress.

"That's me and my parents, Daisy and Bunson Jacobs." Mother sighs. "It's the only photo I have of us together."

The clock on the mantle ticks. The refrigerator hums to life in the kitchen. The TV drones in the background, an Alka Selzer ad. My mind stumbles, unable to understand the words Mother has just spoken. My chest tightens. I will myself to breathe. Questions, hundreds of them, swirl in my head, but my tongue clings to the roof of my mouth unable to form words.

"Rebel, didn't you ever wonder about my nickname, Bunny?" Mother asks.

I shake my head sideways, then up and down. Yes. No. I shrug my shoulders.

"My father, Bunson Jacobs, was called 'Bunny' for most of his horse-riding career," Mother says. "He was a well-known jockey before I was born."

"That's you when you were little?" Mouse stares at the photo.

"Yes," Mother replies. "Daisy had hair that was red and curly like yours, Rebel."

"So that's why Grandma hates my red hair. It reminds her of the sister the family disowned?"

"That's part of it, I suppose," Mother replies.

"Wait a minute. If Daisy and Bunson are your parents, why didn't you live with them? Why do you call Grandma Rose your mother? Does this mean Grandma isn't my… grandma? And the Grandpa I loved really wasn't my grandpa? Is Uncle Waylon really your brother? Did Grandma and Grandpa adopt you? Who am I? Am I adopted?" Once my tongue moves, I can't stop it.

"You're my real daughter, just as Columbia, Amherst and Mouse are. Michael and Rose Cassidy, who you call Grandma and Grandpa, are your grandparents in spirit, but biologically they are your great-aunt and uncle. Uncle Waylon is my cousin."

I don't understand. Why didn't you live with your parents?"

"My parents were free spirits, much like you are," Mother says. "Your grandpa told me they moved from one small racetrack to another.

Bunson didn't win often after he and Daisy married. They didn't have much money. As an infant, I traveled with them. When I was about three, my parents and I visited Francisville. I remember it vaguely. We stayed with Michael and Rose Cassidy. In the middle of the night Daisy and Bunson skipped town on the midnight train."

"They just left you there! Did they tell you good-bye?" I ask.

"No." Mother sniffs away her tears.

"And you never saw them again?" This story is as unbelievable as those on the *Twilight Zone*.

"No. I'm sure that's when your grandma decided to never speak about Daisy again."

"So, Daisy is your real mother. That's why Grandma never gave you these letters isn't it? She's never forgiven Daisy for leaving you with her to raise."

"You're a good mother," Mouse says. "You aren't going to leave me, are you?"

"No way." Mother hugs Mouse.

"This brown dress is all I have from my life with my biological parents," Mother says. "I was wearing it the day they left."

I turn away, feeling like an intruder as she clutches the dress to her chest. The memory of the sad little girl in the brown checked dress standing beside thirteen-year-old Waylon now makes sense. Mother was a frightened lonely child, abandoned. Left with family members who didn't want her. Or at least Grandma didn't want her.

This explains Waylon's behavior toward Mother and me, and Grandma's unkind comments just because I remind her of Daisy. Anger and lies fueled years of deception and unforgiving hearts.

"Daisy hasn't changed much," Daddy says as he hands Mother the photo from the air mail letter.

"Let me see." Mother, Mouse and I hover over a small color photo of a short woman with copper-colored, curly hair standing in a field of sunflowers.

"Rebel looks like her," Mouse says. "I think Daisy loves yellow like you do too."

We are all silent, lost in our thoughts. Then Daddy says, "Bonnie, do you want me to read this letter?"

"Yes. I'm too nervous. I can't believe she's still alive. I wonder if my

Papa is alive too."

Daddy smoothes the letter again and reads.

"Dear Bonnie,

Happy Birthday. I assume Rose never gives you my letters, as I never hear from you or her. Perhaps you're angry with me too. Every time I send a letter, I pray you will read it, and then you'll know how much Papa and I miss you. I know Rose and Lily are angry with me for what we did, but after all these years, I wish they'd talk to me so I could ask for their forgiveness and yours too. I regret leaving you with Rose and Michael, but it was for your own good. You would not have liked moving from one shack to another at the racetracks.

"Bunson and I finally went to Paris last year. Fifty years late, but at last we got here. We like the French countryside. It reminds me of the Midwest. My namesakes are everywhere: wild daisies and sunflowers. We bought a small cottage in the town of Vernon. We have a small yard where we plant vegetables and flowers.

The home of Claude Monet, a famous artist, is nearby. After peeking through the hedges, I understand why he painted the water lilies the way he did. Perhaps his eyesight was failing, like mine is. The lilies on his pond are gorgeous. I would love to show them to you.

Your Papa can't walk without a cane now since his right leg was broken so many times. He should have quit riding horses years ago, but they were his passion, as dancing was mine.

The only photo I have of you was taken when you were three years old. I have touched your smiling face so often I'm afraid the photo will soon deteriorate. I'd love to see you and your family. I assume you've married and have children of your own by now. Tell Rose and Lily I want to see them too. Please write and tell me about your life. I can't believe my baby girl is almost fifty years old.

"As always, our love to you forever and ever. Mama and Papa."

Daddy hands the letter to Mother. "Do you want me to read another one?"

"Not now. I'll read them later." Mother sighs and runs her thumb along the stack of the letters. "So many letters. She and Papa never forgot me."

Chapter 31
New Beginnings

Two weeks before the Senior Prom, Mother says, "If you're going to the Prom, I need to know sooner rather than later. I'm up to my eyebrows in lavender silk and chiffon sewing bridesmaids' dresses for Columbia's wedding this August, but I'll make time to sew your prom dress."

Columbia became engaged to Bobby Benson the day before she graduated from Bethany College. Yes, it was a boring gradation, but the excitement of her getting a diamond ring, and Amherst being accepted at the University of Nebraska Dental College made the day bearable.

"Senior Prom is a must. I'm going but haven't decided who the lucky guy will be. Paul and I have been dating again for the last couple of months. I hope he'll ask me."

"Paul?" Mother shakes her head. "I see you haven't learned your lesson yet. Maybe you should read what you wrote about him in your diary."

I ignore her comment. "Jimmy asked me last week. I told him I'd let him know."

"Rebel, you must go with Jimmy. He asked you first. Ladies don't string gentlemen along waiting for better invitation. That's rude."

"But I don't want to go with Jimmy." Mother doesn't understand that the Senior Prom is special. I want to go with a boyfriend, not a boy who is a friend. I wrote in my diary that I would never have anything to do with Paul ever again, but when he asked me out this spring, my heart betrayed me, throbbing like it would burst from my chest. Memories of our good times made me say "yes." We aren't going steady, but we're dating regularly, so I hope he'll ask me.

"Jimmy's a nice young man. In church every Sunday. I'm sure you'd have a good time with him."

"Yeah, yeah, yeah." I don't want a good time. I want a special evening. Romance, fun, excitement. After all, this is one of the last times my senior class will all be together. Sheesh. I sound like Columbia and Amherst did as they approached their high school graduation. Now I understand how they felt. They were right. I was too young to understand.

After supper when my teen line rings, I grab it. "Rebel, we're going to the prom together, aren't we?" Paul says.

I'm miffed that he assumes I will jump at the chance to go with him. He hasn't spoken to me since our last date, ten days ago, except to say 'Hi' at school. "Jimmy asked me last week."

"So, are you going with Wonder Boy or me?" Paul asks.

Mother's advice about accepting the first invitation jabs me, piercing my conscience, but this is Senior Prom, not just another Friday night dance at the YMCA. "You, of course." I swear I'm possessed. The words leave my mouth despite my best intentions. I hang up the phone, happy and disgusted with my response.

"Start sewing, Mother," I call from my room. "I'm going to the prom with Paul."

"What about Jimmy? Did you tell him?" Mother comes into my room.

"Not yet. I will. But he'll probably hear about me going with Paul at school anyway."

"As you sow, so shall you reap. If you sow the wind, you'll reap the whirlwind," Mother says. "The prophet Hosea wrote that about 700 BC. Still holds true today."

I call Jimmy. He takes my refusal in stride. "I'll go stag. Save a dance for me, Rebel."

"Sure."

"What are you going to wear?" Jimmy asks.

"Mother said I'm old enough to wear black. She's making a black cocktail dress with a tulip-shaped skirt. It has long sleeves, and the neckline is really low in the back. Why do you care what I'm wearing?"

"I'm always interested in what you are doing, Red."

"Uh, really?"

"Yeah. If you change your mind, call me."

"Don't hold your breath. I have to go. I'm helping Mother move Grandma to Shady Rest Nursing Home after school today. See you around. Bye."

Sheesh. Jimmy never gives up. I feel bad about turning him down, but he doesn't need to moan about going stag. He's one of the most popular guys in our class. Girls flocked to him like bees to sunflowers. Well, not this girl, but most girls would jump at the chance to be his date.

* * *

Mother wrote Daisy the day after I gave her the letters. Airmail letters take at least a week to reach Europe and another week or more to receive a response. She's hoping to hear from her long-lost mom any day now.

"Today's the day," Mother says. "I'm asking your grandma why she never gave me these letters."

"I'll drive you to the nursing home, but I'm waiting in the car. I'll visit Grandma some other time."

"No. I want you with me. We might as well be hung out to dry at the same time."

I drive slowly to Shady Rest Nursing Home, dreading this confrontation. Grandma has a private room. She is seated in a deep blue wingback chair. Her right leg rests on a small footstool. The back of the chair frames her snow-white hair. She looks regal and imposing.

"Hello, Mom." Mother extends the packet of letters. "Rebel found these in your dresser the day you broke your hip. Why didn't you give them to me?"

Grandma turns away from the letters as if they exude radiation. "They were sent to my home. I can do whatever I want with my mail."

"But they were addressed to me," Mother says.

"I didn't need her around to complicate our life." Grandma scowls. "And as for you, Rebel, you shouldn't root around in —"

"I never would have found the letters Grandma if you hadn't broken your hip. I don't think hiding someone's mail is right or legal. Since they were addressed to Mother, I thought she ought to have them."

"Enough! I've heard enough." Grandma stamps the foot of her good leg on the floor. "I don't think, that says it all, Rebel. You're just like Daisy. A troublemaker." She shakes a gnarled finger at me. "You look like her too."

"Stop that, Mom," Mother says. "I won't let you spew your anger on Rebel anymore like you have on both of us for years. Neither of us had anything to do with what happened fifty years ago. It's long past time to forgive and forget."

"Forgive! Why should I? Daisy left you like unclaimed baggage in our house and waltzed off in the middle of the night with that jockey. Without so much as a 'please' or 'thank you' she left me with the responsibility of raising you. I can't forget that."

"I was three-years-old. What was I supposed to do? Hunt them down? Ask them to take me back? Get a job?" Mother's lips twitch with aggravation. Her scowl deepens.

"No, of course not," Grandma says quietly. "After several years Michael, Waylon, and I had adjusted to having you in our family. Everything was going well, and then out of the blue she contacted me. Stirring up trouble, like she always did."

"What did she want?" I ask.

Grandma purses her lips until they disappeared inside her mouth. I figure the conversation is over, but slowly she relaxes her jaw, moistens her lips and says, "I received the first letter from Daisy five years after they took off. You were just eight-years-old. Daisy and her jockey were living in New York City. She wanted me to put you on a train to Grand Central Station. I shoved that letter in my jewelry box. Never showed it to anyone."

"Why didn't you let me go?" Mother asks. "They were my parents."

Grandma stares out the window and then slowly turns toward Mother. "We'd raised you for five years with no contact or help from Daisy or Bunson. You were a child. I couldn't send you across the country alone and I had no desire go with you and make a scene in Grand Central Station. I couldn't bear the idea of them dragging you from pillar to post, never having a home, staying in flea bag hotels and flophouses, associating with racetrack and theater trash." Grandma pauses, seconds tick off the wall clock. When she speaks, her voice is soft and shaky. "I couldn't let you go because… because I loved you."

"You loved me?" Mother's scowl changes to wide-eyed surprise.

For years Mother has never been able to please Grandma, seems to be a thorn in her side, and now Grandma says she loves her. This is strange love, indeed.

"More than you can ever know." Tears stream down Grandma's cheeks. "I couldn't have more children after Waylon was born. Michael and I wanted a daughter, and now we had one. You. Daisy had no right to take you back. She didn't deserve you."

"I always thought you didn't want me." Mother wipes tears off her cheeks. I pull tissues from a box on a nightstand, give one to Mother and Grandma, and take one for myself.

"Your dad and I wanted you very much. Whenever Daisy sent a letter, I became jumpy, crabby, worried. Took it out on you. I feared Daisy might show up in the night, the same way she left and kidnap you. I wanted you to be my little girl," Grandma says.

"I am your little girl." Mother pulls her chair close to Grandma. "I don't remember living with Daisy and Bunson. I was curious about them, because they were never discussed. Seeing them won't change anything. You and Dad are my parents. I love you both. I always have."

"I love you too, Bonnie. I'm sorry I hid my love behind a wall of fear and anger. Can you forgive me?" Grandma sniffs. "Bring me another tissue, Rebel."

I hand her the box of tissues and retreat across the room.

"It's all right, Mom," Mother's says. "This is all history, ancient history. Isn't it time you forgave Daisy too?"

"Maybe. I don't know if I can." Grandma sniffs in a very unladylike fashion, a noise like air being sucked through a straw when your soda is gone. "Daisy was a wild child, nothing but trouble from the day she was born, but as sweet as an angel, not at all snippy and spoiled like Lily. I favored her over Lily. Maybe because she was my baby sister." Grandma dabs her eyes and whispers, "Daisy probably won't have anything to do with me since I've ignored her for years."

"That's not true," Mother says. "Rebel, give me the last letter Daisy wrote so I can read it to my mom."

"My Mom. How sweet those words are to me," Grandma says.

I give Mother the letter and leave to buy a ten-cent bottle of Coke from the vending machine in the lobby. Forgiveness is so beautiful. It's like a refreshing stream on a dry Kansas landscape. I wish Grandpa was here.

* * *

This year the Schoenfeld High School staff decides that students who graduated from Schoenfeld High can attend a prom, if they're dating a high school student. So Jaylynn has asked Charlie Birdfoot to attend. He's a senior in college, I expect he'll find the Prom a bore.

"Seems weird to be double dating with my brother," Shirley says.

"Yeah, but it will be fun," Jaylynn replies.

Shirley's date, Pierre Dubois, is an exchange student from France. He's nineteen, having graduated from high school in France before coming to Schoenfeld High.

"He's so worldly," Shirley says.

"Probably knows how to French kiss too," says Jaylynn.

"Of course, he's from France," I say. "If he was from Italy, he'd give Italian kisses."

"That's not what I mean," Jaylynn snaps.

"I know exactly what you mean," I say. "I'm not that stupid." I stick out my tongue.

"Skip and I have a third wheel going with us," Wanda says. "Jimmy's opted to go stag with us. Guess that means no necking for Skip and me after the dance, unless we ditch Jimmy."

A twinge of guilt, actually a sharp jab, pierces me. Jimmy has no date for the senior prom, and it's partly my fault.

"Let's eat dinner together before the prom," Wanda says.

Jaylynn agrees.

"I don't know," I say. "It might be weird for Paul having Jimmy there."

"Weird for you is what you mean," Shirley says.

"Don't be a party pooper," Jaylynn adds.

"Yeah, the more the merrier," Wanda says.

"All right." A twinge of panic makes my stomach growl.

* * *

For Prom, I pull my hair into a chic bun like Audrey Hepburn had in *Charade*. I do not look one bit like Audrey Hepburn, more like the Bride of Frankenstein. A cascade of curls frames my face, though this is not what I wanted. However, my black cocktail dress makes me feel glamourous.

At six o'clock Paul arrives at our door empty-handed. "I planned to buy you orchids, but the florist was out of them."

"That's okay, Paul. They'd wilt before the evening was over." The lack of a corsage is not okay, but what can I do, grab a handful of daffodils from our yard on the way to Paul's car? I pin the red rose boutonniere I bought him on his lapel while Daddy takes photos with his new Polaroid camera.

"Be home by midnight," Mother says as we leave.

The Frontier Steak House has prepared a round table for us in their party room. As luck would have it, I am seated between Paul and Jimmy. Punishment, I'm sure for dumping Jimmy. I hope this is the whirlwind Mother said I might reap. I do not want a night of drama.

After dinner, Paul and I have time for a few kisses at the Holiday Inn parking lot before we enter their ballroom. Island Paradise is the Prom theme. The Junior Class has filled the ballroom with palm trees, exotic plants, and flowers. A live parrot, chained to a stand, is nestled among the plants. Fake monkeys hang in the trees. Jungle sounds from a record player add to the ambience. Tables placed under grass huts surround the dance floor. Hula girls, pineapples, and plastic leis decorate the tables.

"Me Tarzan. You Jane," Paul says. The DJ slips a slow dance record onto his turntable. "You want to dance." I slip comfortably into Paul's arms. The night is perfect, and it has just begun.

After the music stops, we join the rest of the FAB4 and their dates at a table. While we're talking, Marlene Klienmeyer strolls by. Her dress looks like an outfit Wanda's Aunt Mary Jo would wear. The hot pink strapless dress clings to her like a second skin. A slit up the side exposes her leg almost to her hip. She bulges out of the top like an overstuffed sausage. Her bleached hair hangs over her shoulder. She pouts her lips like Jayne Mansfield before speaking.

"Hello Paul. Hello Jimmy. Either of you guys want to dance?" Marlene smiles at me. "I don't think you need two dates, Rebel. How about sharing one with me?"

"Sure," Paul stands. "You don't mind do you, Rebel?"

"As a matter of fact, I do," but my words are sown into the wind. Paul and Marlene are already on the dance floor. After three dances, Paul returns with two glasses of jungle juice sporting paper umbrellas. I take one sip and know someone has spiked the punch.

"Good, isn't it?" Paul chugs his drink and leaves to get another.

"You want to dance, Red?" Jimmy stands and extends his hand.

"Maybe later."

"Okay, but you promised, and I'm not letting you fink out on me."

Jaylynn leans across Charlie and whispers in my ear, "I was just in the restroom, and Marlene was in there crying. Said she wasn't having any fun and was going to leave."

"Isn't that a pity," I sneer? "I won't miss her."

"Yeah, but Paul might," Wanda hisses.

Paul returns with two drinks. "Here, Rebel. Have another."

"No thanks. I'll stick with Coke."

"Fine, then I'll drink yours." He quickly downs my drink. "I'm going to get another. Anyone want one?"

"No thanks," my friends and I mumble.

"You want to dance, Jimmy?" I stand. I want to *Hold Your Hand* by the Beatles is playing.

"May I have your hand?" Jimmy asks and leads me onto the dance floor.

While dancing, I look over Jimmy's shoulder and see Paul pull a half pint bottle of brown liquid from the inside pocket of his suit. He pours some into his glass and offers the bottle to the FAB4 and their dates. They shake their heads. Paul stumbles toward the lobby. Under the crystal chandelier, Marlene tugs on her dress exposing more of her breasts. She reaches for Paul's hand like a black widow luring prey to her web. He puts his arm around her waist. She nuzzles her head against his shoulder. I turn away; I do not need to see more.

Jimmy twirls me so I no longer can see Paul. When we return to the table, everyone is quiet, uneasy. Finally, Wanda says, "Paul left. Said he wasn't feeling good. I think he caught the flu from my dad. You know what I mean?"

I know exactly what Wanda means. Paul is drunk. I have reaped the whirlwind.

"I have something for you in my car," Jimmy says. "Wait here. I'll get it for you." Jimmy strides toward the lobby.

"He didn't come with us," Skip says. "At the last minute he decided to drive his T-bird."

"It looks really cool," Wanda says. "He and his dad finally finished the restoration. There are seats in it now."

Jimmy returns with a box from Snyder's Florist. "Here, Red."

Inside is a lei of tiny orchids. There must be fifty orchids of various colors woven together with jeweled ribbon. It's exquisite. No wonder Paul couldn't buy orchids; Jimmy bought them all.

"Put it on," Jaylynn says.

"How do you rate?" Shirley asks.

"It's gorgeous." I inhale the orchids subtle perfume. It's too beautiful to wear, and I don't deserve it.

"Here, I'll put it on you." Jimmy drapes the lei around my neck. I give him a kiss of thanks on his cheek. Jimmy pulls me to his chest, kisses me deeply and bends me backwards into his kiss. When he pulls me upright, I am giddy. Dizzy. Swept off my feet by a whirlwind.

"Oo la lah," says Pierre. "Amour." Pierre kisses his fingers and gestures toward Shirley. "Shall we dance ma petit fleur?"

"What did he say?" Jaylynn asks.

"I don't know," Shirley says. "It's Greek to me." Pierre leads her to the dance floor.

"It's French not Greek," I call after them.

"Woo hoo. Hot Damn," says Skip. "Come here, Wanda. Let's try that."

"Later, Romeo, later." Wanda blushes.

* * *

Graduation festivities are not boring this year, because I'm the main focus of Daddy's camera. I have no major part in the ceremony like Columbia who sang with the Triple Trio or Amherst who gave a speech. Jimmy is the valedictorian. Jaylynn and Shirley read the class goals and class motto. I'm content to be in the top 10 percent of my class.

Grandma could sit on the main floor in her wheelchair, but she chooses not to attend. "I don't think I can sit that long in one position," she says.

"I'm not sure I can either." We laugh. "Daddy's bringing his Polaroid camera, so I'll have plenty of pictures to show you at my graduation party. You'll be at our house afterwards, for the party won't you, Grandma?"

"Absolutely, and I'm sure your grandpa will be there in spirit."

Neither Columbia nor Amherst attend, which irks me, because I'd been forced to sit through a zillion of their boring events. The graduation ceremonies drag on forever. My friends and I are anxious for it to be over so we can party. We arrive home after 10:00 p.m. In the center of the dining room table is a white cake decorated with yellow sunflowers and the words: Congrats to Redcliffe and Wanda. Gifts and cards are stacked on a chair.

"Speech. Speech," Aunt Bessie says. "Let's hear a few words from the graduates."

"I'm glad it's over, "Wanda says.

"This was worse than your damn dance recitals I used to attend," Uncle Waylon says. "I'm just glad I didn't have to be in the KDOG booth tonight."

"I'd like to say a few words." I make a dramatic bow. Daddy's camera clicks. "A special thanks to Daddy who helped me pass geometry. Mother for always being there to listen to me. Mouse, who has been my shadow for years. I love you Mouse. I'll miss you when I go to college." I sniff. I really will miss her. "As for Columbia and Amherst, who are not here, they owe me big time for missing my graduation."

"Yeah. What about me? I was there. I got calluses on my calluses tonight," Mouse says.

Grandma sighs but says nothing.

"And Uncle Waylon, my favorite uncle, I thank you for keeping your mouth shut, you know what I'm talking about, and Grandma —"

"All right," Grandma says. "That's enough. No need to be so dramatic, but I guess you come by it naturally." She hands me an envelope. "Here, this is for you. Your grandpa would have wanted me to do this."

I slip a nail-bitten finger under the envelope flap and pull out two small, strange multilayered tissue paper items. Delta Airline Tickets. One for Redcliffe Rothberg, the other for Bonnie Rothberg. St. Louis to Paris, round trip.

"Paris! You're sending Mother and me to Paris!" I shout.

Grandma nods. "It's long past time for you to meet Daisy Sunflower."

The doorbell rings.

"I'll get it." Mouse runs to the door. "Your date's here for the all-night graduation party.

I hand the tickets to Mother and run across the room. "I'm going to Paris. Can you believe it, Jimmy? I'm going to Paris."

Epilogue
Today's comments by an older Rebel.

The Big Disclaimer or I Wrote my Book First

As soon as people discover you're writing a book, they maneuver into one of two camps. Camp one wants to be included in your book, so they'll have instant notoriety, a shot at being on TV or if all else fails, grounds to sue you for defamation of character. Any way you slice it, this bunch wants to make money off your hard work.

Group two hopes or, in many cases, prays you'll ignore them as they have no desire to lose their anonymity. This might be because they're shy, on the lam again from federal agents, or have something sinister to hide. My family has card-carrying members in both groups.

No matter what I write, some folks will be angry because I didn't include them, and others will be equally irate because they feel my treatment of them was less than honest. That's what Uncle Waylon told me after he read a rough draft of this book.

Uncle Waylon's exact words to me were: "How dare you treat me and my family in such a shoddy fashion? Who do you think you are? I'm the only one in this family who's ever… uh, who's uh…"

I waited while Uncle Waylon scratched his head, a ploy he uses when stalling for time, hoping to jump start his brain cells into action. It never works. At last he blurted, "I'm the only one who's ever amounted to a hill of beans. I can't remember the last time anyone described me in such unflattering terms."

Of course, Uncle Waylon can't remember. He suffers from selective hearing. In addition, his brain cells have been bathed in alcohol far too long. On Saturdays, if he's not occupying his personalized stool at the Pink Chicken Lounge, he's sleeping off the previous night's binge at KDOG-AM, because his wife, my sainted Aunt Bessie, has locked him out of the house again.

So, it is with fear, trepidation, and my normal barge-right-in attitude that I wrote about my family's secrets. They can deny, dispute, agree, or disagree with anything I've written, and I'm sure they will, but I wrote my book first, so anything they write will merely be a footnote to the true story you have just read.

Redcliffe Rose "Rebel" Rothberg

About the Author
Rebecca Willman Gernon

Rebecca Gernon is a child of the Midwest, born in Illinois but lived most of her life in small Nebraska towns. She currently lives in the New Orleans area with her husband and Spot the Wonder Dog.

Gernon's stories have been published in *Bylines Magazine, Lutheran Digest, Fiction 365, Over My Dead Body,* and *The Weeder's Digest,* and internationally in *Parousia*, an African magazine. She won Awards for her humorous plays in Virginia and Louisiana, and has had plays produced in several Louisiana venues. She won a national food writing contest for *Eggplant Love Affair,* and earned third place in a national humor writing contest with *Surprise Me With Something.*

Amy Signs, A Mother, Her Deaf Daughter and Their Stories (Gallaudet University 2012) was co-authored with her daughter and is in libraries and homes worldwide. Available on Amazon and Kindle.

Her stories have appeared in the following anthologies: *The Best Mom in the World,* (Howard books 2007); *All My Good Habits I Learned from Grandma* (Thomas Nelson 2008); *Love is a Verb* (Bethany Press 2009); and *Expecting Miracles* (Guidepost 2010.)

The Sunflower Letters is Gernon's first experience with self-publishing. She is available to speak to book clubs and other groups via zoom or in person. She may be contacted at rrgernon@gmail.com.